The Samarita

D0005864

2-99

DATE DUE		
10/8/92	DEC 3 0 2010	
JUN 0 3 2000		
JUN 0 7 2005	JUN 3 0 2012	
SEP 1 9 2006	DISCARDED BY	
APR 1 5 2008	FREE LIBRARY	
JAN 1 9 2010		

The Samaritan Woman

A Novel

Eileen M. Berger

HarperSanFrancisco
A Division of HarperCollinsPublishers

FIRST EDITION

Library of Congress Cataloging-in-Publication Data

Berger, Eileen M.
   The Samaritan woman : a novel / Eileen M. Berger. — 1st ed.
     p.   cm.
   ISBN 0–06–060915–X (alk. paper)
   1. Samaritan woman (Biblical character)—Fiction. 2. Bible.
N.T.—History of Biblical events—Fiction. I. Title.
PS3552.E7183S26 1991
813'.54—dc20   90–55315
                                                    CIP

---

90 91 92 93 94 CWI 10 9 8 7 6 5 4 3 2 1

The Samaritan Woman

one

Susanna turned on her bare heel and headed for the door. She held her head high and her shoulders squared. Her cold hands, which had been clasped before her, dropped to her sides, where she forced them to remain unclenched.

She would not let her sister-in-law see her hurt, her fear, her desolation.

The early afternoon sunlight of Samaria bathed her as she left the shelter of the low stone house. Tilting her face upward, she welcomed the fierce heat of the sun to warm and cleanse her.

She was shaking. She had to get away, by herself, to sort out the horror of what had happened these past several days.

As she swiftly turned the corner, she collided with the small hurtling shape of her young nephew. "Be careful, my darling," she cautioned, catching his tumbling body before it could land against the hard-packed golden earth. Without thinking, she gathered David against her breast, and the three-year-old threw his arms around her neck, getting them tangled for a moment in her long, wavy hair.

"Aunt Susanna," he cried, "did you come out to play with me?"

The pain was almost more than she could bear. She wanted to continue holding him but knew she couldn't. The sharp voice spoke behind her. "Susanna! Put him down this instant! Get your things and be gone."

Susanna's dark eyes closed for a moment and her lips pressed together. Then she drew in a sharp breath and, without turning to look at Leah, set the little boy on his feet. Smoothing the rumpled hair and looking into the big eyes, so like those of her brother, she whispered, "David Ben Jonah, I love you!"

He danced along beside her, oblivious to his mother's approach. "Come here!" Leah jerked him back by his arm. David's voice rose in a wail as his mother's hand slapped across his face, and Susanna's feet faltered in their rhythm. "Be still, David," Leah commanded. "Susanna has better things to do than play with you."

Susanna escaped into the small lean-to shed her brother had offered her after her husband Abram had died. This had been only a storage room then, and she'd helped him enclose additional space on the roof to protect the lentils, beans, unspun wool, and other supplies removed to make room for her.

They now had to climb the outdoor steps to get any of these things when needed, and Leah never for a day allowed Susanna to forget the inconvenience her presence caused.

What more could I have done? she wondered. She'd served as an unpaid maid, tended to David and his sister Mikal, fed the goats, spun and wove and carried water and . . .

She yanked her extra tunic from the peg on the wall and reached for her Sabbath head covering and the brightly striped blue, red, and white girdle she'd woven three months before to accentuate her slender waist. Her old sandals were almost worn through, but she'd better take them, also, and she'd certainly need her soft leather water skin.

Wrapping the smaller items within her tunic, she looked around the whitewashed walls for what might well be the last time. Her feet slid into her better sandals, and she bent to tie the laces around her shapely ankles before lifting the long, dark-blue mantle from where it lay on her rolled pallet.

When placed around her shoulders, the woolen robe almost covered her long-sleeved tunic. It often served as a bedcovering, but how would it be used tonight?

Where would she be? On the desert, endangered by wild animals? Might there be as much danger if she slept in some alley here within Sychar? The dogs, which appeared fully domesticated during the daytime, often ran in ravenous packs at night. She had no lantern or light with which to keep them away.

There was also danger for a woman from two-legged animals, as she knew only too well.

She drew in a long breath and exhaled slowly. *I wish I could ask Leah for a little time to make some plans.*

She arranged a soft square of white linen over her hair and pushed aside the striped, earth-toned curtain that had given her some sense of privacy here during the past year.

With one step she was outside her brother's house—only it wasn't her brother's anymore. He was gone even more permanently than she soon would be.

The curtain fell.

The blazing sun raised visible waves of heat from the large worn doorstep and the grassless, packed area behind the house. She noticed that the water pot for the goats was nearly empty and started in that direction. But this was no longer her job.

She forced hereself to keep moving toward the dusty street.

"Aunt Susanna, are you going to the market?" David called. "May I come, too?"

Her lips curved upward for a moment as she turned toward the little fellow she treasured more than anyone else in the world. How often she had wished Yahweh had given her a child like this!

Leah's sharp voice covered the soft beginning of Susanna's reply, and Susanna's eyes filled with tears as she turned again and moved toward the main part of Sychar.

She had walked this road to the market or to do other errands many times. She had also gone this way to the town well on countless occasions.

Her primary problem now was to find a place to stay, at least for tonight, but first she must fill her water skin. Perhaps this would be a good time to go to the well, for not many women would be there this late.

"Oh, Yahweh," she prayed as she had so many times before, "please give me some solution to my problems."

But the first person she saw as she turned the final corner was Mara! She'd have turned back, but Mara had seen her at that same instant and made some comment that caused her companion to turn.

Heightened color attested to her insecurity, but Susanna's step slowed only imperceptibly. "May I please use your rope?"

Mara raised heavy eyebrows in what seemed a mockery of surprise. She had never forgiven Susanna for being the one Shannon had asked to be his wife. "Did you forget to bring yours?"

"I don't have one with me," she said simply.

Could there be a flicker of sympathy in the eyes of Esther, the wife of Ichabod? The fifteen-year-old extended her looped rope, wet from recent use. "Here, Susanna."

Susanna smiled her gratitude and unwrapped her parcel to get her goatskin water bag. Esther offered, "If that's all you need, let me pour some from my pot."

"Oh, not yours . . ."

"I got too much but hate to waste any." The girl would not listen to Susanna's words of gratitude as she reached for the skin and carefully transferred the water. "I would have sloshed out that much before I got home," she added, raising to her shoulder a pot that was unusally large for such a slender young matron.

Susanna pulled the cords tight to keep the precious liquid from spilling. In her desire to get away from Mara, she temporarily forgot her thirst. Even before Susanna had crossed the square, Mara derided Esther, "What a stupid thing to do!"

What was Mara most upset about this time? Was it the usual thing she always brought up?

Or was it that Susanna's brother had just been declared by the priest to have leprosy and been banished?

She almost hoped it was the latter, for then Leah would suffer too. After all, Leah had even slept with Jonah until two weeks ago when he'd first noticed the white area on his leg and, fearfully, had gone to the priest, as ordained in Leviticus. The priest had examined him and, fearing the worst, put him in the small building outside of town for seven days, after which he checked again.

Following another week's isolation, the lesion not only was still there but appeared larger. And so, yesterday, Jonah had been forced to leave the area. He had not been allowed to return to his house even for clothing or farewells. Only Leah and Susanna had gone, separately, to say good-bye.

Grieving but dry-eyed, Susanna had borne through the streets and out through the gate a supply of nails, his saw and hammer, a pencil, and a wooden plane.

He had always been an excellent carpenter. If he could find wood where he was going, with these tools he could make anyplace at least livable.

She shuddered, remembering the trip north at the time of their uncle's death twelve years before, when she'd seen those caves.

"Oh, Jonah," she'd said, "how awful that anyone has to live like that!"

"I suppose they're grateful to have shelter of any kind," her brother said slowly. "Leprosy is a terrible disease, not only because of the physical harm it does but because it breaks up families and friendships."

She squinted and shielded her eyes with her hand. "From here I can hardly tell anything's wrong with the people, except for those who are lame."

And then she sighed. "I'm grateful they're not coming across the stream to beg from us." She'd realized the whole group of travelers was moving a little faster. "I'd be so scared if they did."

Now everyone would be afraid of Jonah!

Her hurrying feet slowed as she recognized that, although she was rushing, it was to get away, first from Leah's house and then from the well; however, she had no destination.

If only her parents were living—but they'd been dead for years. Maybe it was because of his increasing illness that her father had betrothed her to Obediah. He'd agreed she didn't have to go live with the merchant until after her first menstrual period, but how could anyone have known she'd be one of the unlucky girls to become a woman so young?

Four months after Obediah took her she had her twelfth birthday. Nausea still overtook her when she thought of the terrible two years she had spent with that one-eyed, difficult old man.

There was no brother to go to now, either, because of the leprosy, and she'd be unwelcome in the homes of her two older sisters, who had married stable, hardworking men years ago and lived two days' journey away.

To be a widow with no property or money was bad enough, but to have it happen in multiples, and then the divorces as well . . . Her head moved slowly left, then right, in unconscious negation. There was no chance her brothers-in-law would allow her as a houseguest—or even as a servant.

Maybe her elderly friend Deborah would consider having Susanna come to take care of her. After all, Susanna often ran errands for her and checked her needs when on her way to the shop of the oil merchant or to get spices.

She turned into the familiar narrow side street and paused for a long moment before going to the doorway of the small stone house to call, "Deborah?"

A scraping sound and heavy breathing preceding her, the wizened woman pulled aside the curtain with a clawlike hand. Her thin white hair was drawn back tight, and the bones of her head stood out clearly. She had to stand still to catch her breath before asking, "Susanna, how *are* you?"

Susanna's habit of always answering cheerfully almost made her say, "Good," but she stopped in time. "Not good at all, Deborah," she admitted. "I have very big problems."

The skinny arm extended, and her hand almost rested on Susanna's arm but then was withdrawn. The voice cracked in sympathy. "I heard about your brother. I'm sorry . . ."

"It's tragic. He is so young, and he has a wife and two beautiful children." Remembering little David, Susanna felt like weeping.

The old woman coughed spasmodically and clung to the doorpost. Susanna put a strong supporting arm around her and, half carrying the frail body, helped her onto a low bench. Looking around, but not immediately seeing the water pot, she took up her own water skin and raised it to the lips of the aged woman. "Here, Deborah, take a drink of this."

Deborah refused the water, shaking her head and pushing Susanna's arm away. She was wheezing between the coughs. Susanna tried to encourage, "I know it's hard to breathe, but perhaps one little sip . . . ?"

"No, I . . ." Although she could not continue, she made it clear she didn't want to drink, so Susanna retied the cord and set her water bag on the floor by her clothes. She suddenly realized Deborah was afraid she might catch leprosy this way!

The sleeping mats were under the only window in the small one-room dwelling, so Susanna hurriedly grabbed one and unrolled it near where the old lady was sitting. With great care she assisted Deborah to the mat, on which she lay down.

Deborah did not speak, could not, for another minute. When the worst of the attack had passed, she reached to take Susanna's hand in her frail, bony one. "Thank you, my child," she whispered.

"I'm glad I was here to help."

They did not speak for a while as Deborah rested. Finally she asked, "I heard that Leah was sending you away. What will you do?"

Susanna's head scarf had been removed, and her long, waving tresses fell loosely over her slender shoulders. In the muted light within the stone-walled house her dark eyes met those of her friend. "I don't know."

"There must be some answer . . ."

"I pray Yahweh will help me find it."

Again silence. The cracked old voice spoke softly. "If I lived alone, I'd ask you to stay, but Amos would never permit it."

A deep breath filled every bit of Susanna's lungs. "I guess I knew that but . . . but it would have been nice." Her voice was wistful as she gazed with fondness at the wrinkled face of this woman she had known all her life.

"What will you do?" Deborah repeated.

Susanna's hand returned the other's pressure. She hoped Deborah did not realize how hopeless she felt. "I tried to think of someone to whom I could turn, but there is nobody."

"You thought I might be able . . . ?"

"I *hoped* it could be. I didn't really expect it."

"My son has many good traits, Susanna. Even his strong sense of morality and propriety can be considered good, but he seems lacking in the love that should go with them." She paused. "Sometimes I feel deep sorrow, regret, that I was unable to raise him to be more loving and less ready to judge."

"He's like most people in Sychar." If only this were not true!

"I know you, though, Susanna," Deborah said softly. "You are a good woman."

Susanna looked at her for a moment, but there was no sign of mockery in the eyes, face, or in the grip of her hand to indicate anything other than the love and faith she was expressing. Tears sprang to Susanna's eyes, and she wiped them away quickly. How could she weep over kindness when she hadn't cried at the news of her brother's fate? "Nobody has ever said that to me."

"It is the truth!" Deborah stated emphatically. "I know it is."

"But you know nothing of most of the . . . the difficulties of my life." Then she blushed, realizing Deborah, like everyone else, would have heard a great deal.

"There are some of us who don't believe everything we hear, and many of us really don't hear much as we don't encourage gossip. I know of you what I want to know: that you are kind, that you go out of your way to help people, that you are a hard worker, and that you do not rise up and repay with bitterness and anger the treatment you receive from others. I respect you."

A shiver passed over Susanna even though the room was hot and stuffy. "Thank you," she said, realizing how inadequate the words were.

The silence was companionable, easy, but finally Susanna said, "The only possibility I can think of is to go to the Inn of Taharka."

"Have you money?"

She shook her head. "None at all. However, Taharka was a friend of . . . of Jonah's. Perhaps if I go to him and kneel before him and offer to be his servant, to do whatever he needs done at the inn, perhaps . . ." The magnitude of what she was contemplating overwhelmed her. "Do you think he might listen, Deborah?" she asked anxiously.

A brief spell of coughing, not as intense this time, nor as long, interrupted them. "I don't know, Susanna. I am only a woman." But then she must have seen the right corner of Susanna's mouth turn up slightly, for she half-smiled at her own evasiveness. "I have no better suggestion."

Again, there was silence. Then Deborah spoke so softly that Susanna had to lean close to the pale lips. "Go and see. I shall remain here and pray to Yahweh that Taharka may look with favor on you."

Susanna touched her forehead to the back of the hand she was holding, but Deborah gently pulled it away and laid it on Susanna's soft hair. "Bless you, Susanna."

Susanna rose to her feet with the unconscious grace that was always with her. As she moved away toward the door Deborah pushed herself up onto her elbow. "Take your bundle, my child. If all goes well, you will need these things at the inn this night."

Susanna came back and began to fold her mantle around the other items. She didn't look up as she admitted, "I am so frightened."

This time the voice was as brisk as Susanna remembered as a child. "Of course you are. You're not a fool." But then she added more softly, "You must put your faith in Yahweh."

The busy hands paused in their task. "Will He hear the prayers of just women?"

The answer was emphatic. "He hears!"

"Are you sure?"

"I myself have known His care and have seen it in the lives of many more."

Susanna left her friend's house and partially retraced her steps in the direction of the well before zigzagging through streets and alleys toward the western gate of Sychar. She couldn't have gone on had not Deborah prayed with her just before she left.

two

Susanna had to consciously move her feet forward as she came in sight of the very large two-storied stone structure just within the gate. No windows graced the lower floor, and those on the second revealed no movement. Only as evening approached would there be so many travelers spending the night at the inn that the upper gallery would be occupied.

The massive wooden gates with their beaten iron reinforcements and hinges were standing open, and she walked between them, feeling dwarfed by the walls and the large compound inside. Surrounding the open area were doorways and, at the far side, deep open arches would provide shelter for camels, donkeys, and the burdens they had carried.

She was no more comfortable here now than when she'd come years ago with Necho, Taharka's son, whom she and Jonah had met on one of their long rambles through the hills. They had all become close friends and, although a year younger, she had little difficulty jumping streams, climbing trees, or running as fast as the boys did.

Those days were too short-lived, however, for at twelve boys were expected to take on the seriousness of the world in which they lived. Necho, an only son, was soon meeting the caravan masters and dickering with them, his father standing behind him, bare arms crossed over his chest, upholding him in his dealings.

Susanna had rarely seen Necho from then until she heard at the well two years later that he was dying. She had returned the water pot to her house then gone by a devious route to see him.

She still did not regret her visit, even though Obediah beat her for it. After all, she was the wife of a Samaritan. How dare she go into the house of the Egyptian pigs? And to see a *man!*

Although she tried to explain their past friendship, her husband wouldn't listen and swore he could never trust her again. She had not immediately understood the significance of that, but what a difference it made! Spies reported her every move, even to whom she spoke when she went for water.

How ironic it was that Obediah's fatal attack had occurred right outside the gates of this inn, and he had been brought inside these walls to die, here in this "courtyard of infidels."

Looking around uncertainly, she wondered if she should go directly to the several rooms on her left where Taharka probably still lived. Would it be better to ask for him?

Oh, Yahweh, I don't know what to do. Please help me, she pleaded silently. She took several more steps forward as a servant deposited another shovelful of manure onto a two-wheeled cart and came around to lift the short handles. He looked up, seeming surprised to find a woman, alone, within this place. His frank gaze made her grateful she had drawn her veil across the lower part of her face.

"Is your master about?" she asked.

He was a full head taller than she, bigger than she'd thought at first, and extremely muscular. His sun-darkened skin was shining with sweat from the work he'd been doing, and his body was uncovered except for a loincloth. He pointed toward the door she'd considered entering. "He is in his room."

She knew she shouldn't continue to speak to the servant, but she did not want to be embarrassed by going to the door and finding Taharka too busy to see her. "Do you know if he's conducting business?"

A hint of a smile crossed the man's face. "The master is always conducting business."

Her eyes dropped. Had she expected him to lead her across the courtyard and knock at the door? She turned, murmuring a soft, "Thank you."

With her head high, she walked quickly in the direction indicated and within moments was at the heavy wooden door. She raised her hand and knocked twice.

There were footsteps, and the door moved inward on silent hinges. She had dropped her veil, wanting Taharka to recognize her, and was relieved as the tall, handsome Egyptian in his mid-forties greeted her heartily. "Susanna! It's good to see you. Come inside." His right hand was placed firmly under her left elbow to assist her up the one small step to his office-home.

The interior hadn't changed much since she'd been welcomed here as a child and offered strange confections. He led her to one of the seats with backs that he used here. None of her family or friends had other than mats on the floor or low benches, and it had seemed to her and Jonah quite novel when, as children, they could sit leaning back in a chair.

She noted again the cane seats but then quickly forgot them and the unusual thigh-high table with a marble top on which he had apparently been doing his accounts. He was saying, "I just heard an hour ago about Jonah's leprosy. I'm sorry."

Susanna looked into the troubled black eyes. "It's a sad day for him and for his family."

He seated himself in the chair he'd drawn around the table. "Is there something I can do to help?"

Susanna slid from her seat, her small bundle tumbling, unnoticed, to the floor. She had rehearsed all the way here things she might say to him, and he was trying to make it easy for her to bring a petition, but she didn't know how to go about it.

Clasping her hands together, she knelt, head bowed, making herself as small as she could before him. "My lord," she began, her voice quavering in spite of herself, "I am just a woman, and I know I should not come to you seeking help but . . . but my sister-in-law has sent me away."

"To where?" The voice was calm, reasonable.

"I have no place to go," she stated. "My parents are dead, and my brother is banished."

"Other family?"

She shook her head. "There is no relative to whom I can turn." She drew in a deep breath. "I went to the home of an old friend but was unable to remain there. I wondered . . . I was hoping . . . I thought there might be some chance you'd be able to . . . to consider . . ."

How could she have thought this would work? She sank into an even smaller ball of misery. She could see his feet in their leather sandals unmoving before her and the cool, natural-colored linen tunic with its band of scarlet embroidery around the bottom. She wanted to reach out to touch the hem of his garment, to plead her case, but all she could manage was, "Do you have need for another maidservant? Could I perhaps help prepare meals for the people of the caravans or clean or . . . or do other duties?"

The hem of the tunic lowered, but she was unprepared for the two strong hands lifting her by her upper arms. "Do not kneel before me, Susanna," he said quietly. "I want you to sit in your chair, and I shall sit in mine, and we will discuss your situation."

She appreciated his kindness but was confused. He had not rejected her offer, but he had hardly accepted it, either. He asked, "What is in your bundle?"

It looked so small, lying there. "It is all I own, a tunic, mantle, leather water bag, head cover, an old pair of sandals, and a newly woven girdle."

He made no comment on her possessions but went to another subject. "Tell me of your brother."

After her explanation of the rules in the Pentateuch concerning leprosy, he nodded. "It is difficult when one of the gods dictates such an action."

"The one true God does not make rules without reason, my lord, but, in this case, to protect others from getting a dreaded disease."

He countered, "If you believe that others could catch his illness by being around him, then what about you and his wife and children?"

"I can not guarantee I'm free of it, but as far as I know I am. Yesterday I washed the garment I'm wearing, along with my mantle, girdle, and head covering. The sandals and water bag I set in the sun, but I don't know how else to clean them."

His silence and continued gaze made her painfully aware of her problem. "I bathed and washed my hair yesterday as well," she continued almost desperately. "However, I did sleep last night in the little room attached to the house of Jonah, and I ate with his wife and children there this morning." He had been her only hope, and with each word she spoke she felt more certain he would send her away.

A frown caused great creases across his forehead and between his brows. Certainly he was displeased. She moved uncomfortably on her seat, but he raised his left hand, palm toward her. "Stay there. Please." He got up and walked to the door, where he stood looking out across the enclosure. She was afraid to say anything, but turned on her chair to study his back, searching there for some clue as to his thoughts.

"What of your sister's well-being?" he asked.

"I tried to talk with her, to suggest that we could help each other with taking care of her children and working. However, she didn't want my help—or, rather, she said she did not want to have to put bread into my mouth." Her voice was steady, although the hurt was almost as severe as it had been earlier in the day.

"When you went to the house of Jonah after the death of your husband, what were your duties and responsibilities?"

"At first Leah and I shared most tasks, but later it became obvious there were things she didn't like doing. Those became mine."

"Like?"

"Well, she dislikes the tedium of everyday tasks, like grinding meal. She enjoys meeting other young matrons in the morning when she gets the first potful of water from the well each day. However, as we had the ass, chickens, and goats, there was always need for much more water, which I always fetched. I also did the laundry for the household."

He nodded, and she wondered if it was in agreement or if perhaps he'd heard that she had been raped several years before while washing clothes at the river. Her eyes dropped, and she was glad he couldn't see the flush heating her neck and cheeks.

"Cooking?"

She hesitated. "Not much in the house of Jonah, for Leah prides herself on being a good cook. However, I always did all of it for—when I was married," she changed quickly.

"What about sewing, mending, and needlework?"

"I spin and weave and, of course, make tunics, mantles, and hangings for doors and windows. But I've never had the opportunity to learn to do beautiful work like that on the hem of your garment," she admitted, trying to be completely honest.

"Would you be willing to learn to do needlework?"

She nodded, though he was still looking out the door. "I would like to, if that is what you wished of me."

He turned slowly. "Isn't there something in your religion against making any likeness of anything that is in the heavens above or the earth beneath or in the water under the earth?"

She did not indicate her surprise that he'd know Yahweh's commandment. "The clothing of the priests in the synagogue are decorated with needlework," she explained. "If it is permitted there, I see no reason not to decorate a robe for you."

He had moved close to the side of her chair. She had the feeling he was pleased with her answer, though he did not indicate this by word or smile. He looked down at her for what seemed a long time, and the silence stretched her nerves almost to the breaking point. Finally he drew in a big breath, said, "Wait here," and walked quickly from the room.

The soft slap of his sandals receded on the stone slab surface, but because he walked quietly for such a large man, she couldn't tell when he stopped or how far he went. Was he attending to something concerning her, or had he remembered some business matter? The tall servant had indicated he was always busy; she had probably come at a bad time.

The chair was uncomfortable after sitting for so long, but he'd told her to remain where she was. She noted her clothing still on the floor where it had fallen when she knelt before him. By wriggling forward on the chair, she maneuvered it closer with her toe until she could lean forward to pick it up.

She sat still, hands folded primly on top of the bundle. He had not seemed unreceptive, had he? He had not turned away from her or seemed aghast at her suggestion.

An ass was braying and a sheep baaing. Flies buzzed in and out of the window, which, though it had a curtain that could be drawn, was open to the quadrangle.

The door had a similar blue, green, and yellow heavy, woven curtain tied to one side so that any possible breeze might enter. However, in the muggy heat of this day there was no movement of the cloth. She felt moisture on her back, and her tunic stuck to her chair as she leaned forward.

She had been looking at the window to the left of the open door, and now her gaze continued in that direction to a piece of furniture similar to the chair on which she sat, but perhaps five or six times as wide. The waist-high stand beside it held a small, round lamp made in such a way that three wicks, only one of which was burning, were kept separated by the potter's having pinched the wet clay into equidistant channels.

A passageway seemed to lead off at the end of that wall, and she guessed it must go to other rooms in this suite in which, as far as she knew, he had lived alone since his son's untimely death.

Necho had never spoken of his mother, and Susanna wondered about her. Had she died young? Might she have refused to leave Egypt? Or perhaps had she left them to return to her homeland?

14

It was really none of her business, she told herself, shaking her head.

The back wall had a built-in seat long enough and probably wide enough for a sleeping mat to be spread upon; above it were divided shelves.

Lining the wall on her left stood many baskets similar to those often seen on the sides of donkeys, and larger ones like those used for camels. Boxes and crates also were standing two and three deep.

Occupying the last corner was a three-tiered table on which were many rolls. About ten inches long and perhaps three to five inches in diameter, each was tied with a strip of very narrow cloth or fine rope.

Could these beige rolls be papyrus paper? She had never seen so many in her life, not even when she went to the synagogue. Wondering if they all contained writing, she turned her gaze back to the large marble-topped table in the center of the room. Yes, one of the rolls was open upon his desk, and lying on a square of badly stained cloth was the instrument with which he must have been writing.

Jonah had used a stylus on a wax tablet, so she'd never seen anyone use a pen, which she'd heard was simply a hollow reed with a slanted point. She assumed that was a block of gum arabic mixed with soot in the low, saucer-shaped pottery dish; nearby stood a taller container of water with which to moisten this ink.

If only she'd been allowed to learn to read better! Jonah had taught her what he was learning in the synagogue school, until Father forbade it. What did those signs and symbols along the tops and sides of the boxes mean? She was staring at them with fascination when she saw a shadow and heard a sound in the doorway.

She was so pleased to see Taharka that a smile of welcome lit her dainty features before she remembered her manners. She brought her small, capable hands together before her gaze was averted.

His voice was brisk. "Come, Susanna. Bring your clothing, and follow me."

Doing as he said, she paused on the threshold only long enough to adjust her veil. Noiselessly she glided behind him close to the wall along which they moved. She assumed he was taking her to the other end of the large stone building and was surprised when he stopped at a door only two down from that she had just left.

Her arms tightened about the possessions in her arms as Taharka opened the door and led the way inside.

three

It was dark and musty, as though the room had not been aired recently. Taharka swept the curtain aside from the window, and her quick glance recognized this room to be almost a replica of the one she had recently left, although it might be a little narrower and the passageway, if such it was, opened from the far left.

Wide-eyed, she looked at him, and he responded to her silent question. "Put your things in that basket by the door."

Nodding, she leaned over to place her belongings in the bottom of the hand-woven rush hamper, then stood back from the door as the tall servant carried in an oval tub perhaps three feet long and half that at its widest point. By the time he had set his burden down at the rear of the room, four women in plain gray tunics arrived, each bearing a large jug from which water was emptied into the bronze container.

Taharka spoke to them as a group. "That will be all for here. However, it is time to draw water for the troughs. The caravans will begin arriving soon."

Bowing toward him, they left, while Susanna stood, perplexed, in the middle of this room that was nearly as large as Jonah's whole house. "My lord?" She needed to know what was expected of her. Was she to do the laundry?

He must have recognized her uncertainty, for he spoke with a tone of reassurance. "It is all right, Susanna. I had them bring you water for bathing."

She was mortified. He must think her dirty, but she remembered telling him she had bathed yesterday. He turned toward the shelf along the back of the room and lifted the top item from a small pile. Shaking it out, he held up by its shoulders a pale blue linen tunic, which he draped across a heavy wooden table as tall as the one in his room. "This should fit you, shouldn't it? And this mantle?" he asked, displaying a dark blue garment that seemed made of unusually light wool.

A square of filmy material the shade of a clear blue sky was lifted next. "And a head covering," he continued, "and sandals for your feet."

"I'm not sure I understand . . . ," she ventured.

The right corner of his mouth turned up slightly for just a moment. "I am asking you to bathe thoroughly, including your hair. Put your sandals and all of your other clothing with the rest. With your permission they will be disposed of.

"In case your God is right in stating that leprosy can be given to others, though how or why I have no way of knowing, we will take all possible precautions. Everything you brought with you will be removed, including the dust on your sandals and on your hair. When that is taken care of, we will discuss what is to be done." Without waiting to see if she had further questions, he left the room, lowering the door curtain to give her privacy.

She walked over and pulled the window covering closed also. It was suddenly so dark inside that she wished she had asked for a lamp. However, as her eyes became used to the dimness, she slowly removed her head covering and dropped it into the basket.

Her hands moved to her waist and unwrapped the long girdle, which followed the head covering. The mantle was shrugged off, and for a moment she held it bunched up in her hands, then buried her face in its warmth. She had made this long ago with the help of her dead mother's eldest sister, so she could go to her first husband with items she'd woven the material for herself. She had been proud of producing a nearly perfect garment, although it had seemed intolerable to spend those glorious summer days closeted with a loom instead of roaming the hillsides with Jonah and Necho.

She drew in a deep breath, holding it as long as she could before expelling it. Oh, well, the mantle had served her well through these years. She held it over the basket for a moment longer before letting it drop.

Her tunic fell straight down from rounded breasts, now that she'd removed her girdle. Bending, she lifted it by its hem and, pulling it upward, inside out, stripped it over her head. Almost disdainfully she tossed it in and followed it with the right sandal and the left. If all must be given up, so be it.

Slowly she walked toward the tub. She supposed she was meant to get into it to bathe, but that did seem a terrible waste. She had heard that some Egyptians and Romans did this even two or three times a day, but it didn't seem possible. How could they feel dirty enough to take baths that often? Obviously those using water in so prodigal a fashion did not have to go to the well and carry home jugs and pitchers on their heads.

Raising one slender leg, she stepped over the side of the vessel, and the toes of her slim right foot slipped down into the tepid water. She held tightly to the metal tub so that foot would not slide as she brought her other one inside, and then she slowly lowered herself until she was seated.

A smile brightened her face, and her winged eyebrows arched upward. This was very pleasant. She reached for the square of heavy linen draped over the side of the tub and scrubbed herself thoroughly. She wasn't sure how to go about washing her hair in the tub but finally, on her knees, succeeded in getting it completely wet. She rubbed it thoroughly, scrubbing it against itself, and massaged the scalp with her strong hands. She rinsed her hair before the rest of her body and then, almost reluctantly, stood up and stepped from the tub.

With the first of several linen cloths left for her use, she blotted excess water from her hair, with the second she dried her body, and with the third she wrapped her head, turbanlike.

The linen tunic proved to be as fine as it had looked. She raised it over her head and wriggled with pleasure at its softness, as well as to help it fall downward over her still slightly damp body.

The cord tie covered with the same fabric as the tunic felt different from the wide girdle she'd always worn, but she liked the feel of it. She cocked her head to look downward as she knotted it, realizing she would be unable to carry anything within it, as she'd done among the folds of the other. If this was what she'd be wearing, she would have to design a pouch or something to hang from the belt.

She removed the damp material from her hair and reached for the stiff brush lying on the bench. It must be handy to have hair straight like that of most women she knew, for theirs did not seem to tangle as much. However, she thought as she then ran a comb through the hip-length, heavy mass, some people liked hers, and her sister-in-law had actually been envious.

What would Leah think of her being here at this inn owned by a foreigner, a Gentile? How scandalized she would be if she knew of Susanna's wasting all that water on a bath and taking it during what should be a busy time of the day.

How would Leah manage by herself with the two children? Surely she hadn't been thinking clearly, or she'd have realized how much more difficult it would be to take the children with her to the well, to the market, or to the stream when she went to do the laundry.

It had been hard enough for them to live even with Jonah there to earn money and barter, but now . . .

She pulled the window covering to one side and fastened it with the cord, then did the same at the door. Sliding into the sandals, she bent to tie their laces about her ankles. She wondered if she'd have to wear the mantle over her tunic but decided probably not, as the women who had brought water had been dressed appropriately for the heat of the day.

Looking down, she tugged the soft material over her chest so that her breasts were hidden by the fullness of the extra material.

Her hair was definitely going to be a problem. She'd neglected to bring the hardwood pins she often used to hold it in a neat coil at the nape of her neck, though even if she had, they'd have been thrown into the basket. Now she had no way of keeping her hair bound or even covered as the head covering provided was too short.

Loud voices drew her to the doorway, where she saw the first caravan arrive. She watched, fascinated, as the camels and donkeys were led to the troughs beside the well or cistern in the center of the open courtyard. Had Taharka concluded arrangements with the leader of the caravan already? Where was he? She wished she had asked him what he wanted her to do when she'd finished bathing and changing her clothes.

She had been smelling the dust, dung, and animals but suddenly caught a whiff of meat cooking and remembered she'd eaten nothing since sharing bread and a handful of dates with Leah and the children that morning.

There was confusion and activity at the huge entrance gate. A short, bandy-legged Ethiopian came in leading a huge camel so loaded with baskets and panniers it seemed impossible the animal could keep going. And yet it easily stayed ahead of the rest of the caravan, which appeared, camel by camel, followed by a motley assortment of men, donkeys, and family groups.

Taharka came to meet the black man. Each was wearing a short tunic that ended above the knee, and Susanna drew in a quick breath on noting what well-muscled, straight legs Taharka had. Most people she knew did not have more than one or two changes of garment, and, if they did, they would not be wearing short white tunics when conducting business!

Taharka and the other men were in rapid conversation involving words, inflection, and much movement of hands and arms. Although the voices were not muted, there was so much commotion with the beasts of burden and the men tending them that she could make out no words.

Finally she realized that whatever was being said was not in Aramaic or in the Samaritan dialect. Might it be Egyptian? How many languages did Taharka know, that he was able to run this inn for people not only traveling this busy north-and-south road but the east-and-west trade routes as well?

An agreement must have been reached, for the caravan master, with a sweep of his arm and a shouted stream of words, motioned his charges to enter and go to the far right end of the courtyard.

Susanna saw Taharka turn toward his office and, stepping outside, moved quickly, hugging the wall in an effort to remain inconspicuous, so they arrived at his doorway at the same time. He stepped back one pace to indicate she should enter first. She wished he wouldn't do this, for all the men she knew preceded women.

She turned to face him, hands pressed palms together in front of her. "I have done as you commanded," she said.

There was a brief pause, and she didn't know if he was waiting for her to continue. She was about to thank him for the loan of the clothing when he spoke. "That is good. Everything fits, I see."

"Yes, it fits very well. The clothing is lovely—much finer than those I had been wearing."

"And your clothing?"

"In the basket where you said it should be put."

His nod of approval was almost a little bow. "It will be removed as soon as my servants are finished with tending to the needs and accommodations of the travelers."

"My lord?"

"Susanna?"

His tone and inflection mimicked hers, and she felt a blush of confusion. However, she had to ask, "If you are speaking of taking my clothing away, does that mean I am allowed to stay?"

"Do I appear so heartless I'd steal your clothing and send you out on the streets to beg?"

She took a step forward in unconscious apology for giving him a misunderstanding of her regard for him. Her hand was laid for a moment on his bare forearm as she protested, "Oh, Taharka, I never thought you were heartless. If I had, I'd never have come to you."

Suddenly she was devastated by the enormity of what she was doing. She removed her hand from his arm as though she were burned, yet even as she did this she realized she'd have preferred leaving it there. How had she dared to reach out and touch this man? She sank to her knees before him. "Forgive me, my lord. Oh, please . . ."

Again he bent to lift her to her feet. "You have done nothing disrespectful, Susanna. I am not offended. Please, continue to be yourself, and do not be so concerned about proprieties."

The wisp of a smile crossed her eyes but did not reach her lips. "You are very kind. I will try not to make any more social blunders."

His frank appraisal of her as he stood with arms crossed and feet apart was disconcerting, but she didn't lower her eyes. "Young woman, I'm not sure what to do with you."

A set of vertical wrinkles appeared between her brows. "Could I help the women with cooking? I smelled lamb roasting, and I could help turn the spit or make bread or churn butter or—or anything else your women could use help with."

His lower lip was thrust out thoughtfully. "I have not decided how to explain your position here, so it's probably best for you to remain where you are."

"Here?" Her eyes swept the room in which they were standing.

He was looking beyond her shoulder and she became aware that another group had arrived. He started toward the door and answered matter-of-factly, "Or where you bathed."

How nice, she thought as she returned, that such a fine room could be hers. But then she paused, stunned by the possibility he might think she had come offering herself in trade for a place to stay. Perhaps that was why he was not offended at her touch. Perhaps he anticipated more than having her hand on his arm . . .

What would she do if he came to her this night expecting her to receive him with pleasure—or for his pleasure?

Maybe she should not have come after all. What did she really know of Egyptians? She'd loved Necho as a childhood friend and had come to know his father a little, but that was long ago. She was pleased he had even recognized her, but that didn't mean . . .

four

But this was foolishness, conceit, Susanna told herself. After all, he had made no untoward movements or conversation. It had not been he but *she* who'd reached out to place a hand on the other's arm. What must he think of her?

She moved around her room, examining the furnishings. Someone must have loved this place, for the hangings at the window and door were not only beautifully and intricately woven but embroidered as well, with cattle, men, women, and strange-looking long-legged birds.

Walking over to where five scrolls lay on a stand, she unrolled one so some of the handwritten words were before her. Puzzled, she went close to the window, but the late afternoon light didn't help either. Though her brother had taught her the alphabet and many words, she was dismayed to realize that nothing here looked familiar.

Slowly she rerolled the manuscript, replaced it, and picked another. A third and fourth followed, but still she found nothing identifiable. She had not realized how much she yearned to read until the final scroll revealed letters taught her by Jonah.

She hadn't forgotten. Oh, praise Yahweh, she hadn't forgotten!

Eagerly drawing a chair to the table, she followed the lines with her fingertip. Delighted, she recognized whole words, though not enough to make sense of the writing.

It had seemed to her it would be awkward to roll and unroll at the same time, but she realized with wonder that it was easy.

The passing of time was of no importance. Sounds, smells, and sights were nonexistent. She did not even hear footsteps outside her door and answered the knock on the doorpost with only an automatic, "Come in."

Because he was silhouetted by the open door, she could not discern the expression on Taharka's face, but she suddenly realized how dark it was when he said, "You need a lamp in here," and left again the way he had come. She suddenly wondered if he was offended at her looking at one of the precious scrolls. And yet, to roll it up and pretend she'd not been studying it would be a lie. She let it remain where it was on the table but could no longer enjoy it. *Please, Yahweh, let him not be angry!*

Footsteps approached down the passageway, and the light preceded Taharka into her view. She had wondered if this passageway connected the rooms and was reminded of her earlier concern that he might have her here for reasons other than just giving sanctuary and a job. However, his voice indicated none of this. "I didn't know you could read."

"Jonah taught me some of what he was learning when he went to the synagogue school, but I've had no opportunity to look at scrolls."

"I never could see why girls are not taught to read and write, along with boys." He set the lamp on the table beside the papyrus and looked at her with continued interest. "Did Jonah also teach you numbers and how to add, subtract, multiply, and divide?"

Her face lit in a smile, remembering. "Jonah and Necho and I used to play number games while running through the hills or fishing. One of us would call out something like, 'Seventeen times nine is what?' and then whoever got the answer first would get a point."

He must not have known of this, for his interest appeared keen. "And you did this also for division, addition, and subtraction?"

"It was play. Necho was maybe a little quicker than Jonah, but Jonah was always right when he gave an answer, so they got about the same number of points."

"And you?"

She grinned up at him. "I was a year younger, and they couldn't stand it if I got more points. I kept one or two less so they would let me keep going with them."

His right eyebrow lifted as he challenged, "Twenty-two plus seventy-three."

"Ninety-five," she responded immediately.

"Ninety-five divided by five."

"Nineteen."

"Nineteen plus six, divided by five, times twenty," he went on, and she knew he was using numbers he could be figuring easily in his own mind.

"One hundred."

As he came around and sat on the far corner of the table, facing her, his tunic slid upward, exposing much of his muscular thigh. She pulled her gaze back up to his face as he said, "Susanna, you are unbelievable. How are you at *writing* figures and words?"

She sighed and dropped her hands into her lap. "There was never money for paper or other writing materials. Sometimes after a rain I'd tease Jonah or Necho to help me write with a stick in the mud, or we'd write in the dust, but," she shook her head sadly, "no, I have no talent for writing."

"Not no talent, no *opportunity*," he corrected as he rose abruptly and moved toward the window. "Another group is arriving. You stay here. After I make arrangements for these people, we will continue our discussion."

Now what? she wondered. At least he wasn't upset at her knowing how to figure. It was Leah who'd stopped the number game between brother and sister when Susanna first went to live with them. Susanna had been hurt at the time, for she had looked forward to being with Jonah again after not having him around for so long. She'd hoped to renew some of the activities and memories of the good times they'd had growing up.

The game must have seemed to Leah like an effort to shut her out, though Susanna had never meant it that way and would have welcomed the opportunity of teaching her. At the mercy of the other woman, Susanna certainly wouldn't have deliberately tried to make Leah feel resentful or excluded.

But there was no point in dwelling on the past, especially with such an interesting present. There were many words in the manuscript she recognized now that she was becoming more familiar with the writer's hand, but she still didn't grasp much of its meaning. Wouldn't it be wonderful if Necho were still alive or Jonah were able to share this with her?

But Necho had been dead for many years, and Jonah was banished.

Where was Jonah, anyway? Had he made it to the colony of lepers up near the Galilean border? That had seemed the logical place to go, but one never knew if outcasts would welcome another or if he'd be cast out by them, also. Did he have enough to eat? A dry place to sleep? Was he safe from wild animals? Was he afraid?

Deborah had declared that Yahweh did indeed hear prayers by women, so Susanna folded her hands again. *Please help Jonah,* she pleaded, as she had so many times before, but without this much assurance of His hearing. *Please help the leprosy to go away from him completely, and help him to be pronounced clear of it. Let him come back to us—or at least to them,* she amended, afraid to ask too much in one prayer. If she asked just for one thing, the healing, she reasoned, her prayer would have a better chance of being answered than if she also asked to be reunited with them.

She hurt inside when she thought of the children. Little David meant everything to her and had, right from when she came. Leah had been having trouble with her second pregnancy and had to stay on her pallet for the last six weeks. In addition to caring for Leah, Susanna took over responsibility for running the house and entertaining the loving, responsive little boy.

Even though she had helped the midwife through thirty-five hours of the difficult birth, and had tended to the baby, who, though unusually large, was weak from the ordeal, Susanna had never been as close to the little girl, Mikal, as she was to David.

Would they have enough to eat? Would there be fuel for the fire and oil for the lamp?

Certainly Leah's brother, the fuller, wouldn't let his sister and her family suffer real want or destitution, would he? Anyway, Susanna scolded herself, she wasn't going to worry about it. After all, there was nothing she could do to alleviate their problems.

When he returned this time, Taharka looked pleased as he ran his right hand, fingers splayed, through his curly black hair. "That fills all the room we have for large groups, though there are still sleeping accommodations upstairs for individuals or families."

"That must be very satisfying," she ventured.

"We couldn't be better located for travelers from and to all directions." He stretched mightily, his fingertips almost touching the ceiling of the whitewashed room.

Pulling a chair to the side of the table near her, he drew the scroll forward so it could be seen by both. "Read to me," he commanded.

She gasped. "Oh, my lord! I've been trying, but there are more words I don't know than those I recognize." She was dismayed at the prospect of his learning how little she knew.

"So read those you know."

Oh, why had she ever looked at this miserable scroll? Why had she picked it up and opened it and let him see her with it and still have it in front of her when he returned?

"Susanna!"

Her pleading look was met only by firmness. Her gaze fell to the words before her, and the tip of her tongue moistened lips that felt dry and stiff. Slowly she pronounced the words above where her finger rested. "They . . . set . . . out . . . from . . ." Looking up, she whispered, "I don't know that word."

"Gilgal," he replied.

"And . . . and . . . encamped?" glancing up quickly for the assurance he gave with a nod, "encamped at . . ." There were tears in her eyes as she looked at him in despair. "I am so stupid! I don't know the next *two* words."

His hand moved to rest on her head, as gently as she would have touched David, and it was strangely comforting, almost as much as his encouraging smile and voice. "You are not stupid, Susanna. I'm sorry. This particular passage of the Book of Joshua, which my son was reading at the time of his illness, has many difficult words. Let's try it this way: we'll read it out loud together."

"Together?"

"When Necho was learning to read he used to climb up in my lap, and we'd do that. He became a very good reader," Taharka added.

She drew in a deep breath. How could she refuse such a wonderful offer? Nodding, she determined to do her very best, all the while listening to hear how to pronounce any word she did not know.

"They set out from Gilgal and encamped at Elon Morch near the city of Shechem, where they set up the tent of meeting. Then Joshua built an altar of stones on Mount Gerizim as Moses had commanded the people of Israel; and they offered on it burnt offerings and peace offerings. Fire came forth from the presence of the Lord and was consuming upon the altar. Then the Israelites sang many songs and praises.

"And the chief prince of the Levites, Eleazar the son of the priest Aaron, wrote upon the stones the law of Moses in a fine hand as Moses commanded in the book of the law, saying, 'And when you have passed over the Jordan, you shall set up these stones, concerning which I command you this day, on Mount Gerizim, and you shall plaster them with plaster.' And they set them up on Mount Gerizim as the Lord had commanded Moses."

Her eyes were sparkling in the lamplight. "That's *our* Mount Gerizim? *Our* Shechem?"

"It certainly is, Susanna." He nodded, smiling at her wonder. "And there's much, much more in this book and all the others," waving an arm toward the scrolls on the stand.

"But I couldn't read *them* at all," she confessed.

Pushing his chair back, he walked over to look at them. "You poor child, of course you couldn't. It's hard enough to learn the language one speaks without having to learn foreign tongues. This one and that are in Greek, and those others in Latin."

Her shoulders sagged with relief. "Oh, I'm glad to know that. I was discouraged when I looked first at those." And then, remembering her puzzlement as he'd spoken with a caravan master, "How many languages do you speak?"

"Everyone wishing to conduct business has to know Greek and Latin, as well as our own Aramaic," he said. "Because of my background, I know Egyptian, of course, and a smattering of several others, including some of the Canaanite and other dialects."

"How do you keep them all straight?" Her voice, little more than a whisper, showed her awe.

"One learns to think in a different way. For that matter, you usually speak Aramaic, yet I dare say you converse with the spice merchant in Koine Greek and don't get your words or meanings mixed."

"But that's only two languages."

He shrugged. "I started with only one or two, then learned the others."

There were footsteps approaching, and Taharka went to the door. One of the women who had brought Susanna's bathwater was standing outside bearing a tray. "That will be all," he said, removing her burden. "You need not return tonight for the dishes."

Bowing, the woman turned and moved off into the night.

Susanna, rerolling the scroll from each end so she could find the portion they had been reading, placed it at the far corner of the table. She arose and moved backward so he could eat first, but as he set the tray where the scroll had been and took the chair he'd used before, he invited, "Be seated, Susanna. Let's eat before the lamb gets cold."

"But, Master, it's not fitting . . ."

He looked at her quizzically. "Not fitting to eat it while it's warm?"

It seemed he was teasing, but she wasn't sure. "It's not proper for me to eat at the same table-with you, my lord."

He looked annoyed. "This is my house. Who I choose to eat with is nobody's business. So, unless you have something against me personally, please be seated here, and we'll be about our meal."

Slowly she moved forward and, sliding her hands down along her thighs to smooth her dress, took her seat. He dipped his hands into the bowl of water on the tray and dried them on the towel provided, then handed both to her. She followed his example before bowing her head.

"Are you praying?" he asked.

She didn't know how he'd react to her nod.

"What do you *say* to this god of yours?"

Was he sincerely interested, or did he regard prayer as something useless or foolish? "I always thank Him for food before I eat it," she told him.

"Whether it's good or not?"

She smiled. "Almost all food is good when one is hungry."

"Then I hope you're hungry," he stated, cutting a generous portion of meat and putting it on her plate.

"Yes, I am," she confessed. "I've eaten nothing since a small breakfast."

His lips thinned briefly. Lifting a flagon, he held it above the pottery cup. "Wine?"

"I . . . I'd prefer water," she said. "I am very thirsty."

"I'm such a tyrant you couldn't ask me for a drink of water?" he challenged.

How could she explain? "You have been so kind, my lord, and also very busy. I didn't want to bother you."

He laid his knife on the tray. "The next time you have something to say, you are to say it. If I'm too busy or there is reason to say no, I'll tell you."

Her eyes were lowered modestly. "Yes, my lord."

"Susanna! Look at me!" As her long-lashed eyes rose slowly to meet his gaze, his voice softened. "I don't mean to frighten you, Susanna, but you can be a very frustrating person. 'Yes, my lord,' 'no, my lord,' and all of that may be what you were taught and in other circumstances might not only be acceptable, but desirable, but not here.

"You were my son's best friend when he was a child. You and Jonah were closer to him than any brother or sister he might have had if his mother had lived. Incidentally, you have no idea how upset he was when he found that your father had promised you to that old man." He stopped and his mouth twisted into a wry grin. "We all thought of him as elderly, though I'm probably as old now as he was then."

"You don't seem as old as he was," she interrupted. "Your manner, your physique, your outlook on life are much more youthful than his."

"But to continue what I was saying, you never knew what Necho and I had planned just previously. I was going to talk with your father about your becoming betrothed to my son."

five

"**I** never even imagined!" she gasped.

"While yet in the planning stage, we heard we were too late. Nothing could be done except resign ourselves to hoping you'd be happy with Obediah."

"I wish that . . . that it could have been the way you and Necho planned," she said wistfully. "I never thought of him as my husband, but he was my very best friend." She drew in a deep breath and let it out slowly. "It must be wonderful to be married to a dear friend."

"Obediah was not a . . . kind man?"

She shook her head. "Neither kind nor understanding. He wanted a child, a virgin, but he . . . expected impossible things. I really tried to please and satisfy him, but I never could. Also, I found it difficult to adopt his ideas of who was acceptable—"

"Like us?"

Color stained her cheeks. "I'm sorry."

"I'll always remember his charging in here to drag you from Necho's bedside. I've never forgiven him." His brows almost met, and his jaw was squared.

The pause was broken by her admission. "I haven't, either." She remembered all too well how she had been forced to join her husband in the ritual purification for their having been in the inn of the Egyptians. She had almost hated her god for the necessity, and she had hated Obediah for it, though she'd never tell anyone of these feelings.

Did Yahweh truly consider all except Samaritans unclean? Was her being here now wrong? Certainly Yahweh knew she needed a place to spend the night. She had prayed for guidance, and this was what she had thought of. Had it been Yahweh who'd led her here, or was her thinking thus a proof of the evil one himself working in her heart?

The meal was soon over, and Taharka left, saying almost nothing more. What had gone wrong? Why, when she'd thought they were getting along well—with his helping her read the scroll and then eating with her—why had he suddenly turned cold?

Maybe it was her saying she hadn't forgiven her first husband. A good and dutiful wife wouldn't hold a grudge against Obediah. After all, the husband was the head of the household, and who was she, a mere woman, to question his actions?

But she had agreed with Taharka in what she said. She shook her head in bewilderment. She'd had five husbands in these twelve years, and each was totally different.

She hadn't understood any of them except Shannon, who had seemed to truly love and care for her. She'd felt strong affection for him in return, but he had died from a high fever near the end of their six-month betrothal, before they could come together and know one another. She had mourned for her husband Shannon as she should have for Obediah, in spirit and in truth, with ashes spread over her and with professional mourners.

What would it have been like to be one with Shannon? Would she have been able to love him as she wished to be loved? She believed deep within herself, where she had to keep thoughts like this, that marriage should be based upon love—but what was the use of even conjecturing about a good marriage?

Shannon's brother, Gabbai, had talked her into a levirate marriage after Shannon died. She wondered sometimes if he had ever truly wanted to raise up sons to his brother's line, but it was the only acceptable way of having two women at the same time. She was sixteen when he married her; his wife was in her twenties but looked much older.

At first Taphath had not seemed to mind a second wife in the household. After all, with her five living children all under the age of eight, she could use an extra pair of hands and legs!

Susanna did not become pregnant during the first weeks or even months as was expected, yet Gabbai continued to choose her so often as his sleeping companion that she dreaded nighttime. When Taphath's relief turned to resentment and finally to jealousy, he always used Susanna's childlessness as his motive, laughing about it privately to Susanna.

She certainly could not complain of his brutishness to anyone; nor could she indicate how much she wished to get out of this situation. Because a woman couldn't get a divorce except perhaps on the grounds of proven infidelity or in the event her husband had leprosy, Susanna decided to get him to divorce her.

She did her work well and in fact did more and more, until Gabbai praised her and compared Taphath unfavorably with her. And then she tried to indicate to the other woman in many small ways how happy she was with Gabbai.

Finally Taphath could stand it no longer. It was her anger and that of her family, several of whom were of high standing in the community and religious life, that pushed Gabbai into divorcing Susanna.

Jonah was able, in spite of this, to arrange for her betrothal to Elon, who, by anyone's reckoning, was not the best catch in the world. She did not relish the idea of moving from Sychar to the small plot of ground on which he raised grapes, but she hoped to come in sometimes on the Sabbath and perhaps to the market.

She resigned herself to a future with him and had even committed herself to trying her best to make the marriage a success, but this decision was taken out of her hands. On that unforgettably horrible day after her betrothal but before marriage, while by herself in the stream finishing the laundry for Jonah and Leah, she was dragged by those three terrible young strangers into the woods and raped again and again. She returned to the walled town, clothes torn, bleeding and crying—and found that, although some were kind enough to give comfort and consideration, Elon wanted nothing more to do with her.

So she was twice divorced as well as twice widowed. It was years before Abram, who had been a friend of her father, took her to wife. She knew at the time that what he wanted was a nurse, but she needed a place to live as badly as he needed someone to care for him.

There had been no love and actually little friendship, but they got along fairly well, in spite of that. As his illness became more debilitating, his disposition became increasingly sour, but at least she could look back on her activities and manner during this time with little remorse. She'd taken care of him, held her tongue, and served him well.

It was not her fault that when he died his sons sent her back to her brother with nothing. Jonah went to the priest, who insisted on their returning the ten coins that had been her dowry, but Susanna no longer even had them. She'd given them to Jonah when Leah was so sick during her pregnancy with Mikal.

She was now twenty-four years old. Who would want a woman that old when each year many young, lovely, unspoiled maidens were growing into puberty?

It wasn't fair for people to always refer to her five marriages as though she were a common harlot! She'd never even lain down with Shannon and Elon, and Obediah and Abram had both died.

Her pacing brought her to the door, and she looked out. She had been too deeply engrossed with thoughts of herself during these last minutes to give attention to the voices, sounds, and smells of the caravans and groups filling the courtyard. Stepping out into the comparative darkness, she watched with interest as the camels and asses were taken to the troughs, which were kept constantly filled.

By the light of a torch fastened to an upright post at the cistern, she discerned that the person drawing water was the woman who had brought their meal. Susanna saw her stretch her shoulders and neck after pouring another bucketful of water, then rub her right arm before leaning over the wall to refill the leather container.

Susanna ached for her, knowing only too well the pull of muscles with repeated drawing of water. Without thinking further, she moved quickly across the twenty-yard distance and touched the woman on the shoulder. "Rest awhile. I'll do this for you."

The woman, who appeared to be about fourteen, looked quickly over her shoulder. "Oh, no! The master has given me this task and I will attend to it."

"Let me help. I'll return the bucket in just a little while."

The woman relinquished the rope but was far from relaxed. Susanna was surprised that it was so short, then reminded herself this was a cistern, not like Jacob's Well, where she went when she wanted to be alone or when she felt she couldn't stand another snide remark from the women congregating at the town well. There was always the possibility the elders would be meeting at the gate she had to pass through to get to Jacob's Well, but she usually went when it was unlikely they'd be there.

She smiled to herself, realizing how much closer to that well she was now. Perhaps her work could include getting drinking water for the people, for surely they didn't drink this rain water from the roof which was collected in the cistern.

With each lifted bucket of water the woman seemed more disturbed. Finally she pleaded, "Please let me do it. I shall get in trouble . . ."

The tone of fear came through to Susanna. "Are you afraid of Taharka?"

"It would be worse if Putiel finds me not working and you doing my job."

"Putiel?"

"The big man who carried the tub for your bath."

Susanna nodded, handing the rope across. She had many questions but had no right to make queries about the master and his household. "What is your name?"

"I am Sherah," the girl replied simply, stretching over the wall. "I have worked at the Inn of Taharka for five years now, the first two when my mother was living. I stayed here after she died."

"Are you a servant or—a slave?" Susanna asked gently.

The girl's back straightened, and her head was level above her long, slender neck. "I am a free woman. The master forgave the debt of my father and freed both my mother and me."

To have come to the inn of a man this generous was a great blessing. Susanna reached to touch Sherah's arm. "I am glad for you."

Sherah ducked her head in a gesture of humility, and Susanna felt the eyes looking at her carefully in the twilight. "Yahweh has been kind to me."

Another bucketful was dumped into the trough, and then the women moved away as three men brought their camels to drink. Susanna and her new acquaintance slipped, silent as shadows, into the deeper darkness near the wall. Together they moved toward the open doorway leading from the rear of the courtyard into the area outside the thick stone walls.

A spitted sheep was being turned over one large fire, and a kettle simmered over another. Sherah smiled at the youngster who stood there faithfully rotating the sheep and indicated he should rest as she basted the meat with fat from the nearby container. Susanna's eyes followed the procedure. Only a few times in her life had there been money for a sheep. A whole sheep! Even for Passover, neighbors went together to buy one.

The savory smell tantalized her nostrils, yet she knew she couldn't possibly be hungry. The portion of meat Taharka had given her at the evening meal was larger than those she'd usually seen in the house of her brother for all of the family combined.

Taharka must be very wealthy, she thought, then realized this mutton would be sold to the hungry people from the caravans. Sherah turned to the young spit-watcher and said, "Peter, tell the caravan masters this will be ready within the hour." As the boy disappeared through the doorway, Sherah gave the sheep an additional turn. "The first one didn't last long tonight, and many travelers came after it was gone. They will relish this."

"Even though I've eaten, this smells wonderful," Susanna said. "Those who have walked so far must be almost mad with hunger!"

"There won't be enough of this roast left to make a decent broth."

Susanna helped as best she could for the next hour, then assisted as the meat was carved and placed on metal trays that servants then carried through the large doorway. Exclamations of pleasure and satisfaction could be heard from those in the caravans; she was glad the carving knives were very sharp, otherwise she would not have been ready with the next trayful by the time the empty ones were returned.

Baskets of fruits and stacks of freshly baked breads returned depleted as if by magic and were replaced with full ones. She had nearly finished the carving when she heard Taharka's voice, which carried either displeasure or surprise. "Susanna, what are you doing here?"

"I'm helping Sherah, my lord. There is much work to do." As she turned, her eyes looked into his but then dropped modestly as she lowered her head.

There was a long pause. His feet were planted wide apart, and his arms were crossed. She had to look back up and check his expression to see whether she'd done something terribly wrong.

The pounding in her chest was echoed in her head. She was trying to form words of apology when he said, "Very well. Finish what you're doing; then go to your quarters."

"Yes, my lord." She was mortified at having done something apparently so wrong on her very first day here. She was grateful Sherah was silent; Susanna didn't know what to say. They continued their work, but the camaraderie was gone. All she could think of was what he would say when she got back to where she'd obviously been expected to stay.

Sherah straightened and pulled her shoulders back as far as possible. "There! The serving is done for tonight. As soon as I clear away the bones and fat and clean up I'll be ready to go to bed also." Suddenly she turned away, but not before Susanna saw the girl's face become an embarrassed red.

She did not care to consider the reason for Sherah's confusion. "Can I help with the cleaning?" she asked hopefully.

Sherah swung around to look at her with disbelief. "You must not keep the master waiting!"

Susanna wiped her greasy hands on a scrap of cloth then washed them in the water provided. The night was warm, and there was a slight breeze coming from the west. Her hands would air-dry as she walked more slowly than usual, but with head and shoulders high, through the doorway and along the wall the way she had come.

She was nearly back to her room when a short, dark shape waddled toward her and a voice addressed her in a language she didn't know—but with a meaning that could have been no more clear. A beefy hand reached out and squeezed her buttocks, and in that split second she whirled, the straight outside edge of her left hand striking his soft belly with all the force her weight and motion could bring. "Leave me alone!" she cried.

The sharp exhalation of his breath was followed by an expletive she never wanted translated. His companions hurried over from the cistern, and in sheer panic she remembered what had happened to her six years before. She did not cringe, however, and her black eyes circled the three with contempt. "May Yahweh strike you down for your intentions!" she cried in a voice that carried ringingly across the court.

There was no rush of footsteps. Susanna didn't know where he came from, but suddenly Taharka was beside her, then a step forward, his voice hard as marble. "This is how you repay my hospitality? This woman is my guest. Leave her alone. Move to the other side of the courtyard where you belong, or get out of my inn."

One of the men said something, and then Taharka was speaking in the tongue of the three men, his voice cold as he pointed toward the gates, which had been swung shut and barred with a massive beam.

The man who had accosted her was still holding his abdomen but apparently made a countersuggestion, using a soft tone. Taharka had taken the same stance he had when he'd found her carving the meat, but seeing him now, as she pressed her back against the stone wall, she knew that his earlier mood had not been anger and suppressed violence, as was this. Each word he spoke was precise, cut off, and sharp as a blade. The men backed away. A little before they reached the cistern they turned and hurried to rejoin their companions. One of these struck the man who'd pinched her, and the voices showed temper, not teasing, as she would have expected.

Taharka strode ahead of her to open her door forcefully. He preceded her inside, then, as she went around him to stand, miserable, in the center of the room, he closed the door and turned to face her. "I . . . I'm sorry," she stammered. "When he came at me and grabbed me, all I could think of was to make him stop. I . . . I didn't mean to cause a disturbance."

The pale light from the flickering wick darkened the creases from the sides of his nose down around his mouth, and the expression of his deep-set eyes was hidden. Susanna took a step forward, hands open, palms upward, in supplication. "I didn't stop to think, Taharka. It was so like that time six years ago—but I was alone then. There was nobody to hear when I called.

"I guess—I should have known nothing would be allowed to happen here but . . . but . . ." Tears that had been collecting spilled over and ran down her cheeks. "I'm sorry."

He moved forward, and his warm, work-calloused hands grasped hers, holding them tight. "You have no need to apologize, Susanna. It was not you, but the man, at whom my wrath was directed. You have the right to defend yourself—as does any woman on my property. I thought I'd made this clear to all staying here."

"You . . . you're not angry with me?"

"Of course not." His eyes crinkled a little at the corners. "At least not about that."

"Then . . . ?"

"I didn't expect to find you with the mutton."

"I'm not used to being at leisure when there's work to be done," she explained. "I didn't know what were to be my allotted tasks. I saw water being drawn for the donkeys and camels so I went to help there—"

"So *that's* where he saw you," he interrupted. "I wondered, with it so dark along the building, how he had picked you. Doubtless he'd been waiting."

"But Sherah was at the cistern before me. It would not have been safe for her, either."

His eyes narrowed. "Sherah is not you."

"You mean that gossip about my past . . . ?"

"Of course not. You are very beautiful."

"I may have been when I was Sherah's age, but not anymore," she protested. "She has the youth and strength to draw any man."

"It was not Sherah he accosted," he reminded her drily.

"She's still working outside the rear gate. Perhaps when she comes in . . ."

"There will be no more trouble here this night. Word will have been circulated to all the caravans that I'll not tolerate such actions. There *are* caravansaries and inns that not only permit immorality but make money from it." His voice took on the same ring it had outside a few minutes earlier, "But not *my* inn!"

The tears had dried on her cheeks, and her hands had been released when they began speaking of Sherah. She turned slightly and looked around the room. A roll of padded material was lying on the bench built out from the back wall. His gaze followed hers. "That should be comfortable for you. At least I hope so. Is there anything else you need?"

"You have been very kind."

He shrugged this off. "What else do you need?"

"Nothing at all. But thank you—thank you very much."

"Very well." He reached behind himself to open the door and, turning, walked out. "Sleep well, Susanna."

"And may Yahweh be with you throughout the hours of sleep," she responded.

The door was closed, then opened again immediately. "I'm sure you'll be safe, but it is wise to take precautions. Bar your door as I leave." And he was gone.

As she fitted the heavy beam in place, she considered her situation. She still didn't know what was expected of her, but she realized suddenly that she was exhausted. She spread the sleeping roll, noting it was much more fluffy and thick than any she'd ever used. As she lay down and pulled her mantle over herself for a cover, she looked around this room she was already beginning to think of as hers. The scroll she and Taharka had been reading together still lay upon the big table in the center of the room.

How wonderful it was that Taharka had seen fit to let her stay here! She might even learn to read! She could hardly wait to actually see the words Moses had written. All her life she had heard of the Pentateuch, and portions of it were read on the Sabbath and on the holy days. Verses had been quoted to her when, as a child, she'd done something wrong.

Obediah had even used sections of the scriptures to "prove" she should have nothing to do with "foreigners."

What was a "foreigner" anyway? If Yahweh wanted people to be kind to one another and to welcome strangers and help widows and children and to be just, then wasn't Taharka more exemplary than Obediah, who, though he kept the Sabbath and followed dietary laws, loved nobody?

She tried to imagine what would have happened had someone come to him for help as she had to Taharka, and her mouth twisted in a rueful smile. He wouldn't even have let the supplicant within his door!

She rolled over. "Yahweh, do bless Taharka for his goodness," she whispered. "And help me do the proper things and not cause problems. I really did try to do right but I didn't know—I still don't know—what the right thing is. Please give me wisdom. And give Taharka patience. Amen."

six

It seemed as though she'd just closed her eyes, as though she'd only rolled over, when she heard multitudinous sounds. She looked at the window, which, though covered by the embroidered hanging, showed that the sun would be up within an hour or so.

She tossed back the cover and, springing from bed, ran barefoot across the room to draw the curtain. The courtyard was a mass of activity, with each caravan getting its camels and donkeys ready for the day's journey. Most of the beasts of burden had apparently already been watered, for the people with their stock now at the cistern were small family groups who were not important enough to go first.

It would be interesting to go out and be part of things, if only to draw water for the donkeys. However, she had learned she must wait to check with Taharka instead of deciding things on her own.

A short, dark, stocky man looked up and, seeing her in the window, raised his hand and gave a ribald laugh. Mortified, she dropped the cloth. She continued to look through it, which gave her a most unsatisfactory view of the proceedings. But at least she was hidden; it was lighter outside than in here with her one wick. Provided she remembered to ask for more oil, it would doubtless burn day and night.

Her gaze circled the courtyard, trying to see everything, and her ears strained to hear commands, encouragement, even angry quarreling. Taharka's voice was wishing a good journey to the caravan lined up and ready to pass through the huge open gates, and she knew, though she hadn't admitted it to herself before, that it was Taharka for whom she'd been looking, for whom she'd been listening. A smile lit her face, and her heart felt lighter. It was good to be here.

The first caravan moved out and then the second. Small groups, which she surmised to be made up of families, extended families, friends, or even strangers, attached themselves to the ends of caravans, for it was not safe to travel alone.

It might be interesting to go on a long trip sometime, especially if you had a donkey to ride on occasionally. She was sure she'd be able to keep up, for she was strong and active.

She had a bowl and a pitcher containing some water, but no cup. She was thirsty, but didn't want to drink the water she had if it was from the cistern. Perhaps when all the travelers had left she could ask Taharka if she might go to one of the wells and bring water for drinking.

After freshening herself at the washbasin, she ran a comb through her hair and returned to the window in time to see Taharka standing alone in the gateway, hands on his hips, chin lifted as though to greet the morning.

Suddenly he turned and walked briskly toward her, and she ran to remove the heavy bar and throw open the door. "Good morning, Taharka."

"It *is* a good morning. Everyone is on his way, and it's still a short while before the sun rises. There were no broken harnesses or sick donkeys or antagonistic groups determined to settle differences before leaving."

"I was watching as the leaders did their work. They're very good."

"They have to be, or they won't stay in business."

"But how did you so quickly transact your business—collecting payment for the time spent here and the water and food for the men and their beasts?"

"That was taken care of last evening. Most innkeepers do it in the morning, but I don't like that. There are always accusations of unfairness or of cheating in order to get out of paying for services that have already been used."

He moved a chair closer to the table and sat down. "It was hard at first to make them see that this is the way it is here, but I try to be fair and to ask a reasonable amount for accommodations, so I've reduced the haggling, which has always been accepted as a way of life. They know what to expect, as do I. Also, if there's something I need or want I often ask a caravan master to get it for me, and apply that toward his stay."

"What sort of things?" she asked, intensely interested.

"Spices, marble figurines, fine Egyptian cotton, scrolls—"

"You got some of your scrolls that way?"

He nodded. "When Necho became interested in your religion, I felt the only way to learn was to be able to read the writings of your Moses and Joshua for ourselves. So we got them."

"They must be expensive," she ventured.

"But if we were to consider giving up our old gods for a new one . . ."

"The *true* God. The Lord our God is one God, and He is the only one in all the world," she insisted.

Taharka raised one heavy eyebrow, but didn't seem annoyed at a woman's correcting or trying to teach him. "That's the hardest part of all, the putting aside of all the other gods. I have no trouble with accepting Him as a great and good god, but neither of us had reached the point of knowing He was the *only* one."

"And then Necho died," she murmured sadly.

"And when Necho died, I put away the scrolls."

"Did you blame Yahweh for that?"

"I . . . don't think Yahweh would have any reason to cause his death, but the other gods whom we'd come to neglect may have become jealous. Whatever it was or for what motive, Necho is no more."

"But he *is*," she stated. "We believe those who die will be raised again in the last days, and we believe in a Messiah who will come someday and lead us out of the terrible state in which we are now, with the Romans here as overlords."

"Is that in the Pentateuch?"

She nodded. "I know it's there but I don't know where it is. That's part of the reason I wanted so badly to learn to read— although I'd never have had the chance to see the synagogue's manuscripts, anyway," she added with a raise of her shoulders and a small, apologetic smile at her own foolishness.

An inclusive gesture took in all the scrolls. "Now your god— your Yahweh—has provided *these* for you."

"I thank Him for His goodness to me." Taharka didn't appear to be making sport of her, so she took a step forward and looked into the kind face. "And I thank you, Taharka, for your concern and generosity."

His eyes searched hers for a long moment then turned toward the table. "Sherah should be here shortly, bringing the morning meal. Tell me, are there foods you don't like or can't eat?"

She puzzled her answer. "There are no foods I'm allowed to eat that I don't like. However, I *am* a Samaritan—there are foods, like pork and shellfish, which I suppose are on your menu . . ."

He nodded. "Sometimes I serve them, but only when there are guests from foreign lands. And," he added to preclude questions, "so as not to offend the Samaritans serving me, I have these items prepared by Gentiles outside these walls and served by them on their own plates, from their own utensils."

Whether this was fully within the letter of the law she didn't know, but it was very courteous. "I'm sure your servants appreciate your thoughtfulness."

He appeared about to respond when Sherah arrived. Susanna glanced quickly toward Taharka, who said, "Good morning, Sherah. The bread smells delicious. Please put it on the table."

Sherah ducked her head in acknowledgment. After doing as she was told, she stood for a moment looking toward Taharka. "That is all for now, Sherah," he said. "You are free to go about your other duties."

The girl's gaze did not touch Susanna's face as she nodded, turned, and left the room. Susanna felt almost hurt, slighted. "Did I do something to offend her?"

Taharka unwrapped the napkin from around the hot bread and placed the basket of figs on the table so it would be equidistant from the two chairs. He indicated Susanna was to be seated, and explained, "She's not accustomed to my breaking the night's fast with a woman. She's not sure what to do or say."

Susanna hoped Taharka was unaware of the warmth in her cheeks. She became filled with a joy, a gratitude, she was afraid to examine. Taharka didn't keep a woman here with him. She was glad this was so partly because such a person might object to Susanna's presence. She knew, however, that was not her only reason.

Taking her seat, she prayed silently, then broke portions from her loaf to dip into the honey, as Taharka was doing. Honey! It had been at the end of the Passover when she'd had honey last—a special treat with the sharing of the sacrificial lambs. Now here she was—lamb last night and honey this morning! She leaned back in her chair with a sigh of contentment.

Taharka looked at her, a puzzled frown on his face. He noted her hands folded together in her lap. "You *can't* be full already."

"I feel like . . . like the Israelites must have felt after being in the desert for such a long time and then coming here—right here to this very area, to what Yahweh had told them would be a land of milk and honey." Leaning forward again, she tore off another piece of the bread and dipped it into the sweet syrup.

This would have been feast enough without the fruit, but she ate that also. Near the end of the meal she asked about her duties and checked to see where water for drinking was procured. When she found that it was, indeed, brought from the town well, she got permission to assist with carrying it.

"Don't try to do it all yourself," Taharka said when he realized this was her intent. "You have no idea how much we need, not only for those who live here, but for travelers. We provide good water and they are allowed to fill their water skins from our pots."

"May I help with the meal preparations or the cleaning?"

"Not today. Not yet," he said, shaking his head.

From this, she assumed she would soon be adding these tasks to her activities, and as the days passed, her routine became fairly constant. She carried pot after pot of water during the morning, then helped Sherah and the other servants in the evening to prepare food for the travelers.

~~~~~~

Years before, Taharka had obtained a large, smooth oblong of dark stone that he sometimes used, propped against the masonry wall of the cistern, as a messageboard. He wrote on it by pressing against it a softer, light-colored pebble.

Several months after Susanna's arrival, this rock was brought into her room, and in midafternoon the women belonging to Taharka's household were invited in for Susanna to begin teaching them the rudiments of arithmetic. Most of them could shop at the market and could bargain for the best prices, but anything beyond the simplest sums was beyond them.

So Susanna taught them first the numbers themselves and how to write them and then how to add, subtract, multiply, and divide.

Several of the older servants, though cooperative, did not cover well their resentment of this training, which they considered completely unnecessary. However, Sherah and some of the others looked forward eagerly to the lessons, and Susanna soon found herself playing the game she, Jonah, and Necho had enjoyed so many years before.

"What's two plus nineteen, take away seven?" she'd ask as she carved the lamb in the cool of the evening.

"Fourteen," Sherah would reply, eyes sparkling, but it was not long until Peter, turning the spit, was getting into the game. Several other children began coming around, and she enjoyed their enthusiastic participation.

But the time she loved the most, the part she looked forward to with an eagerness she didn't bother to explain away or hide from herself, was the period from midday to early afternoon. Each day when the sun was at its highest, Taharka would come to her door, and they would eat together the meal that Susanna had ready for them. He even told her about some of the satisfactions and frustrations of his business, the difficulties with the caravan master from Ethiopia, worry over the illness of a friend, or concern about the price of barley, which would determine how well the people of the region would fare throughout the next winter.

At first she held back, not wanting him to think she was trying to interfere, but then she realized that when she did speak— when she disagreed with him but had a good reason for doing so—he would listen to her. He asked questions and discussed things with her, not at all like Obediah, who put her in her place with a sharp reminder that he was the man of the house and she only a woman and therefore unable to understand a problem or to come up with a possible solution.

After the meal was finished the tray was removed; their hands were washed and dried carefully; and one of the precious scrolls was spread out on the table.

They were into the seventh week of reading the scriptures when they first read the Ten Commandments together.

"And God spoke all these words saying, I am the LORD your God, who brought you out of the land of Egypt, out of the house of bondage.

"You shall have no other gods before Me. You shall not make for yourselves a graven image, or any likeness of anything that is in heaven above, or that is in the earth beneath, or that is in the water under the earth; you shall not bow down to them or serve them; for I the LORD your God am a jealous God, visiting the iniquity of the fathers upon the children to the third and fourth generation of those who hate Me, but showing steadfast love to thousands of those who love Me and keep my commandments.

"You shall not take the name of the LORD your God in vain; for the LORD will not hold him guiltless who takes His name in vain.

"Observe the Sabbath day, to keep it holy. Six days you shall labor, and do all your work; but the seventh day is a Sabbath to the LORD your God; (in it) you shall not do any work, you, or your son, or your daughter, your manservant, or your maidservant, your cattle, or the sojourner who is within your gates; for in six days the LORD made heaven and earth, the sea, and all that is in them, and rested the seventh day; therefore the LORD blessed the Sabbath day and hallowed it.

"Honor your father and your mother, that your days may be long in the land which the LORD your God gives you.

"You shall not kill.

"You shall not commit adultery.

"You shall not steal.

"You shall not bear false witness against your neighbor.

"You shall not covet your neighbor's house; you shall not covet your neighbor's wife, his field, his manservant, or his maidservant, his ox, or his ass, or anything that is your neighbor's.

"And when the LORD your God brings you into the land of the Canaanites which you are entering to take possession of it, you shall set up these stones and plaster them with plaster, and you shall write upon them all the words of the Law. And when you have passed over the Jordan, you shall set up these stones, concerning which I command you this day, on Mount Gerizim. And there you shall build an altar to the LORD your God, an altar of stones; you shall lift up no iron tool upon them. You shall build an altar to the LORD your God of unhewn stones; and you shall offer burnt offerings on it to the LORD your God; and you shall sacrifice peace offerings, and shall eat there; and you shall rejoice before the LORD your God. That mountain is beyond the Jordan, west of the road, toward the going down of the sun, in the land of the Canaanites who live in the Arabah, over against Gilgal, beside the oak of Moreh in front of Shechem.

"Now when all the people heard the thunderings and the sound of the trumpet and saw lightnings and the mountain smoking, all the people were afraid and trembled; and they stood afar off . . . "

Susanna's voice had become softer and softer, until by the last word it was barely a whisper. Taharka's gaze was upon her as she raised misty eyes to look at him. "Susanna?"

"Oh, Taharka," she breathed, "isn't it wonderful? To actually read the words Yahweh spoke to our father, Moses!"

The smile appeared in his eyes before his lips turned upward. "All too soon you'll take reading for granted."

"Never!" she declared. "I could never read these scrolls with anything but awe and . . . and appreciation." Her small hand moved toward his resting on the edge of the scroll but stopped just short of it.

Then his hand covered hers, and his firm clasp flooded her whole being with warmth and security. His voice sounded husky. "Susanna, you are a joy."

She didn't know what to answer. She had so rarely received compliments that she had not learned how to respond. "You have missed having your son to read with, and now I'm here, giving you a new opportunity to read the scriptures."

His hand suddenly relaxed its grip, then moved away. He pushed his chair back from the table and stood, stretching muscles that had been in the same position for too long. "I must get back to my records. It won't be long till the first caravan arrives."

And he was gone out of the door.

seven

Sitting stricken where he'd left her, she stared at the empty doorway and then down at the unrolled scroll. Oh, how stupid she was! Everything had been so lovely, so enjoyable, until she'd brought to his mind the sadness of the loss of Necho.

Taharka must still hurt terribly to have reacted like that. *Oh, Yahweh, help him not to hurt so much. Help him get over the loss of his beloved son. He is so good, so kind. Help him, please.*

And please help me think before I speak. Help me to be a help in this household and not a hindrance. Help me to . . . to really be a joy.

Thank you for leading me here, and don't let me forget you for a single day, a single hour. Be with my brother, please, wherever he is, and let me have some word from him. Help him and heal him, so he can return to Sychar.

And please bless little David. Help him not to forget me—and, even more, help him to remember his father.

She would have continued praying except that Sherah appeared in the doorway. "Is it all right for us to come now?"

"Of course." She rolled the scroll from both ends and laid it on the corner table so that nothing could possibly happen to the precious document. Little Rachel, the daughter of Putiel, the first person she'd met when she came here, slipped in shyly. Usually she said nothing as she sank to the floor in the front row, but today she came forward.

"I found a different writing stone," she said, looking up at Susanna. "See, it's long and thin and fits in the hand just right. When I scraped it on a rock it made very light marks that are easy to see."

Susanna leaned over to kiss the pale cheek. This child never looked well. Her knees and ankles were always swollen and hot, and one leg was shorter than the other and not as well developed, which caused her to limp badly. Susanna had never seen her run as other eight-year-olds did. "Thank you, dear," she said. "I'll use this for our lesson today."

As she turned toward her flat stone she had a moment of worry. Perhaps she should have at least tested the gift before committing herself to using it. But when she wrote the first number she realized it was clearer than any made with her other pebble. She beamed at the child. "This is a great improvement, Rachel. Thank you."

The lesson proceeded without incident, and she did not have time then or for the rest of the day to think about her conversation with Taharka. By the time she went to bed she was tired and soon fell asleep.

When he ate breakfast with her the next morning Taharka seemed just as always. *Thank you, Yahweh, thank you!* she prayed silently.

That morning she decided to go to Jacob's Well for water. She did this occasionally when the weather was nice and cool or when she had some especially serious thinking to do, or as on this day, because she'd been put on the defensive while at the Sychar well that morning.

"So you're still living with the Egyptian gentile," Mara had begun with a decidedly superior toss of the head.

"I'm at the Inn of Taharka," Susanna corrected, keeping her voice even. "I work there, as do many other Samaritans."

"And you sleep there, too, I'm told."

Susanna wished there were some way she could just get away, but she kept her face and voice as calm as possible. "As do other Samaritans who work there."

"But not all of them live in Taharka's own apartment," Mara purred, her white teeth showing in her smirk of satisfaction at being able to impart this information to the other four women who had come to draw water.

Susanna had the rope, and was grateful she could keep her eyes on the work she was doing. "It is really nobody's business, Mara, but the fact is that I have my own sleeping room." She poured the container of water into her jug and lifted it onto her head.

Mara laughed shortly. "Whether the woman goes to the man or he to her does not matter. After all, we all know . . . "

Susanna looked her full in the eye. "If you paid attention in the synagogue you would know that Yahweh gave the commandment to Moses, 'You shall not bear false witness against your neighbor.' What you are saying is a lie, as Yahweh is my witness. Watch that *you* are not found sinning, Mara."

She always had to walk with head erect in order to carry the jug without holding onto it, but her shoulders were even more square than usual and her step more rapid. She had seen the dark color rising into Mara's face at being corrected, and she heard the angry voice calling after her, but she did not turn or respond. She supposed she shouldn't have risen to the bait, but Mara had been getting more and more disagreeable each time they met.

As she walked through Sychar's gates on her way to the well later that morning she wondered what Taharka would have thought of Mara's insinuations and of Susanna's response. She certainly hoped no gossipmonger would bring him word of it.

What hurt the most was that the only way Mara could have known her room was part of the three-room apartment was if somebody at the inn had told her. Who could have done such a thing? Why *would* anyone do it?

She remembered Sherah's reaction to Taharka's eating with her on the first morning she was here—but she couldn't believe Sherah would try to make trouble. Was it one of the women in her class? Might somebody resent a newcomer's being given privileges and responsibilities that others having lived there for years did not have?

Most people shared rooms. Could her being given her own be reason enough for jealous gossip?

Of course there were also those living in town but employed at the inn weaving, cleaning, grinding, plucking chickens, or doing other time-consuming work. With a toss of her head Susanna decided she'd assume it was one of them, for she couldn't bear the thought that it might be a permanent resident speaking of her this way.

Her first trip was uneventful, but when she was about to leave for more water she was delayed by Rachel, who came limping toward her to show a large splinter in the tip of the right index finger. Susanna used a small amount of wine to clean off the finger and needle, as her grandmother had always done, and then carefully worked at getting out the entire splinter. The wood had come from one of the benches outside the back wall, so it was old and weathered and kept breaking off.

"I'm sorry to hurt you like this, Rachel," she apologized, as she probed for more after the third fragment had broken.

The child held her finger steady. "That's all right. It doesn't hurt near as much as my leg does."

Susanna's gaze flew up to look into the steady brown eyes. "Your leg hurts *now?*"

Rachel nodded gravely. "Now and all the time. No more now than usual."

"But I never hear you complaining."

"It doesn't make it feel better to complain—and nobody wants to hear about how much it hurts."

Susanna's arm circled the bony shoulders. "*I* want to hear about it when it gets especially bad. Perhaps my rubbing it or putting a wrapped heated rock on it might make it feel better."

Rachel did not look as though she thought this would help, but said softly, "Thank you, Susanna."

By the time Susanna finally got the last of the splinter removed and the finger cleaned and bound with a strip of white linen, it was nearly midday. Maybe if she hurried she could get another pot of water before Taharka was free for the noon meal.

At the courtyard entrance she hesitated for a moment. It would take less time to go to the well in town, but she was not over the trauma of meeting Mara there. She turned to the right and went out through the gates.

She walked along hurriedly at first, but as she looked up at the splendor of Mount Gerizim before her, some of that feeling of peace, contentment, and awe she always received from the mountain came upon her. This is what she and Taharka had recently read about. This was the Holy Mountain.

She had never questioned any of the teachings she'd received in her home or in Sychar's synagogue, but how much more real everything seemed now! This was the mountain that had played such a part in the history of Father Abraham and Isaac and Jacob.

She was now on her way to the well Jacob himself had had dug and had drunk from, as had his livestock.

But as she came nearer her joy and peace were diminished, for a man was sitting on the curbing of the well. She hoped he'd get up and leave before she got there, but he didn't. His back was toward her as he sat, slumped slightly, obviously tired. He had probably traveled far, and now, with the sun at its highest, the heat was bothering him.

If that was the case, however, why wasn't he sitting over toward the mountain in the shade of an olive tree?

Then he turned, and she noticed the white tassels attached to the hem of his mantle. This man was undoubtedly a Galilean, a Jew. Well, that took care of several problems. Jews seldom spoke to Samaritans unless they were really hungry, in which case they might have dealings with a merchant, or, if part of a caravan, they might have to stay overnight at Taharka's inn.

But the man spoke, his voice gentle, and asked her for some water. For most people she would have complied with no hesitation, but it was unbelievable that someone from Galilee should be addressing her. She drew back and stared at him. "How is it that you, a Jew, ask a drink of me, a woman of Samaria?"

The smile that lit his strong, tanned face warmed her in some mysterious way, but the words he spoke were perplexing. "If you knew the gift of God, and who it is that is saying to you, 'Give me a drink,' you would have asked him, and he would have given you living water."

Was he an entertainer, a puzzler? She didn't want to laugh at the idea he was presenting, but she had to respond. "Sir, you have nothing to draw with, and the well is over a hundred feet deep. Where do you get that living water? Are you greater than our father Jacob, who gave us the well, and drank from it himself, and his sons, and his cattle?" That should certainly put this man in his place, for Jews revered the patriarchs as much as Samaritans did.

The Galilean did not seem angry at a woman's speaking up and saying what was on her mind. He talked to her as to an equal, as she imagined he might to a man if they were having one of the interminable discussions that took place at the gates of the town. He motioned toward the well, her rope, and water pot. "Everyone who drinks of *this* water will thirst again, but whoever drinks of the water that I shall give him will never thirst; the water that I shall give him will become in him a spring of water welling up to eternal life."

Susanna set her pot on the thick-mortared stone. What a blessing it would be not to have to put down a bucket and pull it all this way up. She had no idea what he was talking about, but it certainly sounded good to her. "Sir, give me this water, that I may not thirst, nor come here to draw."

The man was now facing her completely, his dark brown eyes reflecting the light of the midday sun. He was looking at her with a warmth, a genuineness, that made her unafraid, even though one part of her mind was telling her to get her water and leave. What would Mara say if she heard that Susanna, unveiled, was out at Jacob's Well talking to a strange man—and him a Jew?

It was as though he sensed her thinking that she shouldn't talk to him alone. "Go," he said. "Call your husband, and come here."

Aha, he wasn't so smart after all! "I have no husband," she stated.

But then she was confused and confounded, for this stranger whom she'd never seen before replied, "You are right in saying, 'I have no husband,' for you have had five husbands, and he whom you now have is not your husband; this you said truly."

He talked to her about the five men, knowing them each by name, though she was positive they had never met. She had heard of people who knew the future and the past but had never met one before. She wondered if he might be a prophet.

If he were really a prophet of Yahweh, then he should know the truth and know that the Samaritans were right in their interpretation of the Pentateuch, and, well, she'd just been reading the Ten Commandments . . .

"Sir, I perceive that you are a prophet. Our fathers worshiped on this mountain," she said, indicating the towering, sheltering mountain so near to them, "and *you* say that in Jerusalem is the place where men ought to worship." *I'd like to hear him get out of that,* she thought.

He was obviously not going to argue just for the sake of arguing, as Obediah would have done. His hand was on the top of the wall, and he leaned toward her. "Believe me, the hour is coming when neither on this mountain nor in Jerusalem will you worship the Father." And then, before she had the chance to declare that she would always worship Yahweh here, he continued, "You worship what you do not know; we worship what we know, for salvation is from the Jews."

That's not fair, she wanted to say. *Stop feeling so superior to us, especially while you are here with me, a Samaritan, at the foot of Mount Gerizim.* But that would be rude, and she did not think from the way the man looked and talked that he was trying to be insulting.

He continued, "But the hour is coming, and now is, when the true worshipers will worship the Father in spirit and truth, for such the Father seeks to worship Him."

She liked that "Father" idea. The name, Yahweh, was so holy that she didn't get the same warmth and feeling of closeness as she did when the man said the word as simply and affectionately as though he were speaking of his earthly father. "God is spirit, and those who worship him must worship in spirit and truth," he went on.

He was speaking with authority, yet in fully understandable words. This is what she had hoped for when she'd heard in the synagogue about the one who was to come. "I know that Messiah is coming (he who is called Christ); when he comes, he will show us all things."

And then, wonder of wonders, he sat up erectly, the tiredness disappearing from his face as he declared solemnly but in such a way that she felt she had to believe him, "I who speak am he."

Was it possible? Could he *really* be the One that all of the descendants of the patriarchs had been awaiting? Not knowing what to do or say, she half turned away and saw four men coming from the direction of the city. They also were Galileans, as shown by their clothing and the dialect they spoke with one another.

They looked perplexed or at least surprised to see their friend in conversation with Susanna, and she in turn realized she shouldn't stay alone with all of them.

Besides, suppose this *was* the Messiah. He'd told her to get her husband (knowing that she didn't have one), but there was someone she wanted very much to meet him. In fact, she realized as she found herself running back toward Sychar, there were many who should meet him.

By the time she got to the town gate and then to the inn, she was breathless. "Oh, Taharka!" she cried, hurrying to him as he stood outside the door of his room. "I just met someone who is a prophet at least and maybe even the Christ. He and some of his friends are out at Jacob's Well."

His look was indulgent, as though she were a child. "Susanna, how could you tell that in so short a time?"

She had not meant to get into this but had to now. "He told me all that I ever did."

He frowned thoughtfully and asked a few more questions. Finally he said, "If he's all you say, I suppose I should at least check."

"Oh, he's all I said and much more! He's wise and has a nice way about him, like you, about not looking down on me just because I was born a woman."

His right eyebrow lifted in that little way it had. "By the way, where is your water pot?" And then he laughed aloud at her astonishment that she didn't have it with her.

"I must have left it there. Can you believe that? I was so excited and wanted so badly for you to meet him that I completely forgot the water I'd gone all that way to fetch." She shook her head. "I've never done that in my life!"

"I'm sure you haven't. After all, that's a good mile or mile and a half to the well and back."

"Oh well, I'm returning just as soon as I tell some of the townspeople about him and invite them to meet him."

Taharka did not wait for her to join him. He called Putiel, and the two strode off toward the west. For a fleeting moment she wondered how the Jew in his full-length flowing garment of natural linen would regard the tall Egyptian in his short, belted tunic and the equally tall servant clad in a loincloth.

Somehow she felt they wouldn't be judged, but would be welcomed as friends. Yes, in spite of her skepticism and her arguing, that's the way he had made her feel, not only as though he wished to be her friend, but that this had already been accomplished.

"Sherah," she called, "I'm going to town to tell people about a man I met out at Jacob's Well, and then I'm returning there. Would you like to go with me?"

The girl looked startled, as she had every right to be. Susanna never went anywhere but to the market or to the wells and had never asked Sherah to accompany her on frivolous jaunts. "I would like that," Sherah said, smiling.

eight

At first people did not seem interested in Susanna's account of the stranger, but when she'd told about his speaking to her of her past, many grew eager to meet him. She suspected most were going solely to be entertained, but getting them to meet the man was her goal. He could take over from there.

By the time she and Sherah started from town there was a small stream of laughing, talking people flowing from the gates of Sychar toward the foot of Mount Gerizim.

Oh, thank Yahweh, the Galileans were still there! She'd been afraid even while encouraging people to go that the men might have left.

When she pushed through those near Jacob's Well she heard one of the man's companions call him "Jesus." *What a lovely name,* she thought, *Yahweh saves.* Looking around at the faces, she realized she was seeing something unusual in these troubled days—hope.

Jesus' speaking with ease and familiarity made her forget almost at once that his Aramaic had an accent. He was speaking of water and the value of it to all of them. He continued with the thought he had shared with her earlier, but she still didn't fully understand the idea of "spiritual water." Maybe her difficulty was because she had arrived late. Perhaps Taharka could tell her later what it was all about.

Jesus then spoke of the waters of baptism, and one of his followers standing beside her nudged his friend. "I wish we'd been with the Master when He was baptized, Andrew!"

The swarthy, muscular man answered, "I was, you know. I was John the Baptist's disciple then and was at the Jordan River helping him. I actually saw the heavens open and the spirit of Yahweh, like a dove, descending and alighting on Him. And I heard the voice from Heaven saying, 'This is my beloved Son, with whom I am well pleased.'"

Susanna shivered, even in the hot Samaritan sunshine. She looked steadily at Jesus, who was speaking with such conviction and with such an interesting message that many among the listeners seated themselves in the dusty road and on the bits of grass that had survived the nibbling of donkeys and goats traveling these busy roads.

Where had Jesus come from? South from Galilee? North from Judea? West from the Jordan River? East from the Great Sea? She looked up at Mount Gerizim, rising eight hundred feet before her, and at Mount Ebal to her right. She was at a major crossroad geographically. Might she also be at a crossroad in history? If this was truly the Messiah, the Son of Yahweh, as Andrew had said, the world could never be the same again.

Could it?

Several hours passed, and a few people left, some returning with friends and relatives. There was little restlessness, but Susanna wondered how some of the older or more frail among the crowd stood the heat.

An elderly woman seated on the ground near Susanna mopped her face on her tunic and appeared faint. Susanna edged her way around the disciples and went to the side of the well where she'd left her leather water bucket and rope. Silently she lowered and filled the bucket then brought it back up to the top. A dipper was lying on the well's coping, so she took that and moved quietly around the periphery of the crowd until she could kneel beside the old woman. "Here, drink this," she whispered.

There was no hesitation in accepting the water, and the woman drained the cup. After handing it back, she covered Susanna's hand with her wrinkled one. "Thank you, my dear, for the drink and for your thoughtfulness."

In only a few minutes the cup, dipped into the water again and again by others who were equally thirsty, depleted the supply. Susanna held the empty container on her lap and paid full attention to Jesus again.

With dismay Susanna saw the man named Andrew move close to Jesus. "Master, it's still a long way to Cana. We should be on our way."

Jesus smiled His thanks for the reminder as He rose to His feet and stretched to a height even greater than that of Taharka or Putiel, who had remained standing. He was obviously about to make His farewells, and Susanna felt suddenly bereft.

However, Taharka moved forward, bowed slightly, and said, "Your words and presence have been a blessing to us, and we'd like

You to stay in Sychar. If You would be willing to accept, I would gladly share with You the hospitality of the Inn of Taharka."

A murmuring began among the crowd. Susanna was unsure whether it was at the generosity of the offer or annoyance that the first to come forward had been an Egyptian. However, there was no time to consider the matter further as the smiling Galilean grasped Taharka's hand. "We'd be pleased to come with you."

Andrew also began talking to the two men. Taharka turned and beckoned to Susanna, who immediately rose and went to them. "Andrew, this is Susanna," he introduced. "You two please go make things ready on the gallery for Jesus and His followers. We'll be there soon."

How grateful she was for the opportunity to serve Jesus in this way! Her eyes met those of the teacher and found them smiling down into hers. She knew He had seen her earlier kindness toward the elderly woman when He murmured, "A cup of water given to a thirsty neighbor is a wonderful gift." Although the words filled her with a feeling of joy and wholeness, she knew that few others would have heard.

Starting to leave with Andrew, she was suddenly struck by the enormity of a previous omission. She turned back quickly to say, "Oh, Master, I never gave You the drink You asked for, and that was hours ago!"

As she hurried to the side of the well and again lowered her water bucket on the rope, He followed. "It is all right, Susanna. I have food and water of which you do not know."

Looking around, perplexed, she saw that nobody else had a rope with which to draw water. He went on, "Continue to fill your water pot, and take it with you. I shall drink water with you and the household of Taharka when I get there."

She'd have liked to ask what He meant about having food and water of which she did not know, but she couldn't do that in front of all these men and women. However, she did question Andrew as they walked side by side instead of him first and her bringing up the rear.

He chuckled, a friendly, wholesome sound. "Sometimes what Jesus says has two levels of meaning. Apparently He spoke to you earlier about water?"

She nodded and said sadly, "Which, because of our discussion and then my running back to Sychar to bring people to see and hear Him, I forgot to give to Him." But then her face brightened. "Maybe He was telling me He already has what He offered to me—living water."

Andrew nodded. "And I believe He was also reminding us disciples of something else. We had gone to Sychar to buy food, leaving Him at the well where you met Him. When we got back, Nathanael took the bread, cheese, and fruit to Him, saying, 'Rabbi, eat,' but Jesus told us the same thing he told you. We wondered if you had given Him food, but Jesus, who seems to know what's in our minds all the time, said, 'My food is to do the will of Him who sent Me, and to accomplish His work.' We talked about this for a while, and then, just as the first of your townspeople started this way, Jesus said, 'Do you not say, there are yet four months, then comes the harvest? I tell you, lift up your eyes, and see how the fields are already white for harvest. He who reaps receives wages, and gathers fruit for eternal life, so that sower and reaper may rejoice together. For here the saying holds true, One sows and another reaps. I sent you to reap that for which you did not labor; others have labored, and you have entered into their labor.'"

"I don't understand that," Susanna confessed, looking around at the fields of wheat rippling in the afternoon breezes. "The reapers cut the grain when it is ripe and then, following the drying period, thresh it. There is rejoicing, of course, at the time of harvest. But what did he mean about *your* reaping?"

"He wasn't speaking of the actual fields of wheat. He was not looking at *them* but at the people streaming from Sychar. Most were wearing natural-colored tunics like yours, and the women had on light head coverings. The flow of the people was almost like the rippling of golden wheat. Jesus is always much more concerned with individuals than with *things*."

They walked a short distance in silence. "How did you find Jesus, Andrew?"

"My brother and I had a fishing business at Bethsaida along the north shore of the Sea of Galilee. I began hearing a lot about Jesus' cousin, John, who teaches, preaches, and baptizes, and went to Judea with a group from Galilee to hear and learn more about him. I was so impressed with his words and work that I stayed and became his disciple. But then, after Jesus came and was baptized and John the Baptist proclaimed Him to be truly the Son of God, I followed Him instead."

"Is that when the other three men also joined him?"

Andrew smiled. "I was so excited that I had to share the good news. I went to my brother, Peter—the big man with the shock of reddish brown hair—told him I had found the Messiah, and then took him to meet Jesus. Peter was as impressed as I was, so we stayed with him. It was after we returned to Galilee that He found our friend Philip and asked him to join us. And Philip was the one who brought Nathanael."

"You appear to be so . . . happy," she ventured.

"I am. Very happy," he acknowledged. "I'd thought I was before, but it was never like this."

"Where do you stay?"

"Wherever Yahweh directs us. We sometimes spread our mantles under a tree or in a cave, but if we're in Nazareth we sleep at the home of some relatives of Jesus. If we're near Bethsaida, relatives of mine make room for us. If we're at Jerusalem or Bethany, friends there make us welcome."

"And when in Sychar," she continued, "at the Inn of Taharka."

He agreed readily. "Every morning and throughout the day Jesus asks Yahweh's guidance and help, and then He acts upon it, no matter what the consequences."

Susanna thought there was special emphasis on this last phrase. "Has something happened that made you say that?"

He hesitated. "Well, yes, but as it had to do with the Temple in Jerusalem, it would be of little concern to you." He turned around to look up at the top of Mount Gerizim. "*Your* temple was up there, wasn't it?"

For a moment the old bitterness filled her. "Nothing remains of it—not even what was left after your John Hyrcanus destroyed it!"

His face showed the genuineness of his words. "I'm sorry about that. I really am."

"What right did he have to tear it down?"

He struggled to explain. "There were wars going on, caused by old hatreds, treachery, and misunderstanding between Judea and Samaria. The Maccabees had really done a lot of good in many ways. John was one of the last of these, and I guess he felt, or hoped, at least, that if there were only one temple then perhaps all the children of Israel might be able to get back together again . . . "

"Not when he destroyed this most holy place, which is where Yahweh ordered us to worship Him forever! And where all of us *did* worship until Eli moved the Ark of the Covenant to Shechem, and then David took it to Jerusalem."

"War does terrible things to people and places." He sighed. "Perhaps one of the things I like so much about Jesus is that He is a man of peace."

Susanna and Andrew walked through the gates of Sychar and from there to the inn's courtyard. "He never gets angry?"

"I've seen Him angry only once, and that was in the Temple at Jerusalem, the incident I had not planned to mention. I don't know whether this was done in your temple or not, but in ours there are money changers and sellers of oxen and sheep and pigeons—for the sacrifices, you know.

"Well, when we went up to the Temple for Passover you should have seen the place! The smell was of the barnyard, and the bleating, mooing, and cooing of animals and the shouts of those trying to get the worshipers to buy animals from *them* instead of from someone else made a terrible commotion. Jesus was so indignant when He found some of the businessmen being dishonest in their dealings that He made a whip of cords and drove out the money changers and the livestock and those selling the animals—"

Spontaneous laughter filled her. "Oh, I wish I could have seen that!"

"If so, you could have also seen Him overturning the tables of the money changers and pouring out the coins onto the floor, so that those coming back in had to scramble all over trying to collect their money. They were so busy fighting one another, trying to make sure they got all that was theirs, that they didn't turn on Jesus, as I feared they would."

"Did He say anything?"

Andrew's hand came up to rub the side of his cheek and down along his curly light brown beard. "He told them, 'Take these things away; you shall not make my Father's house a house of trade!'"

She removed the pot from her head and poured the precious water into the large earthenware container from which the drinking water would be dipped. "Wasn't there opposition?"

"Oh, yes, of course, but not all I expected. I thought they would physically drag us from the Temple, but, instead, they argued wrathfully."

"Didn't they ask by what right He did this?"

"They asked Him to show them a sign to prove He had the right to act as He did."

Andrew's forehead wrinkled as he apparently tried to puzzle something out, and she nudged him impatiently. "And then what?"

"He told them something I don't fully understand yet. He said, 'Destroy this temple, and in three days I will raise it up.'"

"He'd rebuild that whole temple in three days?" she repeated. "It's taken many years to build."

"That's what they said: forty-six years so far and it's still not completed. However, He told us later that what He was referring to when He quoted this from the scriptures was His own body—that He would rise again from the dead."

None of this made sense to Susanna, but she had no more time for discussion. Sherah hadn't come back yet, so she hurried out to check the ovens, the grinding of grain, and the cooking of the spitted sheep. Returning to Andrew, she led the way to the stone steps from the courtyard up to the gallery.

She didn't often have occasion to come here, for hired servants arriving each morning had the responsibility of cleaning up after the travelers. "Actually, it's cooler up here than downstairs at night," she told him. "There are windows on the inside and outside, as you see, and there are few partitions to block the refreshing evening breezes."

She unrolled sleeping mats on the floor. "There are just five of you?"

He nodded. "As of now, although I understand Jesus plans to choose more."

"I wish I were a man," she said wistfully.

"There must be many times when it's difficult being a woman, whether you're a Samaritan or a Jew," he said sympathetically.

She nodded. "But I meant that, if I were a man, I would ask to serve Him."

His smile was encouraging. "There are many ways of serving, Susanna. It can take the form of spreading the sleeping mats, of giving a drink in the Master's name, or of healing someone of an illness."

"*You* can heal?"

"Not yet," he admitted, shaking his head. "However, Jesus has been talking about this. I think—I *believe*—He will give us this power."

There were many voices approaching, and Susanna made out those of Jesus and Taharka. "I must go down. There is much to be done."

Jesus did not go up to rest as she had expected but instead seated Himself on a bench, those who followed Him here crowding around to listen to His teaching. How she wished she were free to sit there on the cobblestones and drink in His words, but Taharka was His host, and she'd see that the cooking and serving were taken care of properly.

There was no freedom for Taharka to hear what was being said either, for the caravans had arrived and he had to make financial arrangements and assign groups to their areas for the night.

It was not until after the evening meal when people were preparing for sleep that Susanna remembered she had eaten no lunch or supper. Still, she'd not been hungry. Might this be what Jesus meant when He spoke of having food and drink of which others did not know?

Meeting Jesus and hearing even those portions of His talk as she'd been able to catch was better than honey in the honeycomb and better than the choicest figs.

She smiled to herself as she returned to her room, washed, and stretched out on her mat. She was almost asleep when she realized that she and Taharka had not had their usual reading of the scrolls, nor had she taught the women arithmetic. She yawned sleepily. These had been the highlights of her days, but compared with meeting Jesus, they seemed unimportant.

nine

Taharka didn't eat breakfast with her, but she saw he was with the Galileans, so she could accept her disappointment. However, when the midday meal was about to be served and she still had had no opportunity of being alone with him, she felt a little hurt.

It was she who carried trays of food to those in Taharka's office. As she returned later for the dishes and to ask if anything more was desired, Andrew was inquiring, "Taharka, might there be somebody willing to take me to the top of Mount Gerizim? I've always heard of it, and, if you think the people wouldn't be offended at me, a Jew, going there, I would like to do so."

Taharka turned to Susanna. "*Would* there be objections?"

She shook her head. "What's in a person's heart determines if such is a sin. The priests could not fault somebody's going for understanding. And, besides, the Romans are already there."

Andrew turned to Jesus. "When do we leave for Galilee?"

"We'll start in the cool of the morning."

"So soon?" Susanna asked in dismay. "I was hoping . . . I mean, I would like . . ." She stopped in confusion. It was not her place to interrupt the men's conversation, and certainly it was improper to express displeasure with plans made by them. She had done it again—spoken without thinking! She bowed her head, small hands clasped before her. "I'm sorry. Forgive me."

There was silence until she looked up at Taharka, whose gaze was on the tall Galilean. Immediately she looked toward Him also, expecting displeasure or disapproval. However, there was a gentle smile on His face, and His large brown eyes seemed to be looking into hers with affection. "We have much to thank you for. Without you we would not have been welcomed into your town, nor have been made comfortable in these accommodations. It is blessed to receive strangers in the name of the Lord."

She didn't know what to answer. She did feel blessed, but how could she tell Him that? Fumbling for a different topic of conversation, she turned to Andrew. "If you are leaving tomorrow, we will have to climb Mount Gerizim right away, this afternoon—if you wouldn't mind the midday heat."

"I'm used to being out in it," he stated. "But, did you mean you would go with me?"

"If you wouldn't object to being accompanied by a woman."

Andrew looked questioningly at Taharka, who asked, "You're sure you want to, Susanna? You know I would not ask that of you."

The smile covering her face warmed her whole body. "I'd like to. When Jonah, Necho, and I were children, we climbed up so often . . . " And then, seeing Taharka's face cloud, she was unable to finish the sentence. Oh, why did she have to mention Necho, knowing his father still grieved for him?

Andrew was already standing when Taharka reached for the skin container on his table. "Here, take this with you. That's a steep climb, unless you go by the easier road on the far side of Shechem."

His personal container was always kept filled with fresh water. Reaching for it, Susanna said, "Since we don't have much time, it is probably best to go the shorter way."

Leaving the inn with Andrew, she couldn't help glancing around. She'd rather not be seen with the stranger, but, regardless, she straightened her shoulders in confidence Yahweh knew this was honorable.

Please, Yahweh, let our visit to Mount Gerizim be meaningful for Andrew. Make him appreciative and understanding. Help me to explain things properly, so he will learn the truth about us Samaritans.

She had to walk rapidly to keep up with this long-legged man who seemed genuinely impressed that the well they were passing was the very one Father Jacob had dug so many centuries ago. And there to the right, only a short distance north, at the foot of Mount Ebal, was the tomb of Joseph.

There was awe in Andrew's voice. "I remember from my days in the synagogue school that Moses and his followers returned the bones of Joseph from Egypt to the Promised Land."

"And *this* is where they are buried," she affirmed.

Continuing westward, he motioned toward the valley running east and west between the mountains of Gerizim and Ebal. "What a beautiful area!"

"As you see, olives and figs grow in abundance, along with almond, mulberry, apricot, and other fruit trees. And look at all those vineyards," she added with a sweep of her hand. "Everyone has a garden and each fragment of land is cultivated."

"I've heard this is one of the most fertile areas in all of Palestine."

"I have not traveled much," she said, trying not to show the burst of pride his admiration gave her, "but I know that those stopping at the inn comment upon the beauty and productivity here."

As they crossed a small stream she indicated the steep path rising before them. "Would you rather go the extra mile or so around the side of the mountain to make the less difficult climb?"

His manner was youthful and eager. "I'd prefer using the path you took as a child."

Susanna started to lead the way, but it wasn't long before she realized his preceding her was an advantage. "I wasn't wearing the long dress of a woman when I did this before," she said ruefully, as she again released her hem from some briars. A little later she was grateful when he reached back to take her hand as the smooth leather sole of her sandal slipped on a rock.

Breathless from exertion, she momentarily leaned against the gigantic wall of huge stone blocks that surrounded the summit, and then they continued to circle to the right. "The Romans have rebuilt the wall that John Hyrcanus and your Maccabees destroyed when he pulled down our temple."

A dark shadow of pain crossed the strong face, and she felt sorry she'd worded that like an accusation against all Jews. Her gaze, avoiding his, looked downward along the windswept mountainside devoid of habitation.

A few minutes later they came to the well-made road leading up from the north and waited for a Roman chariot and some horsemen to pass before entering between the massive wooden gates of the city. Andrew breathed softly, "It's beautiful! I had no idea . . . "

"Herod the Great used many of the cut stones from King Omri's palace, our Temple, and other structures here in order to make this city he named Samaria-Sebaste. It didn't matter to *him* that he covered our Holy Place with his temple dedicated to a Roman god!" She turned toward the right, "As you see he also built shops and a theater and, over there, the forum and stadium."

Standing side by side, they continued to survey the busy scene. She tried to see it from his viewpoint—undoubtedly it was a triumph of engineering and beauty. To her, though, the Temple of Augustus, with its massive colonnaded court and worldly glory, didn't represent beauty or majesty. It was a curse, as was the palace.

She moved closer to the Roman temple, pausing to remove her sandals. Andrew did likewise, though he looked at her questioningly. Her voice was hushed. "This is where *our* temple was," she said. "Over toward the north was the courtyard; this section was the temple itself."

She shook her head sadly, "I'm not sure exactly where the foundations were, for everything was destroyed."

Her pulling up of her head covering was not because of the soft breeze wafting over them in the hot sunshine, but to show her humility before God. "The whole top of this mountain has, from ancient times, been the sanctuary of the Most High. Here was the altar upon which our sacrifices were slain and burnt, and I *think* the cistern where the blood and entrails were put is over there."

Turning to face him fully, she explained, "It was here that Father Abraham prepared to sacrifice his son, Isaac, and this is the Bethel of Jacob, where heavenly messengers visited and talked with him."

They took a few steps westward, and Susanna looked around to make sure she was not observed as she indicated a line of rock slabs. "And this is Aasher Belatat."

He obviously didn't understand the significance. "Would you tell me about it?"

How was it possible that Jews would not be taught these important things concerning their heritage? "Do you remember when Joshua led the Israelites across the Jordan River after they had wandered through the wilderness for forty years?"

On seeing his nod, she continued, "As the priests carrying the Ark of the Covenant stepped into the Jordan, the water flowing down from the Sea of Galilee, over there," pointing eastward, "started to pile up in the river higher and higher right there at the place known then as Adam. Not only did the water stop flowing, but the muddy ground became firm. The priests were told by Joshua to walk to the center of the riverbed and remain there until everyone got across.

"Joshua then commanded a representative of each of the twelve tribes to pick up a boulder from the center of the river and carry it across on his shoulder. When everyone got to the other side,

Joshua used the rocks to build an altar, and he let them stand as a memorial so that down through the centuries whenever anyone saw them they would remember that Yahweh truly led His people back to the Promised Land as He had promised He would."

Her companion looked confused. "Wasn't that at Gilgal?"

"It was at first, so they could worship right away. But then the stones were brought here, as commanded."

"As commanded?"

"In the Tenth Commandment that Yahweh gave to Moses," she reminded. How could he forget one of the Ten Commandments?

Puzzled, he looked from her to the row of stones and then back again at her. "The tenth concerns not coveting—"

"I'll show you the scroll when we get back to the inn. It's stated very clearly that Yahweh wants us to worship Him *here* and has wanted it right from the beginning. So they started just as soon as possible, with the Jordan rocks being brought here."

He touched with his toe the edge of one of the flat stones lying flush with the ground. "*This* is one of the rocks?"

No wonder he appeared skeptical. She apologized, "I'm sorry that for your first visit you don't have one of our priests or someone who could explain these truths better. No, *that* is a dressed stone, from some previous ruin, no doubt. Sometime in the past, during one of the sieges, the memorial stones were buried in the sacred soil here and covered with these close-fitting stones in order that they would not be removed."

He nodded slowly, but she didn't know whether he fully believed or understood her explanation.

How could she emphasize for him the importance of this mountain as *the* High Holy Place? "Andrew, do you know the Thirteen Names?"

"I—I'm not familiar with the term."

"Our sacred mountain has thirteen names by which it is called," she said, then recited, counting them on her fingers to make sure she included all of them: "Bitel—the house of God, Bitelwem—house of Yahweh, Ar Akkedem—the old mountain, Ar Garizim—commandments, Ar Anala—*my* mountain, meaning Yahweh's mountain, Gabat Olam—mountain of the world, Luza—Luz or Bethel, Elwem Yereh—Yahweh will see, Makdas—sanctuary, Ad Arem—the *one* mountain, Amakom umeber—the chosen place, Ar Ashekinah—mountain of the presence, and Ar Amaneuh—mountain of gift."

"That's impressive!"

"Our holy mountain *is* impressive!"

"Are all those names from the Scriptures?"

"Oh, yes. The priests could tell you exactly where to find them. Taharka has scrolls, and I recognize some of the passages when I come to them in our reading, but I don't know which are those used by our priests for the list."

Hardly conscious of the people surrounding them, they walked together around the summit, through the carefully guttered streets lined with homes and shops, and out toward the semicircular open-air theater and the huge rectangular stadium, with its oval track and rows of seats.

Finally they climbed steps to the wide, flat top of the city wall and looked westward toward the late afternoon sun. She pointed with her right hand as she placed her open left one above her eyes to shield them from the glare. "Way out there beyond the Plain of Sharon is the Great Sea. There, see the flash of white sails? Perhaps that's a ship coming from Rome or Greece or maybe Egypt."

She turned toward her left. "And there is the coastal area of what used to be known as Philistia, and then all of Judea." She smiled at her companion. "I'm grateful this is such a clear day, for you can make out Jerusalem down there, about thirty miles away."

"I'm not sure . . . ," he began hesitantly. Then, sighting along her extended arm, he said with excitement in his voice, "Oh, yes, *there* it is." In his face was the same reverence for his holy city that she held for hers. "I wish I could show Jerusalem to you," he said wistfully. "It is so beautiful and wonderful and . . . and . . ."

"And your temple is still standing," she finished, but this time she could say it without bitterness.

"Thanks to Herod," he agreed. "We're not happy being under the yoke of the Romans, but they have done some good things, like rebuilding the Temple and making roads, which are opening travel throughout the country—*all* the country of Palestine."

What he said was undoubtedly true, but it hurt too much to agree while standing on the top of Mount Gerizim in what was now a Roman city instead of a Samaritan worship center. With a sigh, she turned farther toward her left, indicating the great Salt Sea. From where they stood, the city hid most of the Jordan River and valley, but they could see the upper portion of the Sea of Galilee.

It was his turn to tell about the area they were looking at. "That's where I'm from," he reminded her. "From the northeast end of the sea, at Bethsaida. I've always loved the water and the mountains surrounding it and the people and the fishing . . ."

"Do you miss it greatly as you travel with Jesus?"

Andrew nodded. "Of course. But I miss my family most of all. My mother is a widow and has stayed with me since my wife died in childbirth five years ago." A cloud crossed his expressive face but passed almost immediately. "She's a wonderful woman and was as attracted to Jesus as I was, right from the start. In fact, she was at the wedding of my nephew at Cana where Jesus performed His first miracle."

Susanna remembered hearing of Jesus' healings and asked if that was a miracle of healing. "Not that time," he answered. He went on to tell of more people coming to the wedding than anticipated and, staying longer, drinking all the wine. The family was distressed, for it was disgraceful to run out of refreshments before the end of the celebration.

"When Jesus' mother, Mary, learned of the problem, she went to her son for help. It was she who told the servants to do whatever He commanded them, no matter what that should be. He had them fill six stone jars with water—a total of about ninety or a hundred gallons."

"And then what happened?"

"Just as soon as the servants had the jars filled to the brim, Jesus told them to pour some out and take it to the steward of the feast. When that man tasted it he was amazed that this wine was superior to what had been served previously. In fact, he called the groom over and commented that whereas most people use the best wine first and then, after the guests are partly inebriated, bring out the cheaper variety, in this case the opposite was true."

"How did He *do* that?" she asked, brow furrowed.

Andrew raised both hands and spread them, palms up. "How does Jesus do *all* of the things He does? I think you knew the answer to that yesterday."

Looking from his hands to his face, with its calmness and strength and yet with its own glow, she asked, "Is He, Andrew? Is He *really* the Messiah? Is He the Savior of the world?"

"What do you think, Susanna?"

She looked off toward the Great Sea; then she nodded, and her gaze turned to meet his. "Yes, Andrew. I believe that."

Reaching out to hold her small hands between his, he stood with her on the wall surrounding the ruined temple to Yahweh on top of the Holiest Mountain in the World, a Jew and a Samaritan, a man and a woman, together in their belief in and love for Jesus as their Savior and Messiah.

ten

Susanna almost came to a stop as she and Andrew passed through the gate of Sychar on their way back to the inn. "What's happening?" she asked, her hand unconsciously on his sleeve at seeing the crowd surrounding the inn's entrance.

A caravan consisting of eleven camels, a large number of donkeys, and uncounted men, women, and children was struggling to get through the throng. The caravan master and drivers were cursing, shoving, and threatening dire consequences if they were not allowed into the courtyard.

"They've discovered the Lord is here." Andrew's voice was quiet, but his face and the tenseness of his arm muscles indicated his excitement. She looked at him with amazement as he continued, "Those people here last night have told others!"

She glanced over her shoulder to note the position of the sun in the clear, royal blue sky. "Oh, dear, I've stayed away much too long!" She hurried forward, skirt swishing about her ankles, long brown hair flung free by her quick motion. Wriggling her way between tightly packed bodies, she hardly heard what people were saying until Mahlon's name was mentioned "What happened to Mahlon?" she asked Judith, a townswoman standing nearby.

"Didn't you see, Susanna?" the seventeen-year-old cried eagerly. "He had a fit, a spell like he has sometimes."

Susanna felt great compassion. How awful for it to happen again—and here in front of all these people!

Judith was not finished. "Jesus walked over to Mahlon, reached down and took his hand, called him by name, and told him to be healed. The evil spirit left him. Immediately he was calmed and got up and—*look* at him!" she commanded, pointing to where he now stood, directly in front of Jesus.

Mahlon had grown to adulthood a few years before Susanna, though his mind seemed that of a child. She used to be afraid of him, for he lived in a world nobody else could enter and he talked to invisible beings.

The familiar glazed look was gone from his eyes. Even his tattered clothes and unkempt hair could not detract from his now being an erect, attractive man, apparently as sane as anyone there.

She stared at Jesus, her whole being filled with awe, with wonder. Then she slowly turned toward Andrew who still stood on the outer fringe of the crowd. Her eyes met his. He, too, must have heard the news, for he was smiling with that same pure joy she had noticed before. Her eyebrows raised in question, and he nodded one time, very slowly, but with an assurance she could not doubt.

She wished she could ask him the same question she had so recently, concerning the changing of water into wine. But then, seeing the adoration with which Mahlon looked at the Galilean, she realized she didn't care *how* it was accomplished: it was enough that Jesus had the power and the generous spirit to do this.

And Mahlon was a Samaritan! Just like her . . .

She must not tarry, though she wished she could stay to hear Jesus' messages. Reluctantly, but with a sense of duty, she forced passage into the enclosure.

Taharka was talking to the leader of the caravan but beckoned to her. "I'm glad you're back." His voice was brisk, though not resentful, as far as she could determine. "There's apt to be more people for the evening meal than we had expected. Would you make sure there will be enough?"

She had wanted to share with him the news of Mahlon's healing but realized this was neither the time nor place. She bowed her acquiescence and almost ran to the back gate. Everything seemed under control. Two sheep were sizzling as they turned over the fire, and Putiel was saying, "We'll lower the height of this spit for a while. Mind you," he said to Peter, whose job this was, "for every turn you give the other sheep, give this one two."

The boy nodded. "I'll see it does not burn. It will be turned regularly."

The tall Egyptian placed a dark hand on the boy's bare shoulder. "That is good."

Susanna wanted to ask Putiel how his daughter's finger was today, but he had moved on to other tasks and she involved herself with helping Naomi mix the ground grain to make bread. "Will we be able to bake it all here, Naomi, or do you think we should send some loaves to the ovens of the baker and pay him to cook them?"

Naomi's industrious hands did not stop their task, though she pushed back her shoulders to relieve the stress of kneeling here for so long. "Our oven is at the right temperature, and Huldah has been tending the baking. She's almost keeping up with me. I believe we will have enough to feed everyone."

Susanna helped knead several batches, formed many loaves of bread, then moved to where Sherah smiled ruefully as she paused to wipe her eyes on a fold of her dress. "I wish leeks were as enjoyable to prepare as to eat!" she said.

"I know," Susanna sympathized, standing back several paces to avoid the strong oniony smell. "That's one of my least favorite tasks, though I've performed it hundreds of times."

Sherah sniffed. "Thousands is more likely."

There were piles of melons to be sliced, but it might be a little early for that. No, she'd better help cut up more vegetables for the stew. When Sherah brought her bowl of leeks to dump into the kettle, Susanna asked, "Have you seen Rachel?"

Sherah looked dismayed. "Not since late morning when she said she felt sick. I told her to go lie down."

"She rarely complains," Susanna fretted. "She must be in a great deal of pain."

"I meant to check on her, but went to the well and then got so busy here I forgot."

Rachel's father was coming back out through the gate, so she called to him, "Putiel, how is Rachel?"

He approached with long strides. "In the middle of the afternoon she was still sleeping. I didn't waken her."

Susanna wiped her hands on a coarse linen towel. "I'm going to check on her right now. It's not like her to stay in her room."

"I'd appreciate that," he said. "You would be able to determine better what her condition is."

Her knock on the doorpost met with no response, so she pushed aside the curtain. "Rachel, are you all right?"

There was only a mumbled, garbled sound, and at first Susanna could see little within this room so like her own. The wick in a small, round lamp burned in its niche in the corner, so she reached for it and went closer to the bed platform at the far side of the room.

The child was moving fitfully, her bent, skinny little legs tossing from side to side. A cover that must have been over her earlier had slipped off and lay tumbled on the earthen floor as tousled as the golden brown hair spread over the sleeping mat.

The child didn't respond even when Susanna spoke more loudly. The glazed eyes did not focus as they looked without recognition from Susanna's face to the light and then, with no change, toward the window. Her voice was husky and slurred, but Susanna thought she recognized several words. "Mama . . . hurt . . . mama . . . so hot . . ."

Susanna smoothed the hair back from Rachel's forehead. "Oh, Rachel, you're burning up!" Setting the lamp at the end of the ledge, she went to the small pot at the right of the door and brought a cup half filled with water. She cradled the child's head on her left arm and held the cup to her lips. "Here, Rachel, drink some of this good water."

Rachel turned her head back and forth, whimpering, not holding still long enough for Susanna to trickle even a few drops between the dry, cracked lips. Susanna spoke soothingly, afraid her words would not register, but hoping the softness of her tone and touch would get through to wherever the child now was. "You must have felt bad last night, too, and all of today to become as sick as you are now," she said. "Let me see your finger, dear," she continued, reaching for the arm, which was hanging over the edge of the bench.

As she touched it, tears formed in her eyes. The arm was very warm, and, as she slid her hand along it toward the wrist, she felt the heat increasing. She laid the child's head back down on the mat and reached for the lamp.

She had been on her knees but now rocked back so she was sitting on her heels. How could this have happened so quickly? *Oh, Yahweh, I tried to remove the splinter correctly, but look at her finger! Look at her hand! It's almost twice as big as the other one. What can I do?* She bent forward until her head was beside that of her little friend.

She remembered Rachel's bringing to her the elongated light pebble she used to write on the teaching-stone. Wildflowers had also been presented to her on those few occasions when Rachel had felt well enough to do more than the tasks of the inn. What a delight the child was in the classroom and out around the cookfire as they did mental arithmetic!

Then Susanna was on her feet, stretching to put the lamp back in its niche before bending to lift the little girl. No, if she held her this way, the swollen arm and hand would be pressed against herself.

She raised Rachel's head and shoulders, then swung her legs off the platform and turned her around so the child's head could rest on Susanna's right shoulder.

It was awkward getting to an upright position with the comatose child, but Susanna managed it. Slowly she moved toward the door, bringing her left arm and Rachel's legs to the doorway first so the curtain could be pushed to one side.

She felt her way out, moving her feet carefully so as not to bump or drop the precious burden. Her gaze circled the courtyard, but Putiel was not in sight.

Where was the Galilean? Certainly if He was able to heal Mahlon He could help Rachel.

It was still light out here, and she looked, aghast, at the monstrous, discolored hand and arm lying across Rachel's tunic. This was even more serious than she had realized when she'd examined it by the light of the small olive oil lamp. The right index finger was swollen so large the skin was tight and shiny, but what concerned Susanna most was that she could now see reddish streaks leading from the finger to over halfway up Rachel's arm.

The child was heavier than she looked—or else it was the dead weight in Susanna's arms—but Susanna corrected herself immediately. She didn't wish to associate the word *dead* with this little one she had come to love so much.

She hugged the limp form closer, then wondered if she'd hurt her as there was an almost convulsive twisting of the thin body. She relaxed her grip slightly but found there was no good way to carry her.

How she wished she could see Taharka or Andrew or Rachel's father!

Jesus was not in the courtyard or at the gate. He must have sent the people home. Had He left with somebody? *Oh, no, Yahweh, don't let Him have gone. We need Him here.*

"Susanna, what are you doing?"

She turned with relief and came to a standstill facing the doorway of the office. Taharka was just coming out. "I am so glad you're here, Taharka! But where is Jesus?"

He raised his chin and motioned with his head toward the stairs leading upward. "The Galileans are resting."

She staggered toward him with her burden. "I know they're guests and it isn't proper to bother them, but, oh, Taharka, look at Rachel. She's so very sick!"

76

He was beside them in a moment, taking in with carefully observant eyes and capable hands the seriousness of the problem. He started to reach out to lift Rachel from Susanna's arms, but, realizing as she had that this would bring Rachel's arm into contact with his chest, he came around to Susanna's side. They carefully shifted the child's weight from Susanna's arms into his.

He did not stop to discuss the need for urgency or to assess the rules of hospitality. "Come with me!" he commanded and moved with long strides to the stone steps, which he mounted two at a time.

Susanna was breathless as she ran up behind him, but she hesitated at the top so Taharka could make their presence known. She heard his words: "Andrew, is your master here? Oh, there you are, Jesus. I'm sorry to bother You when You must be very tired . . ."

The voice that answered was low and reassuring. "It's all right, Taharka."

"I didn't see the miracle you performed this afternoon, but I heard of it from everyone and I saw Mahlon afterward."

Taharka had moved closer to where the mats had been laid, but Susanna could tell that Jesus' voice came from somewhere over near the windows. The footsteps were getting louder now, and Susanna could not stay back in the stairway. She peeked carefully to make sure everyone was clothed, then came onto the gallery where she had been with Andrew the evening before.

When Jesus smiled a welcome, she hurried over to stand by Rachel's head. And then, as He came still nearer, she dropped to her knees before Him. "My Lord," she said in a quavering voice, "little Rachel has a high fever and doesn't hear or know us. Her hand and arm are terribly swollen from the splinter I tried to get out yesterday."

"Why did you bring her to Me?" He asked.

She looked at Him, startled, her gaze sliding past Him to Andrew, then Taharka, and back to Jesus again. "Because, if You can turn water into wine to keep a friend from being embarrassed and You can heal Mahlon so the evil spirits can no longer control him, then You have the power to take away the fever and the swelling and—and the unconsciousness that keeps Rachel from knowing us and from being herself."

His face was intense, but she was sure He was not angry. "Do you really believe that?"

She nodded firmly, knowing it was the absolute truth. "Yes. I do believe."

His seriousness was chased away by a radiant smile that warmed Susanna through and through as He moved yet closer, until the hem of His gown brushed against the soft material that covered her knees. For a moment she was completely content to stay where she was, for there was a peace and assurance coming over her unlike anything she had experienced since she was a small child snuggling in the arms of her father.

Jesus reached out and lifted the unconscious girl from the arms of Taharka. For a moment He drew Rachel close to His breast, then He extended His arms, holding her out as one would hold an offering to the Lord. He turned to look out one of the arched windows, up into the heavens.

His lips moved, but Susanna heard no words. There was no movement, no sound. It was as though the world had come to a moment of prayer as Jesus stood in an attitude similar to that of the High Priest on special holy days: head high, chin thrust forward, arms raised, a look of sanctification covering His visage.

And then Susanna, rising, saw Rachel's eyes slowly turn to look at Jesus. Would she be frightened? Should Susanna move forward to reassure her?

But there was no fear. Jesus' arms lowered, and His eyes fixed on Rachel's, a smile covering His bearded face.

Rachel's left arm came up around His neck in response to His love and acceptance, and Jesus hugged her in return. As He leaned over to set her on her feet, her right arm, also, came up to embrace Him.

Susanna's hand involuntarily reached out to touch Taharka's. "Look," she whispered. "Her hand . . ."

Taharka's grip was so tight it hurt. Tears were streaming down his cheeks as he sank to his knees, his eyes never leaving the two before him. "My lord!" he whispered, his entire being reflecting awe and reverence.

Susanna knelt beside him, drawn down with him, though she would have joined him here of her own volition even if he had released her hand.

Jesus kissed Rachel's cheek and said, "Go to your father. He is concerned for you."

The child turned. She was slight and frail-looking, but appeared to be totally well. Gone was the flushing, the dry, chapped lips, the glazed eyes. Gone was the swollen hand and arm. She seemed herself as she looked past Susanna and Taharka, crying, "Daddy," and ran toward the stairs.

Susanna had not realized Putiel was there. Had he just arrived, or had he been here for a time? She saw him lower himself to Rachel's level, gather her into his arms, and rise again to his full height. He hugged her to himself, burying his face between her head and shoulder then, in sheer joy, spinning all the way around with her in his arms.

"You're all right!" he cried. "You're well again!" And then he looked at Jesus. "She really is, isn't she?"

"Yes. She is."

The happiness, the wonder, seemed to overwhelm the muscular, strong man whom Susanna had seldom seen other than completely composed. With his eyes still on the Galilean, he held his daughter with his left arm and ran the right hand along Rachel's left leg and foot and then the right one. "She ran to me!"

A shiver passed over Susanna. She'd been given to understand that Rachel's problem had begun when she was under three years of age. She'd had recurring bouts of swelling and severe pain off and on through the years, with each acute attack leaving the joints more swollen and difficult to use.

Jesus nodded. "She can now run and climb trees and go into the stream to help wash the clothes."

How did Jesus know about her not being able to help with that—that going into the cool, flowing water had precipitated two of the most severe attacks Rachel had experienced?

Putiel did not relinquish his daughter but with his toes pushed the sandal off his right foot, then the left. Susanna looked at Andrew, remembering how she had removed her shoes on the top of Mount Gerizim that afternoon. Perhaps Putiel, though neither Jew nor Samaritan, was more conscious of the presence of holiness than they were.

She slid her free hand down along her ankle to release the thongs of her own sandal, but Jesus said, "Arise, both of you. It is the Father who should be praised. I have been sent by my Father to do His will. It is not His will that this little one should continue through life so handicapped.

"Go now. Attend to your duties and responsibilities. Another caravan is arriving."

eleven

Susanna heard the unmistakable sounds now, too, though previously she had been as unconscious of them as the others. As they went down the stairs and back to their tasks, the whole episode up on the gallery seemed too wonderful to be true—except that there was little Rachel dancing lightheartedly around, going from one of her friends to another. "Look, Naomi! Look at me. My legs and ankles are as straight as yours. See, Sherah? I can swing around on my toes and lean over and touch the ground and dance and, oh, I can do *every*thing!"

Susanna could not bring herself to insist on Rachel's settling down and sticking to one job on such a marvelous day. Had it been Susanna herself healed like this she could not possibly have kept from rejoicing as much as this child. In fact, there was a constant smile affixed to Susanna's face, and each time she looked at the bubbling, joyous child she felt happier.

When it was time for the food to be served, she called Rachel and handed her the first tray of mutton, on which she had also placed individual warm loaves of freshly baked bread. Before today she would never have asked this of the child, but now suggested, "Would you like to serve the Galileans?"

Rachel's face was glowing. "Oh, *could* I, Susanna?"

She cautioned, "Be very careful now, don't hurry too much—and tell them fruit, wine, and bowls of stew will be arriving soon."

Putiel overheard Susanna speaking and reached for a tray, saying, "I'll carry those."

This was not a job for a man, certainly not for Taharka's chief assistant. But Susanna knew Putiel had a need to serve Jesus, who had done so much for Rachel. She smiled up at him and turned to load this second tray. Proudly he followed the little girl who was moving so carefully, so precisely, toward the stairs.

A man from one of the caravans bawled out an obscenity and demanded to be served first, but Taharka moved quickly to cut him off, and the man stepped back, grumbling.

Rachel never paused, and Susanna, from her vantage point in the gateway, wondered if the child's concentration and delight in doing something for Jesus made her unaware of all lesser things.

Rachel disappeared up the stairs with her father only a little behind her. Susanna felt a pang of what really couldn't be jealousy, could it? No, not really; it was just that she'd like very much to do something for Jesus, too.

And then she had a moment of wistfulness, of longing for something else. If only Jonah could be here! It was unheard of for anyone to be healed of leprosy, but God must know it was possible or He wouldn't have made those rules in Leviticus about showing oneself to the priest for examination and declaration of cleansing. She sighed and went back to cutting the meat.

It was very late that evening when she went to the door of the room shared by father and daughter. "Putiel," she called softly.

The curtain was pushed aside, and he stepped out. "Rachel is sleeping," he whispered.

"I thought she probably was, but I was thinking about her and about Mahlon and . . ." There was no good way to introduce her train of thought. "You know the widow, Deborah? It would not be safe for me to go see her tonight, and there will be no time in the morning before Jesus leaves to get in touch with her."

"What did you want?"

She drew in a deep breath. "Would it be too much to ask of Jesus to heal her, too? She's such a good woman, always trying to help others as much as she's able to . . ."

There was a brief pause. "I hear she is what you say."

"If her son had permitted it, she would even have taken me in when my sister-in-law sent me away."

A muscle twitched in Putiel's jaw. "If you had mentioned this earlier, perhaps something could have been arranged. But the hour is late; it wouldn't be safe for anyone to go, and, as you said, her son is—strict. He would not have sympathy for a messenger from the inn of an Egyptian."

Her shoulders sagged. "You are right, of course. I'm sorry to have bothered you." Her hand rested for a moment on his bare arm. "Sleep well, my friend."

Upon returning to her room, Susanna had difficulty falling asleep. So much had happened this day! Who *was* Jesus? He spoke of His father when they thanked Him for healing Rachel. Could He *really* be the son of the living God?

Maybe it was like being the son of Abraham, the son of Isaac, and the son of Jacob. The Holy Book said that God had made Adam in His own likeness. Maybe that's what Jesus meant—that He was made in God's image, as all men were.

However, if that was all, how did He have the power to heal Rachel? And Mahlon? No, He had to be more than an ordinary man.

Thank you, Yahweh, for letting me see Rachel as she was and now as she is.

Susanna looked up at the plastered ceiling above her sleeping mat and smiled. There would no doubt be skeptics, but whether people accepted the healing of her hand or not, anyone who had seen Rachel would remember the limp and the gnarled joints of her legs, ankles, and feet, which were now straight and whole!

Thank you, Yahweh, for healing her. And for changing the water into wine, as Andrew said. And for changing Mahlon from a perennial child into a man.

She rolled over, facing the wall. Just before she fell asleep she added one more thing: *Thank you, especially, for letting me meet Jesus at the well, so I could talk with Him and bring Taharka to meet Him. Thank you also for Jesus' accepting Taharka's invitation to come.* The smile remained on her face even after her tired body took over and brought sleep.

She awoke refreshed and full of energy. Within minutes she was outside helping the servants prepare for the day. Most travelers carried some food for their journey, but they were tempted by sight and fragrance to buy fig cakes and freshly made hot bread, as well as fresh fruits and vegetables.

Taharka always permitted individuals to fill their water skins without charge, but there was wine for sale, along with dried strips of meat and salted fish. Few of the newcomers bought these, but those who often came this way knew of the availability and quality and planned on replenishing their supplies here.

There was so much to be done that she didn't realize Putiel had been gone until she saw him pushing the two-wheeled cart into the courtyard. She was surprised, then, startled by what she saw, ran in his direction. "Deborah! I'm so glad you are here!"

The bright sparkling eyes belied Deborah's years, although Susanna could hear her wheezing while yet twenty feet away. "Your messenger was very persuasive," she explained drily.

Susanna looked up into a determinedly noncommittal face. "Thank you, Putiel."

He bowed slightly, then glanced up toward the gallery. "They haven't left yet, have they?"

"I haven't seen them this morning."

"Good." He let out a long breath, and Susanna knew he had been racing against time. "I must now be about the master's business," he stated, setting the cart near the inner wall.

Susanna helped Deborah alight, and they walked slowly to the stone seat near the cistern, from which vantage point she could see everything that took place. She tried to answer Deborah's questions concerning the message Putiel had brought when he had awakened her.

She had protested it was too far to walk, and he explained he had brought the cart. "He didn't tell me why you wanted me to come but insisted you were all right—and I see that you are," she added.

"Then why *did* you come, if he told you nothing?"

"I was just asking myself that, too," the old woman confessed. "The main reason, of course, is that I thought you needed me. Also, life gets very dull at times. I get up, coughing, and do a few chores around the house, though I can't even grind the meal for my son and myself anymore. I eat a little and I drink a little, and I take an afternoon nap and go to bed early at night."

She laughed aloud, then had another lengthy spell of coughing. Finally she managed, "It occurred to me that an invitation to ride in a cart pushed by Putiel was an opportunity too unusual and too precious to miss."

Susanna gave her friend a quick hug. "What is *here* is 'too precious to miss,' Deborah," she said and told first of the healing of Mahlon. Then she went on. "Deborah, do you remember the little crippled girl who is the daughter of Putiel?"

Deborah hesitated. "I've heard of her but don't think I know her."

Susanna called across the courtyard, "Sherah, if Rachel is outside, would you send her to me, please?" Within moments the girl came running through the gate. "There she is now."

Deborah looked from one to the other. "You don't mean that is the cripple . . . ?"

Susanna nodded. "There's a story about that, but I'd like her to tell it to you." As the child stood before them, she told about her crippling, which had progressively gotten worse these past years, and then about the splinter that she'd been unable to remove.

"It didn't get better," she said simply. "The next day my hand was very sore and large and something inside made it pound like a drum—you know, *thump, thump, thump,* like that," she explained, hitting her open palm with her balled right fist.

"I tried to get out of bed, but my head pounded like my hand, and I got dizzy and fell to the floor. I was feeling awfully hot, too, and then felt so cold that even with my mantle and blanket I was still shivering. Daddy came to check on me, and I didn't want to worry him so I went to try working, but Sherah told me to lie down again."

She looked up at Susanna. "And that's all I remember until I awoke up on the gallery, in the arms of Jesus."

Deborah was appalled. "You awoke in the arms of a *man?*"

Susanna interrupted to explain this situation that the child would not realize sounded suspicious. "I found her unconscious, with a raging fever, and an arm swollen this big," she said, holding out her hands with thumbs and middle fingers together. "There were red streaks running up her arm, getting close to her elbow.

"I didn't know what to do, but, remembering how Jesus had just healed Mahlon, decided to ask Him for help."

She nodded toward the child, who was obviously waiting to continue her story. "So when I got awake Jesus was holding me and praying, and then He looked at me and I, well I just loved Him and hugged Him . . ."

"With *both* arms," Susanna emphasized, "both of which were completely normal."

"And then Jesus set me on my feet and told me to run to Daddy, and I *did* it," the child cried exultantly.

Deborah leaned over and ran a knotted hand along the straight legs she could see below the short tunic. "Your knees were swollen?"

"And real sore. And they didn't want to bend much."

"Do they hurt now?"

A bubble of laughter welled up uncontrollably, and Rachel danced happily on her toes. "Not at all—not one little bit!"

Deborah's face showed awe, yet confusion and skepticism were there also. Susanna reached to take her hand between both her own. "Last night I was thinking about how good you have been to me, and how I have never been able to adequately repay you—"

"Never repaid? Susanna, you used to bring me things from the market, and many's the time you have filled my water pot."

"Oh, *that*," Susanna sniffed her disregard for these homely tasks. "What I wanted for you was the chance to be healed also."

Deborah was shaking her head. "I don't believe in things like that."

"Don't you want to breathe more easily? Don't you *want* to stop all those coughing spells?"

Deborah drew in a deep breath. "If He were a Samaritan, perhaps, but really, Susanna, this man is a Galilean, you said. A Jew. What would my son say? And my neighbors?"

It had never occurred to Susanna that her friend would not take advantage of this opportunity. "Wouldn't you like to be able to sleep the night through without choking and coughing and wheezing?" she coaxed.

"Of course I'd like that, and I thank you for telling me about the healer and getting me here," and her eyes sparkled again with the sheer fun of being brought on the two-wheeled cart. "But I'm going to leave now. Perhaps if I don't go directly home but to the well first, nobody will know where I've been."

Susanna felt herself flushing and bit her lip. Deborah must have seen the tightness of Susanna's face, for she reached to put her arms around the younger woman. "Susanna, I'm sorry if I offended you. I know you were trying to help."

"Yes," softly, "I was. I'm afraid it was I who was an offense to you, as it turned out."

"Love is never an offense, dear—but people with small minds can appreciate neither the bigness of love nor the idea of wanting the best for others."

Deborah shuffled toward the gate, and Susanna walked beside her. "Could Putiel take you back?"

Deborah's already much-wrinkled face acquired two deep horizontal creases across the forehead, and Susanna realized that the delayed answer was not consideration of a yes or no, but of how to phrase her negative answer. "The sun will soon be up, and people will be about. Too many questions would be asked if I'm seen on the cart. One would think that at my age I could do what I want, but I still have to live with my son and neighbors."

"Yet you thought it would be all right for me to come here," Susanna reminded.

"Because I knew of nothing better to suggest."

Susanna stopped at the edge of the road and looked at Deborah. "He is a good man, Deborah."

"Taharka?"

"Um-hm. You may have wondered about . . . about our living arrangements . . ."

Deborah stopped her with a hand tenderly placed against her friend's cheek. "It is not my concern, Susanna."

"But I *want* you to know that we have done nothing wrong. I meet Mara at the well sometimes, and she's always making remarks."

"Everyone knows Mara! She's a gossip and she's mean. Try not to let her upset you."

"She *does* upset me," Susanna confessed. "And yet, isn't it interesting? It was because of her that I met Jesus."

Deborah's interest was keen. "How was that?"

"She was so nasty when I went to the well two days ago that I decided to go to Jacob's Well, instead, on my next trip. Jesus was there, and after we talked I came back and brought others with me to meet Him. Taharka heard His words and asked Him to come here for a few nights."

Deborah obviously did not want to talk about Jesus. Requesting Susanna not to accompany her, she started the slow return home.

Susanna could do nothing more. She had tried, as had Putiel, but now her responsibilities were to help with the morning meal and prepare for the departure of the caravans.

A northbound caravan was almost ready to leave by the time the five men came down from upstairs. They accepted with gratitude the gift of food for their trip, but Susanna did not have time to speak with any of them except when Andrew crossed the courtyard to say, "I want to thank you again for climbing Mount Gerizim with me yesterday."

"It was a pleasure for me, Andrew. I didn't realize how much I'd missed roaming, now that I'm a grown woman."

His eyes crinkled at the corners. "You are a lovely person, Susanna. I pray my sisters will grow up to be as fine as you."

"But they are Jewish and I'm Samaritan," she reminded him.

"With Jesus, that doesn't matter. It is what's within the heart that's important."

Suddenly she remembered. "He told me the time was coming when people would not be worshiping either at Jerusalem or Mount Gerizim."

"And we will all be brothers and sisters," he added.

The first of the camels and donkeys were beginning to move through the open gates, so Susanna walked with Andrew in that direction. Taharka was ahead of them, accompanying Jesus and listening intently.

Susanna would have walked with Andrew to the gates of the town, but Rachel came running to say she was needed in the weaving room. Before returning to her duties, she reminded Andrew of Taharka's invitation to Jesus' group to stop here whenever they were traveling through Samaria.

When, two hours later, she had the opportunity to thank Putiel for fetching Deborah, she found him amazed that Deborah would leave without seeing Jesus, even if she hadn't wished to ask Him for healing. Putiel looked again at his daughter, who couldn't get enough of running and dancing and flitting from here to there. "Thank Yahweh *you* had enough faith to ask for a miracle," he breathed.

~~~~~~

She had assumed Taharka would eat the midday meal with her as he had grown accustomed to doing, but such was not the case. Later, she would have liked to ask Putiel if he'd seen the master, but Taharka was certainly not accountable to her. Or to Putiel. Or to anyone.

Late that afternoon Taharka greeted the late afternoon caravans with courtesy and graciousness, as he always did. Susanna was still amazed, when she had time to notice, that the caravan masters responded so well to this. Taharka simply stated what he expected and what he was offering, and they almost always accepted his terms. In all the time she had been here, she had seen only a couple of groups turn around and go spend the night outside the town's walls. At least one of these had stayed here at the inn on its next trip and continued doing so.

Things returned much to the way they had been before Jesus came. The days were busy; the nights were slept through; people came and went.

But Taharka no longer ate his meals with her, and he didn't come to read the holy scrolls with her.

She longed to invite him, but how *could* she without appearing forward or presumptuous? Had she offended him? She tried to think what she might have said or done to make him angry with her. He had seemed to like the Galileans and had spent much time with them, so it seemed unlikely that her meeting with Jesus at the well had upset him.

And it had been he who had carried Rachel up the steps.

He absented himself more than before, but whatever was drawing him away from the inn during the middle of each day remained a mystery to her.

Might he have found a woman friend? Could he be calling on her during the only hours when he was free?

By the sixth day, she had to know. There was a question she could ask him. Perhaps the way he received her and her request would give some indication of where she stood with him.

It was almost time for the first arrivals when he returned to the inn and went directly to his office. Within a few moments Susanna was at his door. "Taharka, may I please come in?"

As she responded to his invitation, she was distressed by his haggard appearance. "Are you ill, Taharka?" she asked solicitously.

He rubbed his hand across his face as he leaned back in the caned chair. "No, I'm fine."

She had not intended to become so personal, so domestic, but found herself moving toward him and laying her small hand on his forehead. "You don't seem to have a fever," she said, gratefully. "I was afraid carrying Rachel when she was so sick might have made you ill."

He smiled at her concern. "It's nothing, Susanna. I'm just tired." He leaned forward, arms resting on the table. "Now, what was it that brought you here this afternoon?"

She remembered now. "I was wondering, do you suppose it's possible for Jesus to heal . . . leprosy?"

He squared his broad shoulders. "I've been wishing I'd asked Him that while He was here. There were so many other things to talk about . . ."

She wondered what those other things were, but could hardly ask. "Do you suppose there's a chance?"

"Is it harder to heal the skin than the bones? To heal deep sores than the mind?" he countered.

She shook her head. "It doesn't seem that it should be—but then I've never before known a healer."

He looked at her intently. "I think—I believe—He's more than a healer, Susanna."

"I feel that way too." And now she had to ask her favor. "Taharka, would it be possible to ask the leader of a caravan to check for me on . . . on . . . ?"

"You'd like to know where Jonah is? Whether he's with the leper colony near the Galilean border?"

She was unconscious of clasping her hands over her breast. "Oh, could you?"

"I already asked Mibzar last evening. But don't get your hopes too high," he cautioned, as a delighted smile spread over her face. "It may be impossible to find him, and perhaps when they get there Mibzar might reconsider getting close enough to inquire."

She didn't tell him why she had to know, although she supposed he must have guessed. Meanwhile, she'd bide her time and do everything in her power to help this man who had done so much for her.

twelve

Almost two weeks passed before Mibzar's caravan returned from Damascus. He had left it long enough to personally verify that Jonah was, indeed, among the unfortunate group of lepers near the border.

Jonah had sent word back that his entire arm was affected by the leprosy, and there were sores on both legs. Otherwise, Mibzar reported, he appeared well, appreciated his sister's concern, and asked for any word concerning his wife and children, as well as her.

During the weeks until the caravan would come north again Susanna formulated a dozen letters in her mind. However, although Jonah had taught her to write numbers and had worked with her on letters, she found herself woefully unprepared for writing words.

She got out the precious scrolls again, searching through them for words she needed and copying them on the dark rock. Leah's name was there, for a Leah had married father Jacob, but David's name was nowhere she could find in the Pentateuch or the Book of Jonah, nor was Mikal's. In despair she went to Taharka for help in writing the first letter she had ever attempted.

She found him understanding and considerate. When she felt she could write the words satisfactorily, he gave her a scrap of papyrus on which to formulate them. After correcting this for her, as she asked, he gave her a new reed pen and fresh writing material so she could copy it.

And then she waited, trying not to grow impatient. One morning when Susanna saw Leah and the children at the well, as she did occasionally, little David's face became one big smile and he started running toward her, but his mother jerked him back with a firm, "You stay with me!"

He looked hurt and perplexed. Moisture collected in Susanna's own eyes at seeing the tears rolling down his cheeks. "Good morning, David," she said gently before greeting his mother and sister.

At first she thought Leah wasn't going to even acknowledge her, and Susanna wondered if she should bother relaying Jonah's message.

Thanks be to Yahweh, she didn't have to make that decision, for Leah nodded when Susanna asked to speak with her.

At first Leah didn't seem to care very much how her husband was faring, but as they walked a dozen paces away from the well where other young matrons were coming to draw water, Susanna realized that wasn't the case. "Don't tell him about . . . how hard things are," Leah requested.

"What *would* you like him to know?"

Leah's gaze circled the square, seeing the small stone houses, the dry-baked earth, barefooted children in short clothes playing in the streets. "Just say we are all well. David had a bad cold two weeks ago but is fine again, though his sister now has it.

"The hens have stopped laying and are losing their feathers, for it's that time now. The garden is producing all right . . ." her voice trailed off.

"Shall I tell him you miss him?" Susanna prodded.

The look she received was almost pitiful, and Susanna ached for this woman, who may have been cruel to her but who was also alone, confused, and in such pain that right now she was trembling.

"Yes, please." She cleared her throat and added, "We still have grain and some oil, so I suppose I should be thankful," she said, but her voice didn't sound that way. "I'm helping my sister-in-law some days and my brother when he needs an extra pair of hands."

Susanna did not know the fuller very well but could well imagine he would be a hard taskmaster. When Leah said she must hurry there with the jug she had just filled, Susanna did not detain her.

It was Taharka who penned the additional messages on Susanna's letter, for, being unused to writing, she could not make the characters small enough to be squeezed into the narrow border of the papyrus sheet.

She had leaned across the table, watching his flying reed pen, her lips silently forming the words as they appeared before her. "Isn't writing wonderful?" she whispered as he finished.

He smiled up at her, his smoothly shaved face responding to her glow. "It takes you to remind me this is so."

"You said once that I'd get used to reading and it might cease to be exciting, but I don't think that it, or this, could ever be dull," she stated.

He pushed back his chair as she straightened, and then he was walking around the table, so close that his short tunic brushed hers. She placed her hand impulsively on his bare forearm. "Taharka, thank you again for all you do for me and . . . and for being the wonderful person you are."

And then she feared she'd gone too far. But he *was* wonderful and kind and always doing things for her and others.

His dark brown eyes looked into hers with a gaze so intense, so concentrated that she felt herself drowning in them. His arm trembled beneath her touch, and his lips parted to say something but then closed in a straight, firm line. The tip of her tongue moistened her suddenly dry lips, and she realized they had parted slightly.

And then they heard the call from one of the servants. "Master, the first camels are entering the gate."

The fourth caravan to arrive was Mibzar's.

∼∼∼∼∼

The next morning she was just stepping from her doorway when she heard Taharka's voice out of the semidarkness. "Susanna, gather together enough provisions for two people for a trip of two days, and also make a package containing a new robe, mantle, sash, and sandals as well as grain, oil, and dried and salted meat."

She looked at him questioningly. "How much of those foods?"

"Enough to last a man for a couple of months," he said tersely, already beginning to move away.

"Taharka?"

"What is it?"

"Shall I do this immediately, or shall I help with the morning work first?"

"Do it right away. Come find me as soon as it's accomplished." And he was gone about his duties.

Rachel danced over to give her usual good-morning hug, as she called it, and Susanna, returning the caress, longed again for a child of her own. But that could not be.

She busied herself with collecting the items Taharka had requested. Probably one of the caravan masters had ordered these and would need them to take when he left soon. These men led strenuous lives and needed sturdy materials, so Susanna went to the weaving room where not only loomed cloth was stored but also some completed garments.

. She wished she knew how tall the person was who was buying these. She shook out one of the folded tunics, a colobium made by one of the women whose specialty was the long, closely fitting garment of one piece of cloth, not sewn together. Yes, this would fit anyone of average height or above.

From the pile of heavy woolen cloaks or mantles she chose a blue and gray striped one that had not had its tassels attached yet. If the purchaser were a Jew, he would want white ones sewn on; a Samaritan would need four blue ones; but if he was Syrian, Egyptian, or something else, he might be offended to have any at all.

As she entered the food storerooms she marveled again at how much was kept here. It took only a few minutes to get the items prepared for the two bundles, but then she also scooped up some beans, lentils, and dates in additional containers, in case Taharka might wish to include them with this special order.

Taharka turned from talking with Putiel just outside the opened gates. "Everything is ready as you requested," she reported. "I've put the things in your office."

"Good. Now, go fill water skins for you and me, and get some breakfast. We'll be leaving soon."

She gasped, eyes wide in amazement. "We—you and I? Where are we going?"

Putiel turned away to hide his amusement, but Taharka smiled. "I thought it a good idea for you to see your brother and deliver your messages, food, and clothing in person. However, as it is not good for you to travel alone with the caravan, I shall accompany you."

She was thrilled and excited. Only once had she traveled with a caravan. To have Taharka go with her was an especial blessing but—"Can you be spared here?"

He nodded. "Putiel knows everything I do. He can manage well for this night."

She could not protest. She had thought about Jonah so much, prayed for him, worried about him, and dreamed of him. Now she would get to see him.

And Taharka would be with her!

As it turned out, her news was already known by the servants, who had been sworn to secrecy since Taharka had told them of the idea late the night before and talked with Mibzar.

Taharka offered a donkey for her use, but she chose to walk. They couldn't travel very fast because of the number of animals and walking people, so she didn't feel unusally tired when at noon they ate their midday meal and rested under some trees.

Susanna had realized Taharka would not be walking beside her so was neither surprised nor disappointed at his talking with great interest to the men who had various caravan responsibilities. Before, she'd seen mostly the freedom of the people as they relaxed in the security and provision of the inn, but now she realized how well the group functioned.

Mibzar was everywhere, it seemed, checking a donkey's hoof, a camel's bridle, or the condition of the old man who seemed to have trouble even staying on his little donkey but was too proud to accept the offer to ride in an open cart.

Susanna knew that wives of the men sometimes accompanied them, but she'd made no attempt to meet or talk with them before. Now, however, there were hours of time and not too much to see other than the well-cultivated land off to the right, nearer the Jordan River, and sheep grazing over toward the west, where it was more mountainous.

People were harvesting dates and grapes, and the olives were ripening. "What a wonderful area we live in," Susanna exclaimed to the young mother whose older child she was carrying for a while. The two-year-old girl had not had enough time for a nap when they had stopped earlier for lunch and now slept against Susanna's shoulder, the warm little body completely relaxed.

"I hope Galilee is this nice," the little widow murmured. Adiah was on her way to the parents of her husband, who had died at the age of twenty. He had been a younger son, and Susanna knew how frightened and insecure the girl must feel about making this move, which would probably be permanent.

"I understand it is," Susanna tried to reassure her. "There are supposed to be pleasant towns and good agriculture and—and there's fishing on the Sea of Galilee," she finished lamely, remembering that Andrew and Peter had once been fishermen.

"I don't think I'm going that far," Adiah said, continuing to nurse her baby as they walked. "From what my husband said, and also from the caravan leaders, I believe Nain is a town not many miles beyond the Samaritan-Galilean border."

Later, when asked how far she herself was traveling, Susanna said it wouldn't be much longer, but she saw no need to tell more than that she was going to visit her brother. She didn't want the girl to pull away from her or take back her child just because Jonah had leprosy.

The shadows were lengthening appreciably by the time Taharka waited along the line for her to catch up with him. "Mibzar says it is just over the next hill," he told her.

She shivered in the hot sunshine. Was she prepared for what was about to come? Would Jonah be so changed that she might not recognize him? Would he be glad to see her, or might he be so embarrassed or depressed that her visit would only make him feel worse?

She forced herself to smile into Taharka's eyes, which appeared troubled. Was he worrying also? "It will be good to get there, Taharka."

"Are you terribly tired?" he asked.

She laughed. "The travel has not been hard, and the child," she said, looking reassuringly at Adiah, "is not as heavy as my water pot at home."

For a short while he walked with her at the end of the line but then grew impatient. The dust from the beasts of burden and the many walking people made a permanent cloud about them, and much of it stuck to their perspiring faces and sweat-dampened clothing. "Let's move to the front of the line," he suggested, stepping out to the right.

She really did not want to leave the security and friendship she had found here. "Would Mibzar mind?"

"No, I'm sure he wouldn't," he assured her, so she handed the awakening youngster to her mother.

"You'll have to walk, dear," Adiah told the now refreshed child, who set off on stocky short legs, waving a farewell to Susanna as her mother directed.

They were cresting the hill by the time they passed all the people and animals to come abreast of Mibzar on his long-legged horse. He pointed ahead to their right. "The leper colony is there, on the other side of the small stream."

Was this the same spot she'd thought she remembered? It looked so different—but perhaps that was because she now knew somebody here. There were caves in the hillside and two wooden structures between them and the creek. As they closed the distance, which could have been no more than a mile from the hilltop, she saw a few people moving about over there, while others sat or lay in the scant shade provided by the cave entrances, buildings, and a few bent, twisted trees.

Susanna decided that Taharka's brief nod to Mibzar must have been a signal, for the lithe, middle-aged leader said briskly, "We'll make a stop in those trees a half-mile up ahead. There's a spring that feeds a stream for refreshing the stock. Everyone can use a rest."

"We appreciate that, Mibzar," Taharka said feelingly. He took several bundles from the donkey next to which they'd been walking then, turning, said, "Susanna, you set the pace. We'll cut across here toward the caves."

Suddenly she was frightened. She had lived on hopes for so long that she almost preferred to just keep on going. But she couldn't tell Taharka that.

She reached for the bundle of clothing she had prepared with no thought it would be for her brother. Although she offered to carry more, Taharka refused. Carefully avoiding the worst of the brambles, they threaded their way downhill between rocks and tall weeds.

Susanna was surprised there appeared to be so little interest in their coming. Several men shifted position so they could more easily watch these strangers, but others simply glanced away or tried to cover their limbs better with their threadbare clothing.

Taharka set his packages on the ground and bracketed his hands about his mouth. "Jonah," he called. "Jonah, brother of Susanna, we would speak with you."

Susanna could feel a pounding within her chest and an unaccustomed breathlessness. She looked intently from one leper to another, and then from around the side of one wooden building came the emaciated relic of what had been her brother. "Oh, no," she moaned.

Taharka looked at her with a frown, and she accepted the reprimand gratefully. She must not show dismay at Jonah's appearance. She willed a delighted smile to her face. "Jonah, we've come to see you."

His face was a study as it went from puzzlement to surprise to joy. He hurried across the open area and down the bank but did not, of course, come across.

"Susanna, how wonderful!" His arms stretched out, then dropped with the uselessness of his desire to touch this sister to whom he had been so close. "And Taharka," he added. "Thank you for bringing her. And for checking on me before."

The Egyptian nodded. "I didn't want her coming alone. But I shall leave you together for now. Later, I want to talk with you."

Susanna was touched at his thoughtfulness. However she assured him, "There is nothing we could say that you would not be welcome to hear."

Jonah likewise invited him to stay, but the big, agile innkeeper climbed back up to the road and sat on a flat rock watching the caravan as it broke up into its many parts at the woods.

Susanna tried to tell Jonah of the many things that had taken place in Sychar while he was away, including births, deaths, accidents, and sicknesses. She tried to gloss over being sent away from his home the day after he'd gone by saying Leah had thought it best for her to find a home elsewhere, and this had worked out well for her.

It was providential that she had talked with Leah only the day before, for she could now tell him how well his family looked. It was unnecessary to bring up the fact that Leah had previously avoided her, and, in fact, usually turned away when they had been unfortunate enough to meet at the well or the market.

He had enough to be troubled about without fretting over differences between his wife and his sister.

And then he told Susanna of his life. They barely had enough to eat, and the clothing of some who had been here for years was reduced to rags. "One of the depressing things about having this disease, in addition to being forced to leave all those we care about, is that after a while people forget us."

"I'd never forget you," she declared.

He shook his head sadly. "Not now, maybe not even for several more years, but the time will come . . ."

Suddenly she remembered the main reason she had wanted to see him. "Jonah, I must tell you about a man by the name of Jesus." He listened intently to the beginning of the story, but she soon realized he thought her too gullible in her reaction to and belief in the Galilean. "Did Taharka see the miracle with Mahlon?" he finally asked.

She shook her head, the long hair sweeping across her back. "Caravans were arriving, so he didn't actually see what took place," she admitted. "But everyone in Sychar has seen Mahlon since. He's not the same person, Jonah."

He grinned. "That's an improvement, anyway. The old Mahlon wasn't of much help to anyone, including himself."

"Well, he is now," she insisted doggedly. "You remember his father is a shepherd, but Mahlon couldn't help even with that. One never knew if he'd remember which way home was, much less be able to lead the sheep toward shelter, food, or water. Now, however, he's working with his father and not having spells of falling, foaming at the mouth, making strange sounds—or anything."

"But if he's out on the hillside with the sheep, you know only what's being told. Maybe the family wants so much to have him normal that they make believe he's recovered."

She sighed. "I know it's hard to believe, but it is true. He often comes to the inn and helps with anything that needs to be done. I assure you he's as sane as I am."

He laughed out loud. "There were times when we were children that I wouldn't have thought that proof at all," he teased.

She wrinkled her nose at him, but smiled, too. It was good to have him say something funny. "Even if you can't believe *that*, let me tell you about Rachel, the daughter of Putiel."

He remembered the Egyptian. There weren't so many people in Sychar that he wouldn't have known Putiel and have seen the crippled child. As Susanna gave the account of that memorable evening when Rachel was healed, his face became pensively wistful. "You *saw* this take place?"

Her answer was clear and emphatic, "Not only did I see the miracle, but I can vouch for the fact that this child, whose joints were almost twice as big as they should have been and who was unable to move without pain, is now running and climbing and dancing as freely as you and I ever did."

There was a long silence, and then, "He's a Galilean?"

"But that doesn't matter," Susanna reassured, telling of Jesus' speaking with her and then of Andrew's conversation as well. "I believe He's the promised Messiah," she concluded.

He slowly shook his head. "Be careful to whom you make that avowal, dear sister," he cautioned. "We've waited for centuries for the Messiah to come."

"I know, but don't you see? All the signs are pointing to the time being *now*."

"But 'now' could be this year or twenty years or two hundred years from now—or maybe even some time in the past when we didn't recognize Him."

She shook her head. "It is *now,* and He is Jesus," she declared.

"But the Galileans thought Judas of Galilee was the Messiah and they rose in revolt. Look what happened to them. It's not even twenty years since that rebellion took place and Sepphoris, the capital city of all Galilee, was completely destroyed by the Romans following a siege. By the way, is your Jesus a military man?"

She smiled, remembering. "Definitely not. He's a very gentle man. Even His name tells something of Him."

"Well, His name may mean 'Yahweh saves,' but, really, Susanna, your name means 'Lily,' and you're hardly a flower," he said, trying to reason with her.

She had to convince him, had to make him realize this was his one chance to be cured of leprosy. Finally she called Taharka—perhaps he could persuade Jonah. After all, he had talked with Jesus and the disciples for many hours. For a while she stayed with the men, then, when they accepted her offer to leave them alone—though she'd hoped they wouldn't—she went to sit where Taharka had waited for her.

They seemed to be discussing something intently. Was it still Jesus, or did it have something to do with her or the past that she and Jonah had shared with Taharka's son?

When she was invited back for the few minutes before they would have to hurry to join the re-forming caravan, she saw that the food and garments they'd brought had been given and received.

She wished she could touch her brother, but that was impossible. She knew there were many more things she had meant to talk with him about, but she couldn't remember them now.

All too soon she and Taharka were climbing the bank together and turning again and again to wave or call back over their shoulders.

"I'll be watching for you tomorrow," Jonah promised, recognizing that they would be returning with the first southbound caravan they'd meet.

Tears blurred her eyes, and she stumbled over a rough spot on the road. Taharka moved closer and put his strong arm around her slight shoulders. She wanted to bury her face against his chest and sob out her frustration and hurt at her brother's condition, but she couldn't let either man know how miserable and weak she was.

Taharka had gone out of his way, even leaving his inn for the entire night, so that he could come with her. The least she could do was to behave like an adult.

She tried to put on a happy expression as she looked up at him. "Did you have a good visit with Jonah?"

"*I* think so." But he didn't volunteer anything about it, saying only, "I liked your brother when he was a child."

She sighed, thinking of the fun of childhood, the freedom, the good times. "The first time I came to your inn I was very young and you were very big," she said, and the remembrance filled her with a soft glow. "You were sitting in your cane chair at the table, and you received us as though we were equals, offering chairs that seemed frightfully uncomfortable to us, who had always sat upon the floor."

He looked startled. "I'm sorry. How inconsiderate that must have seemed!"

"Oh, no. It was just that you lived in a world entirely different from the one Jonah and I knew. It was very exciting for us. I remember your even giving us a sweet candy of some sort, the best treat I'd ever had."

"I remember your first visit also," he said slowly. "My son had never before brought a girl to the inn. You sat there with your huge brown eyes meeting mine as we talked. You weren't bold or forward, but you weren't afraid of me, either, or of your surroundings. I found you remarkably mature for one so young."

He was walking beside her now with his usual long gait, arms swinging easily at his sides. In a way she wished he were continuing to give her physical support or touching her, but of course that wouldn't be proper. "I didn't feel mature," she confessed, not looking at him now.

As they caught up with the caravan just across the Galilean border, he moved forward along the line, and she tried to fit back into the easy relationship with the young widow. But it was as she had feared: because she had visited a brother with leprosy, she was now an undesirable companion.

She was grateful when Ephrathah, the wife of Mibzar, came to walk beside her for a time. This woman could have been anywhere from thirty-five to fifty years of age. Her clear brown eyes seemed to miss nothing of the surroundings or what was going on among these travelers.

When Susanna commented on her traveling with her husband, Ephrathah explained simply, "He's seldom able to stay at our home in Damascus for more than a day or two at a time." A broad smile crossed her leathery face, which had known more sandstorms, wind, rain, and sun than Susanna ever could. "By coming with him I have my husband through much of the night, and I can see him throughout the day, as well."

"You are a wise woman," Susanna commended.

"But you also are close to Taharka throughout the day and night."

Susanna looked at her, startled. "We are not man and wife," she said. Then, lest that give the wrong impression also, she added, "nor do we live together as man and wife."

The woman apologized. "A thousand pardons. You seemed to have authority over the servants at the inn, and Taharka appeared to defer to you—and he came along with you to find your brother."

"He is a good man and a kind one. His son, before he died, was the best friend of both my brother and me."

But then, realizing that her few words hardly told the whole story, she added, "There was a message I felt I had to give to my brother, some hope for him to be cured."

Ephrathah stared at her. "A cure for leprosy? Susanna, you are asking for a miracle."

"Yes, I am."

"What?"

"That *is* what I'm asking. You see, I've met a man . . . ," and she went on to tell what she knew about Jesus.

She would not have been dismayed had her companion expressed more doubt and was thus pleasantly surprised at her saying, "I wonder if that's the same Jesus we heard about the last time we went through Galilee. We were told of a prophet or teacher from the town of Nazareth who was going around preaching and doing miracles."

"Like what?" she asked eagerly.

The older woman shrugged. "I don't remember exactly. It was a good story, and I enjoy hearing new and different things. One gets tired of walking day after day, and anything which varies that is appreciated."

"Do you know if there were healings?" Susanna prodded.

"I'm fairly sure there were, but I don't recall what they were."

What a wonderful opportunity! "Ephrathah, could I ask a very great favor? If, while passing through Galilee or Judea, you hear things concerning Jesus of Nazareth, would you please pay close attention, then tell me about them?"

"Of course. But don't expect too much. His glory probably won't last any longer than all the other self-proclaimed prophets who keep appearing on the scene."

Susanna glanced around to see who might be listening, then dropped her voice. "I think He's the Messiah we've been waiting for all these centuries."

"Because he knew something about your past? A smart person can make wise guesses, or he may have talked with somebody . . ."

"He didn't speak like a fake or a fraud."

"A good one wouldn't *be* good if he sounded like one," she reminded wryly.

"Well, I still think that's who He is. Who else do you know who can drive out the spirits of madness and heal a hand and arm that were poisoning the child and, at the same time, heal joints that were so swollen and hot they barely moved?"

"I've never seen such a thing," Ephrathah admitted. "Well, Susanna, if I meet Him or if I hear anything about Him, I'll let you know."

The wife of the caravan leader went back to talk with Adiah, her two children, and other caravan followers before moving forward again. Susanna suspected that by the time the group got to Damascus there'd be nobody she had not met and talked with.

How kind she was. How friendly. Taharka had said Ephrathah was skilled at taking care of travel injuries, and Susanna wished she herself had more competence at that and more knowledge of herbs and medicines. If the woman came back this way Susanna would ask about some of the treatments she used.

Her knowing various healing methods might make Ephrathah more skeptical concerning Jesus but, on the other hand, she would be aware even more than most people how often even the best treatments failed.

In the far distance Susanna saw another caravan approaching the town they were nearing. Would Taharka know this caravan master as well as he knew Mibzar? She hoped they would all stay here overnight before traveling south again, for she was getting a bit footsore. Working around the inn all day was a lot different from tramping over the dusty, stony roads of Samaria and here in the southern portion of Galilee.

~~~~~~

So this was Nain, the new home for Adiah and her children. It appeared to be a pleasant small town with narrow streets, stone houses, and a centrally-located well. In fact it was much like many of the villages in Samaria. The provinces of Galilee and Samaria had both been part of the territory of the original ten tribes that constituted the kingdom of Israel, as separate from the land of the two tribes in the south that was now Judea.

Wasn't it sad there was all this misunderstanding and enmity between people? Was it just that they didn't have the opportunity to get to know one another better? Certainly since meeting Jesus, Andrew, Nathanael, Peter, and Philip she would never again be able to see all Galileans in a negative light.

Besides, Jesus had told her the time would come when there would be no difference between them, at least insofar as worship was concerned.

She hoped that time would come soon!

Nain did not have an inn big enough to take care of the people or livestock, so tents were raised outside of town, and fires were started. Susanna was glad she'd brought meal already ground so it didn't take long to prepare the flat thin loaves. Some were already cooking when Taharka came to tell her he had been to see the leader of the southbound caravan that was camped on the other side of the town. Arrangements had been made to leave with them early the next morning.

She was ready for sleep by the time the stars came out. She stretched out on the ground wrapped in her mantle with a blanket nearby for when it got cooler during the night.

She could not help smiling to herself. It was not long ago that her sister-in-law had forced her to leave and she'd worried herself sick thinking about how awful it would be to lie out under the open skies.

Well, it would have been terrifying then, and it would be now, too, were it not for the security of being with the caravan. It helped even more to know Taharka was lying here beside her, so close she longed to reach out and touch him.

He must have fallen asleep already, for he wasn't moving at all but was breathing regularly, apparently completely at ease. What had he talked to Jonah about? Why had he come himself and not just sent Putiel or one of the other servants? Could it mean that he cared especially for Jonah? For her?

Or would he have done this for *any* of his servants?

She lay awake for a long time listening to the sounds around her, seeing shadowlike people silhouetted before the fires, smelling the pungent odor of the camels and donkeys and hearing their grunts and braying.

The humming and buzzing of insects were hardly worth note, for they were present at the inn, too. She pulled the end of her robe over her face and went to sleep.

The morning activities began long before sunup, as she had known they would. She rose when the others did, and, although she didn't have animals to care for or load, making the fire and cooking the bread kept her busy until Taharka returned. "Shishak's caravan is getting ready to move," he announced, a note of expectancy in his voice.

"Good. Everything is ready here." As they ate, she waited for the new caravan to arrive, and watched the group she had been with the day before as they gathered into their comparatively tight formation. At the last moment she ran over to remind Ephrathah, "Please wave to my brother on your way back. And get any news you can about Jesus."

The woman patted her hand. "I'll be interested too. But at your busy inn you may get information before I do."

~~~~~~

As it turned out, Susanna learned nothing more until Ephrathah's return. They met in the courtyard soon after the caravan's arrival and embraced like long-separated friends. Ephrathah was obviously excited. "I could hardly wait to get here. When we arrived at Nain last evening I went into the town and asked questions about your Jesus. I got a lot of different opinions, but one story that seems to have met with everyone's belief is His healing of the son of one of Herod Antipas' officials."

"He healed a Roman?"

"It seems that the child, who lives in Capernaum, was very sick and at the point of death. The court doctors as well as others in the area tried their very best, but the child kept getting worse and worse, until the family knew he would die. I don't know how they heard of Jesus, though He seems to be traveling around and speaking in synagogues and wherever He finds people. Anyway, He was at Cana, twenty-five miles from Capernaum, so it wasn't just on a whim that the father set out to find Him. He traveled all day, and it wasn't until nearly sundown that he found Him at Cana and begged Him to come to Capernaum."

"Did they start right away?"

"That's what I'd have expected, but He didn't do that."

Susanna felt a stab of disappointment. "He didn't heal the child?"

"I didn't say that," Ephrathah broke in, shaking her head. "He looked around at the Galileans and said something about unless they saw signs and wonders they wouldn't believe Him. When the father, terribly upset, pleaded with Him to come heal the boy, Jesus turned and commended him for the faith that had brought him all this distance and then simply told him to return to Capernaum, for his son was well."

"Just like *that*?"

"Just like that. Well, the officer was delighted and would have started back home that night except that his companions talked him out of it. It's not safe for *anyone* on the highway at night, as you know. Besides, he was exhausted from the long, hard trip. They stayed overnight with somebody in Cana and were halfway home the next day when met by servants with the report that the child had completely recovered early the night before."

"Oh, how wonderful!"

"I don't doubt this is a true story, but I'll check further when we stop at Capernaum on our next trip north," she promised.

In the little time she could further spare, Susanna asked about the trip itself and thanked Ephrathah for her courtesy when Susanna had traveled with the caravan.

Now she fretted that if she had only asked, Jesus might have healed Jonah even at a distance. But how could she have known He could do that?

thirteen

That Taharka still did not eat or read the Scriptures with her troubled Susanna greatly. She'd have liked to ask him about that, but shortly after their return from the trip, he had requested that the scrolls be brought to his room, as he wished to study them.

She missed them. And she missed him. However, he was still thoughtful and each day pleasantly asked how she was.

He never mentioned, though, what was still taking him away many afternoons or what kept him in his rooms so much of the time.

A screen covered the passageway connecting her room to his, but sounds carried easily. Long after she went to bed she would hear him pacing his floor. Something was obviously troubling him greatly. How she wished she could help, but, because she didn't understand the problem, all she could do was continue working to the best of her ability and keep things running smoothly at the inn.

Several long weeks passed before Putiel brought her the message as the women and children left her room after studying arithmetic. "The master has need of you."

Rolling up the last mat from the floor, she said, "Thank you, Putiel," and went outside, turned right, and knocked on Taharka's doorframe. "It's Susanna," she called, hoping her voice sounded more assured than she felt.

She entered hesitantly in response to his bidding, then hurried quickly toward where he was resting on the elongated, bedlike caned piece of furniture. "You're ill!" she cried, seeing that his face had that sickly, greenish-white pallor seen only on the dark-complexioned.

Breathing deeply, he started to sit up straighter against the pillows on which he was propped. His eyes closed to hide pain, and his lips pressed tightly together for a moment. "No, Susanna, I am not sick."

"Thank Yahweh you don't have a fever, but you *do* have much pain, don't you?" she asked, her hand on his forehead.

"More even than I'd anticipated," he admitted.

He had not shaved, something he did without fail before he began his day. "Can I get something for you?"

A weak smile tugging at his lips, he said, "Yes, please. Your needle, thread, and four blue tassels."

Her head was cocked slightly, and her brow wrinkled in the effort to understand. "Four blue tassels?"

"Yes. Get them right away and bring them here."

She did as requested, though she wondered whom they were for. Only Samaritan men wore them; Jews used white ones on the corners of their mantles. This reminded her that she hadn't taken care of that for her brother's robe. Maybe Taharka was about to send another one to him, or perhaps just a needle, thread, and tassels would be delivered by one of the caravans.

Quickly she reprimanded herself. She was being very self-centered in thinking of her brother as the recipient of more of Taharka's generosity. After all, tassels made here were justifiably recognized as being of the best quality wool, with the longest strands.

Hurrying back, she stood before him, uncertain what to do. "Take my mantle, which is folded there on the table beside you," he directed, "and sew one tassel on each corner."

She looked from him to the robe and back again. Nodding, she lifted the heavy garment and sat down with it on her lap. Neither of them spoke during the entire time it took to attach the tassels, but that should not have seemed strange. Often in the past they had enjoyed a companionable silence.

If only he'd tell her what this was all about! Perhaps she'd never learn, but that thought gave her pain as she remembered his past sharing of many plans, dreams, and ideas.

Biting off the thread, she patted the cloth into a neat rectangle on her lap and smiled at him. "I'm finished, Taharka."

He winced as he pushed himself up to a rather bent standing position and then straightened. "Bring it to me."

But when she rose and carried it across to him he requested, "Help me put it on."

She started to protest, to remind him that he was not permitted to wear the robe with these tassels, but he was obviously sick. She had better humor him, she thought, unfolding the finely woven garment that she recognized as one she had made. She helped adjust it over his left shoulder and then he just stood there, holding on to the back of his chair. "What do you think?" he asked.

How could she answer such a question? "It looks very . . . nice," she managed. He leaned over to see the tassels, which were brushing the tops of his sandal-clad feet. "I think so, too."

His gaze was so intent upon her then that she could not help but wonder if he did, indeed, have a fever that she'd failed to recognize. "Susanna, I have to talk with you . . ."

He seemed to be swaying slightly. "I'd like that, but couldn't you sit down to do it?" she asked, coaxing as she would a child.

"Not now. Not until I say what I've . . . summoned you to say." He was breathing heavily, and the muscle at the side of his cheek twitched.

She had a moment of sheer panic. Suppose he was tired of having her here. Perhaps he was standing to show his authority as he told her to leave his house. She bit her lower lip to still its trembling. *Oh, please, Yahweh, don't let him send me away!*

"You thought it was kind of me to go with you to see Jonah," he began, and she nodded silently. "But it was not kindness, it was sheer selfishness. I had been thinking about it even before Jesus came, and then when I talked with Him . . ."

"About Jonah?"

He shook his head. "About many other things. Anyway, much of what I'd studied with my son and had read with you began to make sense. I started going to the rabbi in the afternoons with many questions I couldn't figure out for myself, and I began reading the five books again and again, memorizing those portions he recommended."

She waited, breathless, not sure if she was going to cry or laugh with joy. "And then, Susanna, we went to see your brother. He is now the head of your family, and I wanted to ask him—to see whether, if and when I were to be accepted as a proselyte into the Samaritan faith, he'd be willing for me to ask you to be my wife."

It was all she could do to keep from running to him. "Today I am accepted as a Samaritan," he announced. "My beard will take a while to become respectable," he said, running his hand over the stubble on his chin, "and there's still much I don't fully understand, but *now* I can ask my question. Susanna, will you marry me?"

She threw herself into his arms, rubbing her face against his scratchy one, then found herself being gently pushed away. "I'm sorry, dear one," he said, and his eyes, as she looked up, confused, showed love as well as pain. "The priest just performed the circumcision an hour ago, and I am so terribly sore!"

"Oh, how thoughtless of me!" she apologized. "You tried to tell me, didn't you? Please, Taharka, sit down or lie down or do anything that might help . . ."

He chuckled. "I had to stand, wearing my robe with its four new tassels, while I asked you my question. I cannot lie down until I receive my answer."

She reached for his hands and held them against her cheeks. "Taharka, I've loved you ever since soon after I came here, and that love has grown with each kind word, each gentle act, each look, each touch . . ." Words failed her at the immensity of what was happening, what he had told her.

"And so your answer is?"

"You could not doubt that I would say yes."

"Then say it, Susanna," he urged.

She drew in a deep breath and released it as, looking into his eyes, she stated, "Yes, Taharka, I greatly desire to become your wife, to live with you and care for you and be all that you wish me to be."

He leaned over and kissed her, his hands holding her shoulders. "My dear, beautiful Susanna. Thank you for accepting. But now," turning and shrugging off the woolen robe, he eased himself back onto the couch, "I must lie down before I fall down."

As she knelt beside his couch, the fingers of her left hand strayed upward into the curly hair she'd longed so often to touch. It was soft, as she'd known it would be, and his chest was hard where her face rested against it. She could hear his heart thumping within his chest and could feel his breath against the wavy tendrils of her hair.

"I could stay here forever," she whispered, expecting him to rise as the sound of the first arriving caravan was heard.

However, his arm remained around her, and his open hand held her head where it was. "Putiel will take care of things tonight," he said. "He knows how it is with me. I could not stand out there and greet people and take care of all that must be done."

Finally they had time to talk of many things, including their marriage, which they decided should be as soon as possible but without fanfare. They would invite only the people from here at the inn and perhaps Deborah as witnesses, and they would have it in the daytime if that was all right with the priest, because that was when everyone could be free.

"I have no dowry," she reminded him sadly some time later.

"You *are* the dowry," he declared, squeezing her hand even more tightly. "I have plenty of money, cloth, and jewels and wish for nothing more. Just you."

She smiled mistily. "I wish Jonah could be here!"

"I wish that also. We'll just continue praying for him every day and hope he gets to meet Jesus."

She had neglected to tell him of Ephrathah's report of the long-distance healing of the son of the Roman official, and did so now. Later, it seemed significant to her that, even at this time of her greatest happiness, Jesus was a part of their conversation.

She had just given him a drink when she brought up a matter that troubled her. "Taharka," she began hesitantly, "did you remember about my previous marriages?"

"Of course. You've told me about them."

"Well, you recall that I have been—known—by three different men, although the one was only for a short time, until his wife got him to divorce me. The problem is, I've never had a child, nor ever even conceived. Perhaps, Taharka, it would be better for you to marry a different woman, one who could give you children."

He seemed to be giving the matter some thought, and waves of sorrow threatened to overwhelm her when he asked, "Have you somebody in mind?"

Her throat was dry as desert sand. "Perhaps . . . Sherah?" she suggested, looking down at the floor so he could not read the agony in her eyes.

"How would you feel about that, Susanna?" he asked. "Susanna? Don't look away from me."

She was afraid to raise her eyes, but she could not disobey the gentle voice. "I . . . I would try to be happy for you."

"But?"

The tears would not be controlled. "I think I would . . . would die."

He held out his arms, and she threw herself down on her knees again beside him. He wiped her tears and kissed her. "My dear little Susanna. You worry much too much about too many things. Don't you think I'm aware that you have no children? However, although my only son is dead, I've never before considered taking a second wife in order to perpetuate my line. If it should be the will of Yahweh that we have children, we would rejoice together in that happiness. However," shrugging, "if such should not take place, I'd be no worse off in that regard than I am now."

"But you are still young enough—" she began.

"You are the only woman I want for my wife," he said, touching her lips with the tip of his forefinger to request she not bring it up again.

It was all she could do to leave him after that, but before long she went to help the servants.

She said nothing to them about Taharka's proposal, of her acceptance, or about his becoming a Samaritan, although her mind was so full of these wonders that she could scarcely think of anything else.

"Susanna," Rachel pouted, "you're not listening to me."

She started, almost knocking a spoon from the wooden bench. "I'm sorry, Rachel, what did you say?"

"I asked if you would play the numbers game with us."

She tried, but everyone was soon teasing her, for she made mistakes and was not as quick as usual. After one error she looked up to see Putiel in the gateway. She would have expected him to be harried with the responsibilities that had been thrust upon him, but his grin as he looked at her was almost conspiratorial.

"You're looking very handsome and official in that short white tunic," she complimented, walking toward him.

He had always been aloof and seldom spoke to her until after Rachel's healing; since then things had become much more relaxed between them. "Taharka thought it made me look more like his representative this way." He nodded toward the busy group before him. "I assume you have not told them?"

"It is the master's place to tell them—whatever he chooses to," she finished softly.

"Not many women could keep from spreading that word."

"It's not that I'm not tempted to do so."

His smile was a benediction. "May I say that I am well pleased —for both of you?"

She touched one of his crossed arms. "Thank you, my friend."

The work of the evening seemed to get done with unusual ease as Susanna had boundless energy, and yet, in another way, the time dragged, for she wanted so badly to look in on Taharka. It would be good to touch him, to hold him, to help him forget his pain in her nearness.

Finally the work was completed, and she was free. Her knock was little louder than the footfall of a mouse, but he heard. "Come in," he called, laying the scroll down beside him.

"Shall I put it on the table?" she asked and did so when he willingly handed it to her. "Taharka, I'd like to ask a very big favor of you."

His brow was raised quizzically. "What is it, little one?"

She knelt beside him, arm around his waist, hand under his shoulder as his fingers slid up along her neck and out through her hair, the long, softly waving strands slipping slowly through his fingers. "When we are married, could we please—when it's convenient for you, of course—begin to read again from the scrolls?"

"You liked that, didn't you?"

"So very much!" she exclaimed. "It was like heaven to have you there beside me, teaching me the words and reading with me."

"Yet you have not once asked me to do it since—since the Galileans were here."

"It wasn't my place to ask it of you, but I missed it, and you, very much."

"I grant your favor, although, as I enjoy it as much as you do, it's not really a favor to *you*, is it?" he said, smiling crookedly. "But I think we should establish some other rules before we get married. I think that if you have some desire, need, fear, or something that should be discussed between us, you should tell me about it."

She hesitated. "I'm not sure I always can, Taharka. I've been taught that the man is to make decisions and it is his will that must be obeyed. And certainly in my other marriages I couldn't discuss problems."

"I'm like your previous husbands?"

"Oh, no, not at all!" But then she had to be fair. "Well, perhaps the one who died before we knew each other was a *little* like you, but it's hard to say, for Shannon and I were not together much. What prevented my coming to you before was that I didn't know if I had done something wrong that made you wish not to eat with me or read with me."

He raised his head from the pillow to kiss her again before he explained. "I didn't spend time alone with you because I didn't trust myself. I didn't want to frighten you, and I didn't want to make promises or requests I wasn't free to follow through with. So I thought it best to see you only out in the courtyard or outside the gate where others were around."

She snuggled closer to him, delighted to know he cared as much as she did, but then she had to shift position as she saw a spasm of pain cross his face.

"I've wondered if you would prefer keeping your room as the bedroom for both of us," he asked much later. "Or would you rather move into the smaller one I now use, which would leave your present one for your teaching and for you to rest or work in while I'm here in my office."

She didn't even have to consider the answer. "I'd prefer coming to you in your room," she answered immediately and then realized how that sounded.

"I love seeing you blush," he teased, which only made her cheeks get hotter.

They both knew she would have to go to bed soon, or morning would come before she was ready for it. She brought him a cup of water, but there seemed little more she could do. She walked with him to his bed, which was long, wide, and made of cane, like the chair and couch. She fluffed the wool-filled pad and straightened the blanket for him, then insisted on washing his feet. "It will make you feel more fresh and ready for sleep," she coaxed.

At first he refused, then, seeing that it meant something very important to her, as the first service to her betrothed, he permitted it. When she leaned over to kiss him good night after he'd stretched out on the bed, he said, "At least tonight you're perfectly safe putting me to bed."

"Yes, I know," she said demurely, but her eyes were dancing.

Her heart was, too, as she went on down the passageway to push the screen aside and enter her own room.

～～～～

As soon as the caravans had left the following morning, Taharka requested Putiel to gather everyone near the cistern. He put on a white tunic and the robe with its four newly attached blue tassels and walked out before them.

Susanna watched him come, admiring his fortitude in not wincing as the material brushed his body. "I have several announcements to make," he began, looking from one to another until he had met each eye. "First, and this may come as a surprise to many of you, I have now become a Samaritan. I have studied long and hard and have had many sessions with the priest and the rabbi. And yesterday I was circumcised," he added.

The women's dropping their gaze was not from embarrassment, as they were aware that all Samaritan males had to be circumcised. However, they knew how painful this procedure was for an adult. They looked up quickly, however, when he continued, "And the second *very* important announcement is that Susanna and I are to be married in a few days."

Suddenly there was shouting and laughter, and everyone crowded around her with expressions of joy and wishes for her happiness. It was a few moments before Susanna's eyes turned again toward Taharka where he stood alone except for Putiel. He had a smile on his face as he raised one hand, palm forward, as though giving a blessing, then turned and moved slowly toward his office.

The following days were crowded with activity. "We will be married shortly before midday on Friday," he announced. "That way we can have the wedding feast at noon and enjoy singing and dancing until sundown."

That was the first it had occurred to Susanna how much it was costing Taharka financially to become a Samaritan. He was going to be unable to host travelers from sundown Friday until sundown Saturday each week. Would the leaders of caravans become angry about this and stop coming?

The law was clear. She had memorized this part of the Ten Commandments: "Observe the Sabbath day, to keep it holy. Six days you shall labor, and do all your work; but the seventh day is the Sabbath to the LORD your God, you shall not do any work, you, or your son, or your daughter, your manservant, or your maidservant, your cattle, or the sojourner who is within your gates; for in six days the LORD made heaven and earth, the sea, and all that is in them, and rested the seventh day: therefore, the LORD blessed the Sabbath day and hallowed it."

"That was one thing I had difficulty accepting," he admitted when she spoke of it to him. "Although I could understand that I, as a Samaritan, should not be working, it did not seem necessary to apply this rule to the non-Samaritan servants."

But then he shrugged and smiled. "I finally concluded that if Yahweh could create something as great as the entire world and also someone small like me, He must know what's best. He gave the laws to Father Moses, and through all the centuries, through wars, uprisings, fires, and floods, these words have come down to us. He must have meant it for me, Taharka, an Egyptian

Samaritan innkeeper, just as much as He does for an Arab carpenter or a Jewish merchant."

She loved him when he talked like that. She also loved him when they sat quietly together, which was not often enough, and she loved him when she saw him directing the travelers to where they were to stay.

She loved him all the time.

It seemed strange to her when people from the town made comments about Taharka's becoming a Samaritan so he could marry her. As much as she prided herself on being a Samaritan, she knew if he had asked her, she would have married him even if he weren't one. After all, ever since she had come to live here, she'd been unable to worship in the synagogue.

Would she be allowed to now?

The priest didn't give her a clear-cut answer to that question when he came to talk about the marriage. It was obvious to her that he stayed outside the inn's gates because he didn't wish to be defiled, although the servants were already cleaning and scrubbing everything.

Susanna herself scoured Taharka's bedroom and took the blankets to the creek to be pounded clean on the rocks then draped over bushes to dry in the fierce sun. This had not been her job since she'd come to live here, and she would normally have avoided it if she had the choice.

She still found herself looking over her shoulder, remembering the rape of several years before.

But this was Taharka's bedding, which, tonight, would be shared with her. She shivered, not from the coldness of the water in which she stood but from the deliciousness of knowing that in a little while she would be his.

Returning to the inn, she found that Putiel and the women had brought in and filled the big tub she had used her first day here. It was not strange anymore, and she enjoyed the luxury of being wet all over at the same time and being able to feel totally clean.

She got dressed in the new gown of the softest, whitest linen she had ever seen. She relished knowing that, without even hinting to her about it, Taharka had asked one of the caravans to bring it for her. That was another proof that this marriage was something he had seriously thought about for months.

Her hair, which was parted in the middle as usual, was combed to hang down her back to dry into soft waves.

"May I come in?" Taharka called.

Under usual circumstances, the groom's men would go to the bride's father's house and take her to where the groom was waiting in his home or that of his father. This is where she would be expected to live for the rest of her life.

However, because they already lived in the same place and the marriage would be a much more private affair, they would not be so formal.

She ran to the door and pulled him inside. Their arms were around one another, and she whispered against his ear, "Oh, Taharka, I'm so happy."

His lips brushed the smoothness of her cheek. "I'm glad you are. I am, too."

"Thank you for this lovely tunic and the new sandals and girdle," she began, but he stopped her with a kiss.

"My love, it is you who grace the clothes, not they you."

She could feel her cheeks getting hot again and was more flustered when he grinned at her. "I suspect you will get over blushing before long, but I think I'm going to miss it."

He removed a small packet from his girdle and untwisted the cloth. "I've brought something, Susanna, which I treasure very much." The sunlight streaming through the open door was broken into tiny dancing fragments by the many facets of a large ruby pendant. "It belonged to my mother and to her mother and her mother before her, back so far nobody knows from where it came originally."

Fascinated, she watched as it swung back and forth. "It's beautiful," she breathed softly, reaching out her forefinger to gently touch it. She bowed her head to make it easier for him to put the golden chain about her neck, then looked up at him slowly. "It is the finest gift I have ever received. And you are the finest man I have ever known. I pray to Yahweh that I'll be worthy of all these blessings."

He held her close. "You *are* worthy of all good things, Susanna. I hope *I* can be worthy of *you*." With a hand on each of her shoulders, he stepped back a pace. "Stay here until Putiel comes for you."

"I will be waiting."

"And don't be frightened," he cautioned.

Her hands framed his face and pulled it down to meet hers. "I can't fear anything when you are with me."

The ceremony itself was finished quickly. If not for the long portions of scripture that the priest recited and the prayers that were said, it would have been over with little more than her stating her intention of being a faithful, obedient, industrious wife and his of taking care of and loving her.

Dinner was superb and the food and wine plentiful. It seemed almost indecent to not be doing something productive in the afternoon, but this was a holiday and they were all going to enjoy it.

Then Susanna and Taharka went together to the room where Taharka had slept alone for all these years since his wife had died.

He would be alone no more.

fourteen

Awaking before he did, she relished the feeling of his body curved around hers, his arm about her waist. She smiled in the darkness, and her arm pressed his more closely to her. She could feel his breath against her ear, and turned so her bare arm could come around his shoulders.

He started to awaken, and she became perfectly still. He needed his sleep, for he worked very hard and kept long hours. He shifted his position a little but did not release her. She sighed. *Thank you, Yahweh. Oh, thank you!*

When morning came he didn't get up right away. "It seems odd not to have camels snorting and their tenders bawling out orders," he commented, stretching to his full length.

"Yes, it does. But it's especially nice this morning to have it that way," she said.

He laughed softly, running a finger down the line of her nose, then outling her lips. "You feel very brave saying that, when you know I'm not completely healed."

She moved nearer her side of the bed. "Very well," her voice became very prim, "I shall behave myself and be a proper lady."

"Oh, please! You don't want me to be sorry we married, do you?" he said, drawing her back to him.

And then she was clinging to him, the joking lost in the depth of her love for him. "Taharka, please don't ever, *ever* be sorry you married me."

He proved very satisfactorily that he was not.

~~~~~

Each day he got around more easily, and by Tuesday was again in charge of the inn. He told Susanna how much more secure he felt now that Putiel had some experience in running the business, for he had worried since the death of his son what would become of the inn were he to become ill even for a short time.

As the days, weeks, and months passed, he often had Susanna sit with him as he went over accounts and made records on the long scrolls. He also gave her exercises to help improve her writing of letters and words until the day came when he dictated messages and records of financial transactions as she wrote them, either on wax tablets or scrolls.

Everything about the business intrigued her. She started going to the market with the servants, teaching them how to distinguish the quality of particular goods, how to get the best prices, and also how to make sufficient notations so that records could be kept of all purchases.

Even so, she still set for herself the responsibility of going to the well each morning, and continued holding classes in the early afternoon for those wishing to attend. She had learned that this was an unpleasant chore for some, so school was made a privilege and not an obligation.

The saddest thing for Susanna that first year was Deborah's death. Susanna had gone to see her several times, but with her varied duties and her desire to enjoy as much free time as possible with Taharka, the months had passed quickly. She was told the news when she went to the well one spring morning. Esther's sweet young face and voice were sorrowful. "Poor Deborah tried so hard to keep going. She even cooked the evening bread for her son, though she was racked with coughing all the time. He told her to go lie down, but when she tried that, it got even worse."

"I hope it wasn't too difficult a death," Susanna said, remembering her grandfather's suffering torment for days before his release.

"She knew she was dying. And she was able to make the Confession of Faith for her very last words."

"Oh, I'm glad! That will be such a comfort to her family. She told me once she feared she would die coughing, and how could she then say, 'The Lord our God is one Lord'?"

Esther nodded, "She had to really struggle and tried many times before she managed those seven words. She lived for an hour afterward but would say nothing more. They were, as she'd planned, her final words."

By the time Susanna arrived at Deborah's house for the burial, which must be done within twenty-four hours of death, the purification by washing the body with clean water had been performed. The two three-wicked lamps she brought were placed with those that, as a token of respect and honor, were lit at Deborah's head and feet.

Deborah was wrapped in a cotton shroud and placed in a wooden coffin made of planks roughly nailed together. She made such a small bundle, unmoving and still. It seemed incongruous that only hours before she had been a living, breathing, working, vital being.

An old man stood at the side of the room reading aloud from the Law, and continued this even when the coffin was lifted by four young men and the procession formed to carry the body several miles to the place prepared at the foot of Mount Ebal.

The paid mourners wept, wailed, and raised their voices in anguish. Susanna thought, *Though I loved her dearly, my eyes are dry, yet tears are raining down the cheeks of these women who hardly knew her.*

At the grave, Susanna moved quietly, shadowlike, until her hand touched the rough boards. *I'm sorry to lose you, Deborah. You were a wonderful woman. May Yahweh be the friend you always thought He was. You told me on a day that now seems long ago that He hears even the prayers of a woman, so: Please, Yahweh, be merciful and loving and take her home with You.*

If only Deborah had stayed that morning and talked with Jesus . . .

If only she could have reached out to Him by herself, for herself, instead of fearing what others might have to say about it.

If only his being a Jew had not bothered her.

Sighing, Susanna turned away, walking by herself most of the way to Sychar, hardly noticing the wildflowers beside the stream she passed or the children climbing the steep side of Mount Gerizim, where she had gone with Andrew.

Poor Deborah. But maybe it wasn't she who should be pitied. Might she be with Yahweh right now? How Susanna hoped that was true!

Even when she got to the inn she hardly looked around, although she could not help but notice that a large caravan had already arrived. And then a short woman with a weathered, pleasant face bustled toward her. "Susanna, how are you?"

She brightened immediately and went to greet Ephrathah with a tight hug. It was a few minutes later that she said, "I'm sad today because of the loss of a very dear friend."

"I'm sorry. We never have enough of them but that the one taken is sorely missed."

"That's true." She laid her hand on the arm of this most unlikely friend and indicated the inviting doorway. "Come to my room, and we'll have refreshment."

They walked companionably to the place to which she'd been brought as a homeless outcast. She showed Ephrathah to a seat and reached for the skin she kept here for rare visitors. "Share with me this wine that is humbly offered for your enjoyment."

As they sipped the beverage and ate small sweet rolls made with honey and dates, Ephrathah told about some of her interesting experiences since they had last been together. In return, Susanna spoke of changes in her life.

"I wish I could read," Ephrathah said wistfully. "Girls were not allowed to be taught when I was growing up, and there's been no opportunity since."

Susanna started to offer to teach her, but they both realized there was too little time when Ephrathah stayed at the inn and the visits were too far apart to do much good. "Thank you for offering, anyway," the older woman said, smiling. "If I ever decide to settle down and stop following my husband from Egypt to Damascus, perhaps I can hire a tutor."

"Settle here in Sychar, and we can read together as Taharka and I do."

"It does sound wonderful. But as long as I'm well and Mibzar has the caravan I will be traveling." Then she added, "I've been eagerly waiting all the way north from Jerusalem to tell of my meeting with Jesus of Nazareth."

"Oh, I've been hoping you might know something more. You actually got to see Him?"

"Yes, I did, for the very first time, though I've heard additional stories about Him since I last talked with you."

"Where did you meet?"

"I wasn't more than the width of this room from Him right there in the Temple."

"Was He teaching?"

Ephrathah snorted. "Hah! Not with the Pharisees there. You see, they were very angry with Him."

"Why? What had He done?"

"It wasn't *what* He'd done that upset them, it was when He did it."

Susanna's brow wrinkled in puzzlement. "I think you'd better tell me from the beginning," she suggested, but then, as Ephrathah leaned back in the chair preparing to do that, she raised a hand. "Let me see if Taharka's free. He'd like to hear what you have to say."

Taharka couldn't come right then, so Ephrathah repeated for him later that evening the story she'd told Susanna. Hearing it again, Susanna sat perfectly still, hands clasped tightly together in her lap, watching the excitement on Ephrathah's face and listening to the sound of it in her voice.

"An older man carrying his bedroll through Jerusalem's street on the Sabbath was met by two Pharisees. 'It is the Sabbath, it is not lawful for you to carry your pallet,' they told him.

"But he answered right back that the man who healed him had told him to take up his bed and walk. Needless to say, this upset the leaders. They wanted to know who had healed on the Sabbath, especially because they didn't approve of somebody's encouraging a Jew to break the Sabbath by carrying a burden; that was *work*.

"Anyway, the man explained he didn't know who it was that had healed him, for the tall Jew had turned away into the crowd immediately after the miracle was performed.

"The Pharisees were upset about all this, but they must have realized they could get no further information from him, so they let the man go, after reminding him of the Law.

"The man had been crippled for *thirty-eight* years, Taharka, and was truly grateful for what had happened, so as soon as he took his bedroll home and told his family the news, he washed himself and went to the Temple to give thanks. And it was there that Jesus came right up to him and gave him a big smile and said, 'See, you are well! Sin no more, that nothing worse befall you.'

"When the Pharisees saw the healed man in the Temple, they asked him again who was responsible for the healing, and he joyfully told them it was Jesus of Nazareth.

"Now this first part I didn't actually see, but it was right about then that Mibzar and I, hearing and seeing the commotion, crossed over to that side of the Temple. I asked someone what was going on, and, when we learned who was involved, we stayed to see what would happen."

Her bright eyes looked from one to the other. "They started berating Jesus for working on the Sabbath, but then I heard Him say quite softly that it's all right to do good on the Sabbath. 'My Father is working still,' he said, 'and I am working.' "

She raised her strong, capable hands and flung them outward to express explosiveness. "They were outraged and accused Him of blasphemy. He was claiming that Yahweh was His Father, as though He were someone special to Yahweh. I thought He'd back down, that He'd apologize to these powerful men, but He did nothing of the kind. In fact, everything He added only made them all the angrier.

" 'Truly, truly,' He began, 'I say to you, the Son can do nothing of His own accord, but only what He sees the Father doing; for whatever *He* does, that the Son does likewise. For the Father loves the Son, and shows Him all that He himself is doing; and greater works than these will He show Him, that you may marvel.' "

Ephrathah, too excited to remain in her chair, walked back and forth as she continued. "They couldn't let that pass, of course, and they tried to make Him take back what He'd said. However, Jesus kept adding more and more things, each of which offended them more.

"He talked about personally seeing all the marvels that His Father does and said that He can do them as well, even to raising the dead—"

"Raising the dead?" Taharka repeated.

She raised her shoulders and spread her hands. "That's what He said. As I recall, it was like this: 'For as the Father raises the dead and gives them life, so also the Son gives life to whom He will.' He also spoke about the judgment of the Father, and that this has been given now to the Son, for His honor. And then He added, 'He who does not honor the Son does not honor the Father who sent Him.' "

Taharka's eyes sparkled in the lamplight. "Even if I hadn't respected and admired Him before, I'd have to applaud His sheer courage. I don't know if I could stand up to such men, even if I were a Jew."

Susanna smiled at her husband, then said to Ephrathah, "I'm not sure I understand that about Jesus' Father working."

"I think what He was saying was that although the Law states that Yahweh rested on the seventh day and we should do likewise, it isn't really that Yahweh stops working each seven days. I saw your friend Andrew there, and asked him about it. He says that it is right to do good on the Sabbath, and not evil. For example, it's permissible to keep a farm animal from drowning or to help others, but not to go around doing evil or things only for our own amusement, for that means we're less separated from the world and thus are not as close to Yahweh as we should be."

"That's an interesting interpretation," Taharka murmured, but he didn't have time to discuss the matter further as Putiel came to consult him about some difficulty between two of the caravans about lodging for the night.

All too soon Ephrathah left also, after again inviting Susanna to come to their room early in the morning to see the ivory figurines being transported under their personal protection for a wealthy Syrian.

"Could I pay you to deliver a bundle to my brother?" Susanna asked, after admiring the tall, slender carvings the next day.

"If you gather it quickly. Our caravan will be leaving soon."

Susanna hugged her friend spontaneously. "I was hoping you'd agree, so the bags are packed and ready," she confessed.

They talked together as the shouting, boisterous men went up and down the line that seemed so disorganized, so unwieldy, yet was part of a purposeful, vibrant whole. Susanna was glad she'd had the opportunity of traveling with the caravans those two days, for it meant much more to her now as she watched the bedding, cooking supplies, and tents attached with carefully balanced thoroughness to the short-legged donkeys. The merchandise and valuables that were the very reason for the caravan were being stashed on other asses and camels.

Finally, all bindings rechecked, word was shouted back down the line, and out between the wooden gates everyone passed. They turned right, through the massive, thick, ironbound portals of the town, and then northward into the mists of the morning, toward Galilee.

Galilee. Just south of there was her brother. And north of the boundary was the town of Nain, where the young widow probably lived now.

How was she doing? Had her husband's parents and family welcomed her, or was she left to fend for herself and her children?

North of Nain was Nazareth. Did Jesus spend much of His time there anymore? She had heard reports of His travels throughout Galilee, but Ephrathah spoke as though Jesus and His disciples were often in Jerusalem, too.

Did He travel through Samaria to get back and forth? It was certainly the most direct route and theoretically the simplest, but most Jews would cross the Jordan just below the Sea of Galilee and go south through the Decapolis and Perea, fording the Jordan down near Jericho to climb the steep route up to Jerusalem.

If only He would come this way again soon. Certainly He knew He was always welcome at this inn.

It was almost a year since Jesus had been here, and much had taken place! Especially outstanding had been the trip to see Jonah, and her marriage to Taharka. And now, well, now she had a secret, or *maybe* had a secret, that she didn't want to share with anyone until she was absolutely sure.

She went to fetch the special water pot kept now in her room since the one she'd previously used had accidentally been broken when bumped from its shelf by the door. It was earlier than usual for her to go for water, but she didn't feel like helping with those tasks she usually set for herself.

She walked briskly down the path, her flat-soled sandals hardly raising dust because of the dew. It was decidedly cool, but she relished shivering just a little bit, for she knew that in a short time it would be very hot.

She got to Jacob's Well and was drawing the last bucket of water to fill her pot as the first sliver of sun cast her shadow westward. She drew herself to her full height, head tilted upward, arms spread out and lifted before her. She drew in a big breath and let it out slowly while a wonderful feeling of being right with all the universe filled her.

"Good morning, sun," she greeted softly then, feeling embarrassed, looked around quickly. *Oh, thank you, Yahweh, for not letting anyone see me do that. Someone would be sure to think I was following the Canaanite worship of the sun, and I wasn't, You know. I am just so thankful You made this world so beautiful and that You let me be born and live in Samaria, which must be the most wonderful part of all You made.*

She turned slowly to check on where her shadow fell, and her gaze continued upward across craggy outcroppings and the patches of brush, weeds, and grass that had taken up residence there. A courageous goat was nibbling its way across the northeast section of Mount Gerizim, coming toward the path she and Andrew had climbed.

According to Ephrathah, Andrew was still traveling with Jesus. Had he ever learned to heal people, as he had desired?

She lifted the heavy water pot, positioned it carefully on her head, and returned to Sychar with a brisk tread. She wanted to get back to the inn, to see Taharka, to touch him, to know visually and physically what her mind knew but that was still almost too marvelous to believe.

The love they shared was growing deeper with each passing week, and their delight in each other was so great she was filled with wonder whenever she thought of it.

And now there just might be—there *must* be, though such a blessing had seemed impossible—an added gift from Yahweh.

She longed to reveal the good news to Taharka but told herself she must wait a little while yet. If she still did not have her monthly bleeding by the quarter moon, she would know for sure.

Oh, Yahweh, please let it be true!

She did not see her husband as she entered the courtyard and went directly to the large container used for drinking water. Carefully she removed the close-fitting lid and folded back the tightly woven cloth covering the opening. She lifted down the pot, from which she had not spilled a drop, and poured the precious liquid in with what was left from yesterday. Tomorrow she would start filling the alternate receptacle so this one could be scrubbed thoroughly.

The empty jug was light enough that she carried it in her arms back to her room, or what she still thought of that way, in contrast to Taharka's office or "their" bedroom. It was not furnished much differently from when she'd first seen it, although the mat on the ledge where she had slept then was now a padded, needleworked one, made more for decorative purposes than for serviceability.

She looked at it longingly, surprised that, although she had felt eager to get up and around only two hours earlier, she was tired already.

Maybe if she ate some breakfast she would feel better, but that thought was rejected by her body at once. She had not lost any meals, for which she was grateful, but she often felt half-nauseated. Such was now the case.

She'd just lie down for a few minutes, and then, whether or not she felt completely herself, she would get up and help tend to tasks involved with keeping the inn running smoothly.

Unfolding the cloth, she spread it out on the stone slab, then, lying down, pulled a portion of it over herself. At first she was on her back, with arm raised to cover her eyes, but this was uncomfortable. Turning on her side, away from the window and door, she bunched the cloth so it kept out the light. She was not accustomed to lying down while there was light outside. Not only did it feel strange, but she felt like a slackard.

It would only be for a few moments, until her stomach felt a little better . . .

"Susanna?" She heard the voice saying, and then, again, "Susanna, my beloved, are you ill?"

She was dreaming. She was on a long trip, walking at the end of a very great caravan so long she was unable to see its front. She was heading north, with the morning sun on her right, but the cattle would not stay where they belonged with the drovers, and they were jostling her, pushing on her shoulder.

"Susanna, can I help you?" the voice was asking, and the note of worry, of genuine concern, got through to her. She knew she should reassure the one calling her, so she turned, but a little moan came out as she did. The softness of his curly beard was against her cheek and, turning, she reached both arms to hold him close.

A little smile came to her lips before she even opened her eyes. "I love you, Taharka."

"I love you, too," he assured her, but he had to know. "What's wrong, dear?"

Her smile faded as she struggled to rise, ashamed that he had found her asleep during the morning. "Oh, I'm sorry, Taharka. I got back from getting water from Jacob's Well and I felt tired, so . . . so . . ."

His eyes, in the dim light as dark as midnight, did not miss a thing. "That's only part of it."

"I thought I'd lie down a few minutes, but must have fallen asleep." She was still trying to sit up, but he held the covers around her, keeping her down.

"You're not as well as usual, are you?" he persisted.

She wanted to assure him that all was well, that there was nothing wrong at all, but to her dismay, she felt tears well up behind her eyelids. Oh, how weak of her body to do this! She started to speak, but then, finding her lower lip trembling, she bit down to control it.

Lifting her as easily as though she were a child, he turned and sat where she'd been lying. She was on his lap, his arms holding her tight. "Tell me about it, Susanna. Please," he coaxed. "I do not choose to think there's anything you can't tell me. Is it something bad?"

Her voice was muffled as her head burrowed between his shoulder and neck. "I hope you won't think so."

"Do you think so?"

It would be perfect to stay just where she was, held by this man she loved, but she had to see his face as she told him what she knew must be said now instead of several days later. "I think it's wonderful—if *you* do," she started.

He looked at her with such concentration that the furrowed brow almost gave the impression of anger, but then his expression relaxed and his mobile mouth turned up with the smallest of smiles. "I think it's time for you to tell me, dearest," he encouraged.

"I've daydreamed and thought many times of how I was going to give my news, but I never planned it to be like *this*," she said ruefully. Suspecting he already had a good idea of what she'd thought was a secret, she traced the outline of his lips with her first finger. "What I'd rehearsed was to say that I hope our firstborn child will be a boy and he'll look and be just like his father."

She watched, enthralled, as his joy and fulfillment were mirrored on his ruggedly handsome face. The lines at the outside of his eyes deepened, and his dark brown eyes sparkled with happiness. "Wonderful?" he repeated what she'd said before. "I do think it's wonderful! And I want you to think that, too!"

His lips parted in a wholehearted smile showing his even white teeth. "I'd like to have a son so my line could continue, but also so this inn could remain in our family. However, should Yahweh give us a daughter, so be it. If she is as lovable, dear, sweet, and intelligent as you, I'll love her as much as any son."

She clung tightly to him. "I've never been with child before, Taharka, and I didn't want to speak with any of the women until I'd told you—I had to tell *you* first of all, since our love was responsible for the conception."

Apparently he had to interrupt her at that point, but she rejoiced in his kisses, caresses, and reassurances.

It was not in the telling, but in his special care of her, his insisting she not carry heavy burdens, that made everyone at the inn suspicious, and then sure, that their master and mistress were expecting an addition to the family.

"Yahweh is so good," she murmured to Taharka as she lay in his arms one night.

He chuckled. "I've noticed."

She enjoyed his running his hand across her bare shoulder and down her arm, but that had not been what she meant this time.

"Through the years I've wished I had been blessed with a baby, but Yahweh knew better than I when the time was right. It would have been wrong to bring a child into a home where there was no love, but now . . . this baby will be the result of our love and not just for . . . for . . ."

He laughed softly. "Dear little Susanna. I'll bet your face is as red as though burned by the sun, as embarrassed as you sound." She started to try to explain more, but he put his finger on her lips. "I understand. I really do. I thought I'd never have another child after Necho's mother died. I never saw a woman I cared enough about to want to live with or even share a bed with, until you came to the inn."

She clung tightly to him. "I never knew what love was before, Taharka. Marriage was never a choice for me but made for the convenience of others. Thank you, oh thank you so very much for loving me and teaching me to love."

"You are an apt pupil, my wife."

"And you are an excellent teacher, my love . . ."

fifteen

The days had passed quickly ever since she'd come to the inn, but now they flew by. Complying with Taharka's wish that she discontinue her water-carrying duties, she busied herself more with weaving and sewing, in addition to helping him with the record keeping. It was several months later, while looking through some of the previous scrolls, that she said, "Taharka, there aren't nearly as many caravans stopping here of late. Is it entirely because of the Sabbath?"

He nodded slowly. "It has become a serious problem. Even many who came for years are not as faithful." He rose to pace back and forth across the office. "And I can't really blame them. If I were leading a caravan and found that the inn where I'd planned to stay was closed from sundown Friday until the same time Saturday, I probably wouldn't keep going back, either."

"Would it help to *explain* the reason for it?"

"To a Jew or a Samaritan this makes sense, though either of them truly practicing his religion wouldn't be traveling then. However, to a Syrian, Ethiopian, or Egyptian this seems not only unbusinesslike but stupid and inconsiderate."

"I can see how it would appear so . . ."

"As time goes on, some don't send a man ahead to find out if we're welcoming people on a particular night. Instead, they camp outside of town, and, if they need to replenish provisions, they find other places to do it."

"If only we could accommodate more on Saturday—if they would arrive after sundown," she said wistfully. "Or if the commandment didn't read that even the servants are not allowed to work."

He came to a stop just inside the door, looking out. Slowly he turned toward her. "I keep thinking of something, and I'm not sure whether it's of Yahweh or of Beliel."

She wanted to protest that the devil could not be bothering such a fine person, but he needed to tell someone about this. He continued, "Remember Ephrathah's talking of Jesus' answer to the Pharisees concerning work being done on the Sabbath? Well, is it possible that could apply *here?*"

She wished she could tell him it was all right, but she really didn't think it was. After all, the commandment was very specific. "I . . . don't know, Taharka."

"It isn't just that I'm not making as much money," he went on, "but I've worked for years to develop this business. When I came, my uncle had far fewer caravans than we have even now, but he didn't keep things clean, and the food available wasn't well cooked and seasoned, and it wasn't warm and fresh. I vowed I would make this the sort of place I'd like to stop at if I were a tired traveler. And I think I succeeded."

He started pacing again, head thrust forward a little. "We can't get everyone settled in by the time Sabbath begins at sundown Friday, and it's too late on the next evening for people to come *after* sundown."

She knew this was true. It had been nice for her in that they could go to the Friday evening and Saturday morning service on the Sabbath and sometimes even the special Saturday afternoon one. Also she had time alone with her husband this way—but it wasn't good business practice. Taharka rubbed his head with his fingertips. "I don't know how we can keep going this way."

Susanna asked, "How do other Samaritan and Jewish innkeepers manage?"

He shrugged. "Most of them wink at the Law."

She didn't want to be in the position of leading him from the Law. "Have you asked the priest about it?"

"Yes, I had to. It's perhaps well that I didn't, though, until after I was taken in as a proselyte," he said. "He was so upset he almost fainted."

"Did he suggest anything you can do?"

"Nothing helpful. He couldn't see why people wouldn't come early on Friday or wait outside on Saturday until it was sundown and time to come in!"

She raised her brows. "He doesn't know how independent people on a caravan are, does he?"

"No, but they are. They have to be. They're responsible for safely delivering all the merchandise and animals, as well as people.

They have to make decisions on the basis of what's best for *them,* not for the innkeeper."

"Yet I've heard many speak well of our accommodations and the safety that is afforded . . ."

"And the gallery rooms where groups can be together and yet have at least a little privacy . . ."

"Also the fresh water to drink and the good food at reasonable prices."

He smiled at her as he turned slowly. "You've had a lot to do with all of these."

"They were cooking almost the same amount before I came," she started to protest.

"True. But you have a talent for seasoning, and the small amount it costs for the herbs and spices you use is amply justified."

She was still touched by his frequent compliments. She'd tried to learn not to make some self-belittling comment on these occasions but still didn't know how to accept praise gracefully. Her left hand reached out to rest on his. "You can't know how much I love you, Taharka."

He drew her to him. "I think I can. It's about the same amount that I love you, which is also more than I have words to tell you."

〜〜〜〜

Susanna realized many times as the weeks and months passed that they were probably powerless to make changes. And it *was* nice to go to the synagogue for scripture readings, prayers, and interpretation of the scriptures by the priest or by any of the local men who could read well enough and were able to prepare a commentary.

Several times Susanna was pleased to hear men from other parts of Samaria, and on three occasions individuals with caravans staying at the inn were the speakers. Each of these latter had been educated and reared in the Samaritan community at Elephantine in Egypt, and she was delighted to find that the scrolls that had meant so much to her here had been painstakingly copied there in Egypt.

Taharka had told her that his mother had been from Elephantine, but somehow Susanna hadn't realized that she was a Samaritan. Having married an Egyptain, however, she had refrained from openly worshiping Yahweh and had not had her sons circumcised.

"But she never rejected Him," Taharka hastened to explain. "She told me about Him and about the children of Israel and all He'd done for them. Being an Egyptian male, I must admit I didn't think too highly of the stories of the Exodus she told me, but even as a child I was intrigued with the idea of a god who was really interested in a people—and equally interested in single individuals."

Susanna knew the story about Taharka's childless uncle requesting his sister to send her second son to Sychar with a caravan so that he could learn the trade of innkeeping. Later Taharka was legally adopted and eventually became master of this business.

"I wish he were alive so he could see what you've done with the inn," Susanna said wistfully.

"I wish that, too. Also, although he never tried to influence me in spiritual matters, I think he would be pleased that I'm now a Samaritan in every sense of the word."

Susanna looked up from smoothing one of the wax slates so it could be used again for writing class. "How did *he* manage the inn and still remain a Samaritan in good standing?"

"My uncle talked being an upstanding Samaritan better than he lived it. To him there were two kinds of laws: those that made sense and those that didn't. The latter he just forgot about, but the former he fulfilled to the letter."

"Like what?"

"Like taking his tithe to the synagogue, and observing all holy days, especially Passover." He handed her another of the rectangular wooden forms that had been filled with a shallow layer of wax. "And he had a fine sense of honor and respect for his fellowman. He willingly gave alms to the needy, but if the need continued he wanted to know why and what could be done about it. Then he'd go out of his way to help solve not only the immediate problem but the underlying ones also."

"As you did for Sherah and her mother?"

He frowned a little. "Did she tell you?"

"Right after I got here. You know, my love, she thinks you are the finest man who ever lived," she said, smiling up at him.

"She shouldn't."

"It is no small thing to be freed from slavery."

"She is working just as hard for me as a servant."

"But for a different motive. Not because she's forced to, but because she wants to show you she's truly grateful. Of course, I appreciate how she feels, after all you've done for me."

He looked down at her, seeing the reflection of the lamp's flame in her eyes. "I hope, Susanna, that your being grateful is not why *you're* working so hard."

Her full lips curved upward and parted slightly as she pushed back her chair, rose, and came around the table and into his arms. "No, Taharka, it hasn't been just gratitude for a long, long time. I'll never be able to thank Yahweh enough for bringing me to you—and letting you love me and me love you."

—◦◦◦◦◦—

Many changes had taken place in the running of the inn since Taharka became a Samaritan, and the women were most conscious of them. There were now two sets of dishes, pans, and utensils, one for meat and the other for milk or milk products. The sheep, chickens, and goats had to be killed and pronounced clean by the religious leaders, also.

Even though fewer people came than formerly, five days of the week as well as Friday until sundown and on Saturday evening they were still busy. The servants enjoyed the unaccustomed twenty-four hour freedom, and some of them, with families or friends living nearby, found time to visit or make new acquaintances.

As for Putiel and Rachel, their favorite pastime was to go for long walks, something seldom done before because of Rachel's disability. Susanna enjoyed watching the changes in the child, the most noticeable being that her face and limbs were fuller and her lips and cheeks pink with the vigor of youth.

Every time she returned, Rachel brought something for Susanna, like a shiny rock, a gnarled piece of weathered wood, or a brightly colored butterfly. The day she brought the single, long-stemmed lily she said simply, "I think of you when I see the lilies of the field."

Susanna's finger gently moved upward against the softness of the petals. "Because that's what my name means?"

"Oh, no. At least that's not the main reason. It's because it's so pretty and soft and gentle, and it's right there where Yahweh put it, looking beautiful and smelling good whether anyone's there or not." And then, realizing what she'd said, she looked, embarrassed, at the floor.

Susanna hugged her. "Thank you both for the flower and for the compliment, Rachel. You are a lovely person. You know, if our baby is a girl, I'd be happy if she were just like you."

The eyes were sparkling. "Really?"

"I certainly would," she affirmed, then added, "the baby's very active today. Would you like to put your hand on my stomach and feel the movements?"

"Oh, could I?" As her small hand rested against Susanna's linen-covered abdomen and she felt the thrust of the unseen infant, her expression was one of wonder. "He feels so *strong*."

Susanna laughed. "Sometimes he kicks so hard he wakes me from a sound sleep."

"Does it hurt?" Rachel asked with quick sympathy.

"Oh, no. It makes me feel good knowing he's strong and healthy." She did not tell her young friend of her worry in previous years that she might never have a child.

Various travelers who frequented the inn had become friends, and Susanna made a point of speaking with them whenever possible. At first when she'd mention Jesus of Nazareth she was met with a shrug or a simple statement that He was unknown. However, as time went on, some began telling her of things He was reputed to have said or done.

She listened carefully to each account but was particularly enthralled when the wife of a Greek teacher on her way south from Sidon told of a cousin's experience with the prophet. It seemed that Miriam's small daughter was possessed by a demon, causing her to do and say irrational, foolish, and dangerous things.

One day word went around the neighborhood that the healer was staying with people only a few houses away. Miriam would have preferred taking her daughter to see Him, but the child had been violently throwing herself about to the point that she'd had to be bound to keep her from hurting herself.

Frightened but determined, the mother approached the house and entered, over the objections of the servants. She knew immediately from His bearing and the deference of those in the room whom to turn to, so she hurried across and knelt at His feet. "Have mercy on me, O Lord, Son of David," she cried. "My daughter is severely possessed by a demon—"

Before she could go on, the household servants and the master's disciples tried to draw her away, while others begged Jesus to tell her to leave at once.

It looked as though He were going to do as they said, for He told her He was sent to minister to the Jews and not to outsiders.

When she desperately pleaded with Him for help, He explained, "It isn't fair to take the children's bread and throw it to the dogs."

Under normal conditions such a rebuff would have hurt so much she would have crept away, but now, remembering her little one restrained on the bed at home, she looked directly into His eyes and said, "Yes, Lord, yet even the dogs eat the crumbs that fall from their master's table." There were tears streaming down her cheeks as she realized this was her last hope. If Jesus would not heal the child, she would surely die.

Jesus leaned over then to help her to her feet, and He was saying in a voice that was soft yet able to fill the entire crowded room, "Oh woman, great is your faith! Be it done for you as you desire."

Whether it was His touch or His words she would never know, but immediately she was filled with the assurance that everything would be all right. She whispered her thanks and, turning, worked her way through the throng between her and the doorway. Holding up her skirt, she ran quickly to her house.

With only the light from the open door, she had to walk to the far corner before she could see distinctly that her six-year-old was lying calmly on her bedroll, still wrapped from neck to toes in the blanket, which had been securely tied with cords.

The brown eyes meeting hers were intelligent and aware and the voice greeting her was completely rational.

Was it possible? Jesus had said, "Be it done for you as you desire." Well, what she desired above all else was for her daughter to be completely normal.

She unwrapped the blanket, and the child stood and walked and embraced her mother and did all the other things a six-year-old should!

Miriam's prayer *had* been granted.

Susanna asked, "Had you seen the child during the possession as well as after?"

"Yes. I don't know how He did it, but she truly was completely changed. The demon that was within her is gone."

Susanna then told of the miracles of Mahlon and Rachel and called the latter so the woman could see how healthy the child was.

"Mahlon is frequently here also," Susanna added. "I guess he feels that if Jesus had not stayed here that day he would not have been healed, so he comes and offers to help with anything that needs to be done."

Many reports were also brought concerning Jesus spending much time in teaching and preaching. His stories and parables were often repeated around campfires or while people were eating. One day Taharka invited an itinerant metalworker to his office to give Susanna an account of being at an outdoor meeting where Jesus talked of many things.

Susanna was to mediate often on Jesus' advice not to lay up treasure here on earth where thieves could break in and steal it but to lay up treasure in heaven where it would be safe from rust, moths, and robbers.

The prayer the man had learned from Jesus was taught to Taharka and Susanna, and they began including this as part of their morning scripture reading and prayer.

"Our father who art in heaven," it began, and Susanna always felt warmed by the use of "our" instead of "my," "Hallowed be thy name. Thy kingdom come. Thy will be done on earth as it is in heaven.

"Give us this day our daily bread; and forgive us our debts, as we also have forgiven our debtors. And lead us not into temptation, but deliver us from evil."

Another portion of Jesus' teaching that she especially liked was His saying, "Whatsoever you wish that men would do to you, do so to them; for this is the law and the prophets."

She wished He had not mentioned the prophets, though, for although the Jews studied and revered them, the Samaritans did not. There was nobody like Moses, who was the one true prophet of the Lord. She was unwilling to believe—unable to—that there were others as valid.

As least she had felt that way until she met Jesus, who *had* to be the Messiah foretold by Moses in order to accomplish all those miracles!

With her active participation in things concerning the inn and her conversations with travelers from outside her town and province, the nine months of her pregnancy passed much more quickly than she had anticipated.

Her labor, however, did not.

sixteen

Susanna's first contraction came long before dawn on that Thursday morning. It was little more than she had felt with some of the baby's movements, and she smiled as she shifted position.

For the past several mornings she had said to herself, "Perhaps today our child will be born." So when these sensations within her body passed those resembling bad gas pains, she rejoiced.

She had often marveled at the way Taharka's inside clock awakened him at the same time each morning, and today was no exception. He yawned, stretched, enclosed her within his embrace, and laughed softly. "It's a good thing I've got long arms."

She hugged him in return. "It is indeed, my love."

"He's really active this morning, isn't he?" Taharka noted, not recognizing the difference between normal movements and contractions.

"He should be, as industrious as his father is."

He kissed her. "You are every bit as busy as I, Susanna. And speaking of busy, I must get up and dressed. Some of the caravans will soon be making preparations to leave."

He suited his actions to his words, and Susanna lay in bed, one arm pillowing her head, watching him. She usually arose with him, but the last several hours had made her fairly sure this would be a long day for her. "Would you think me slothful if I stay in bed a little longer?"

He turned, body tense. "You're not feeling well?"

She didn't want him to know yet. His first wife had died in childbirth and there was no point in making him worry about her yet. "I'm fine," she assured him. "I didn't sleep well the latter part of the night, and I'm feeling lazy."

He finished washing and replaced the rough washcloth in the basin of water that had been brought the evening before. "You know how you feel, Susanna. Take the best possible care of yourself and the child of our love. Stay in bed all day if need be."

She reached out toward him, and he came to take her hand, then, sitting on the side of the bed, leaned over to gather her close. "I love you so dearly. How grateful I am to have you for my wife!" he breathed huskily into her right ear.

She knew he could feel her nod. "I love you so much—so very much!"

Then he was gone, after stopping on the threshold to say, "I'll check on you later, but will try not to awaken you if you're asleep."

She smiled and thanked him, but didn't mention she was sure there would be no sleep for her that day.

Before the last caravan left, she was beginning to wonder if she should get out of bed and let Taharka or Sherah know of her condition. But everyone would be busy, she told herself, and first babies seldom come quickly or easily.

By the time Taharka returned, however, she could no longer disguise the pain she was feeling, though she held back the groans that had several times broken the silence. He ran to her. "It's your time?"

She bit her lower lip as this contraction went on longer than the earlier ones. As it ended she answered his question in a voice that was much smaller than she'd intended or expected. "I think the midwife should come."

He took only long enough to brush the hair back from her forehead and plant a kiss there before hurrying to the door and bellowing, "Putiel! Putiel, come quickly!"

Even as another contraction began, Susanna couldn't help smiling. Taharka never yelled or raised his voice and was usually soft-spoken even when being firm. His concern for her was obvious as he called to his second-in-command, whose response and running feet were heard by Susanna. "Go get Kezia at once. Tell her Susanna needs her."

Now everyone at the inn would know, and she was glad. Perhaps some of them would think to pray for her and for the baby, who was trying so hard to be born.

Although Kezia came immediately, the baby did not. By midday the pains were almost constant, but the middle-aged Kezia reported little progress. She was shocked when Susanna requested that Taharka be allowed to come in to be with her. "It is not right for a man to see a woman in this condition," she stated firmly.

"He's my husband," Susanna coaxed. "Please let him in." The midwife refused and Susanna had to bite back words that would have overridden the other's as Taharka came to the door for perhaps the twentieth time to ask about her.

"You must cooperate," the midwife commanded her patient. "When I tell you to push, you must do that, but only then!"

There were tears on Susanna's cheeks as she nodded. "I'm trying. I honestly am. It's just that it h-hurts so *much!*" In spite of herself, the last words rose in a wail as another massive contraction contorted her body and face.

For much of the afternoon she was conscious only of her own body. She barely realized when the caravans began to arrive and hardly cared. Had Taharka ceased coming to the door, or did she not hear him anymore?

Her world was a blur of excruciating agony. "Help me! Help me," she pleaded again and again until Kezia spoke sharply to her.

"I'm doing all I can! The baby isn't in the right position."

"Will he be all right?" Susanna asked, bald fear in her voice matching the terror within herself.

The answer was too quick. "Of course he will. I've delivered many babies."

Susanna did not dare ask how many of those babies had been born dead—or what had happened to the mothers.

Sherah came several times with cold water fresh from one of the wells, and Susanna drank it eagerly. She'd been sweating profusely from all this effort and found herself to be constantly thirsty. Sherah, returning again after serving the evening meal to the people of the caravans, stayed to talk awhile. "Your friend, Ephrathah, is asking about you. I told her you're having a difficult labor, and she wanted to know if she could help in any way."

Kezia jerked upright as Susanna said, "Ask her to come to me."

"I don't like people around when there are difficult births," the tall, thin woman stated flatly.

As Susanna tried to soothe the midwife's ruffled feathers, she saw Sherah slip around the curtain covering the doorway. It was hard enough being in labor without having a temperamental midwife to deal with!

Ephrathah must have been waiting right outside, for she pushed aside the striped curtain and stepped in almost at once. She was short and stocky but covered the distance to the bed in quick strides. Laying her hand on the bare abdomen, she stood there silently as another enormous contraction took all of Susanna's attention.

With her free hand she had taken Susanna's and did not wince as the patient clung to it convulsively.

Kezia remained tenaciously in her position at the foot of the bed. "Are you a midwife?"

Ephrathah's open face wrinkled into a smile. "I have delivered babies on many occasions. There are seldom midwives traveling with our caravan, and there have been times of great need."

"I suppose you help the camels, asses, horses, and sheep as well," the sarcastic voice continued.

But the desired result did not come. With a low chuckle, the newcomer responded, "More often than you would believe."

"Well," sniffed Kezia, "the baby trying to get born here is not a foal or a lamb!"

Again the soft reply surprised Susanna during that moment before she was thrown into agony again. When a bit later she became conscious of things outside herself, she saw Ephrathah just coming to an upright position. "The baby is not in a position to be born," she was saying.

"That is what I told Susanna." Kezia was gratified that the stranger agreed with her. "I keep hoping he will turn around."

Susanna asked, "*Can* he turn around?"

Kezia looked at her more kindly than at any time so far. "We hope so."

When Taharka again came to the door, Ephrathah went out to speak with him. She still looked very serious when she returned, although her voice held what seemed to Susanna false enthusiasm.

Susanna lost all track of time, but later heard Sherah's voice asking Kezia to come to the fireside for some lamb and pottage. Kezia's immediate reaction was to request Sherah to bring the food to her here as she couldn't leave her patient.

"Go along," Susanna encouraged. "As slowly as I'm progressing, I'll still be here when you get back." She surprised herself by realizing that what had started as sarcasm came out as humor, and Kezia amazed her even more by agreeing to go when Ephrathah, staying with her, promised she would call immediately if there was need.

Within a half-minute of her leaving, Taharka slipped like a shadow into the room. Susanna's arms came up to hold him as close as he was holding her. "I'm so sorry, Susanna," he whispered, and his voice as well as the tears on his cheeks attested to his deep feeling.

Ephrathah, however, did not let them use any of the precious time she had free of Kezia's presence. She had taken off her outer robe and briskly washed and dried her hands and arms, all the way to above her elbows. Now she came back to where Kezia had been moments before. "Sometimes a foal is turned so it cannot come out, and it also happens with sheep and goats. In those cases I've sometimes been able to reach in and move the baby into a proper position.

"Susanna, your baby cannot be born the way he is now, and you are not strong enough to continue as you are. Taharka," she commanded as firmly as though he were a slave boy instead of master of the inn, "you hold her tight, and, all the time I'm working here, you be praying."

"I have been praying," he said meekly.

"I'm sure you have," she stated. "But this time I want you to do it out loud." She was looking at him as an equal, even though he towered above her. "Jesus says that when two or more are gathered together in His name He will be in the midst of them. There are three of us here, all of whom love Him. I want you to pray *in Jesus' name*. And I want it to be aloud, for Susanna and I are too busy right now to do it on our own."

For a moment he looked confused, then nodded slowly. With the coming of further terrible waves of pain Susanna did not get to hear much of his prayer, but she caught fragments. "Oh, Yahweh, hear our prayer . . . Help Susanna and the baby . . . Be with Ephrathah in what she's trying to do . . . Don't let Kezia come back too soon . . . Thank you for the baby . . . Thank you for Ephrathah's coming at the right time . . . Thank you for love . . . In Jesus' name, amen."

Susanna could not tell what Ephrathah was doing, for her pain was so great it obscured other sensations. "Keep praying!" the woman commanded when Taharka paused, so he continued, using some of the same themes he'd already used but adding others.

He even included the prayer Jesus had taught, and Ephrathah, without pausing, glanced up briefly in recognition and prayed the words out loud with him.

Finally, just after an extremely severe contraction left her drained, Susanna heard a sigh of satisfaction. "There!" Ephrathah withdrew her hand and stood to her full height. "I *think* your child can be born now."

She went to the washbasin and scrubbed the blood from her hands. "Taharka," she said, holding the bowl out to him, "finish that particular prayer then dispose of this water. It would be well not to have to explain what I was doing while Kezia was away."

". . . In Jesus' name, amen," he finished, then, turning toward her, he added, "But if this works you should get the credit for it."

"No!" she interrupted. "You are to tell nobody."

"But *why?*" Taharka asked.

"Jesus says that we should do good not for the credit we might receive but for the joy of serving Him. That if we do things for Him and for others in secret, He honors that and will reward it in His own time and way."

"I don't understand."

"We'll talk about it later." She cut him short. "Here. Empty this, and fill it with clean water. It may have been meant for washing the baby before rubbing him with salt."

Taharka reluctantly left his wife to meekly empty the basin outside the walls of the inn. He then carried it toward the cistern but veered to his left in order to get water from the container holding water from the wells. This son or daughter of his should be washed in fresh water and not in rainwater collected from off the roofs.

He handed the bowl to Ephrathah then started toward Susanna, who was moaning and turning her tortured face from side to side. Ephrathah directed him toward the door. "There's no time to lose. Find Kezia, and tell her that," a smile transformed her weathered face, "there is need for a midwife here."

"I wish you'd continue."

Her small, square hand on his arm gave him a friendly shove. "I'd like to, but Kezia has needs too."

He looked at her and bowed his head. "I'll do as you request," he said and left.

He returned, a pace behind Kezia's running form, and would have followed her into the room that held all that was important in the world for him, but Ephrathah stopped him, motioning toward his office. "Wait for me there," she ordered and hurried out across the courtyard. Within a minute she brought Mibzar, and the three prayed steadily until they heard the wail of the newborn infant.

Taharka's head turned toward the passageway, and his hands gripped the marble tabletop so tightly that his fingertips blanched. Mibzar beamed at the innkeeper. "Congratulations, father."

"Father"! Yes, he *was* a father again. He felt warmed by the knowledge, but then he shivered. "I wonder how Susanna is."

Ephrathah countered his anguish with assurance. "She'll be fine. I promise you." She excused herself to go see if she could help with infant or mother.

It was the midwife's honor to bring the newborn, wrapped in a linen blanket, to his father, and she could not immediately break away from watching Taharka who, smiling contentedly, at first held him cradled on his arm and then laid him on the table to unwrap and inspect.

Yes, all the toes and fingers were accounted for, and the dark eyes looking up at him seemed fearless and wise. As he wrapped his secondborn to keep him warm, he wished it would not be necessary for the little one to go through the circumcision in eight days. He'd already been through so much that he had bruises on his hips, back, and shoulders. Taharka started to return him to Kezia but changed his mind, bringing him against his shoulder and patting his back.

It did not seem long ago that he had held Necho like this. But Necho's mother had died giving birth to him, and, had he lived, he'd have been roughly the same age as this baby's mother. "How is Susanna?" he insisted on knowing.

The midwife looked well pleased. "She was torn from the difficult birth, and she's been in the last stages of labor for many hours. She'll be tired for days but will have no lasting problems."

She reached for the infant, but Taharka continued holding him close to the warmth of his body. "Let me keep him awhile. When Susanna is ready for him, I would like to be the one to place him in her arms."

This was not the proper procedure, but she, too, was tired. Perhaps it would be all right for the father to hold him awhile. When she returned to the other room Ephrathah was just returning a cloth to the bloody basin. "I hope you don't mind," she said, "but while Susanna and I were talking I thought I'd wash her for you."

For a moment Kezia was annoyed then apparently decided to accept the deed as a favor. "Thank you," she said grudgingly and busied herself with changing the bed linens and assisting Susanna into a clean garment.

Susanna wondered if she looked as totally exhausted as she felt. She was so tired it was an effort to help get her clothing changed. She had always thought it must be wonderful to have a baby, but had never seriously considered the possibility of having trouble like this.

"May I see our baby now?" she asked. If she didn't soon she would be asleep, and that would be inexcusable.

Kezia was brushing the tangles from Susanna's long hair. "As soon as we have you looking a little more presentable," she promised.

Susanna's eyes met Ephrathah's, but she suppressed her smile. She knew Taharka would not be troubled by tousled hair, but she need not convince the other woman of that.

When Taharka followed Kezia into the room the infant, with one fist against his mouth, was making loud sucking sounds. "The little fellow's hungry already," Taharka commented, and Susanna was surprised to find that her enlarged breasts responded to the sound by an outthrust of the nipples and a feeling of fullness. Oh, how marvelous it was!

She'd wondered how Taharka would carry the baby and was pleased to see her son held against his father's breast. "Is he . . . all right?" she asked.

"He's perfect," Taharka declared as he leaned over to place their child in the curve of his mother's arm. Their faces were close, and he could not resist giving her a kiss, which she returned. It was only later that she realized that this also was not proper in front of Kezia and Ephrathah.

But she was not ashamed.

The next morning Ephrathah came for a short visit before leaving and responded to Susanna's gratitude that she had happened to be at the inn at the right time. "It's even more miraculous than you know, Susanna, for we weren't due at Sychar until tonight. I thought it was my own desire to see you that made me coax Mibzar to leave Jerusalem a day early. I knew if we came Friday we'd have to stay outside of town, and it's more pleasant and convenient to stop here. But I've never done this before, so I now think it was Yahweh who led us here at the time you needed me."

Susanna's voice was soft as she shifted the baby slightly. "I believe that also, and I praise Yahweh's name."

"And the name of Jesus, also."

"Yes," she agreed, "the name of Jesus, also."

seventeen

Susanna had not expected to be so completely fatigued, but the women coming in to see her and the baby the following day assured her it was because she had gone through an especially difficult delivery and had lost much blood. How did people manage when they had *days* of suffering like this? How had Leah survived her travail, which had begun early and run so long?

As she held her son, she felt a strong wish to see David again. "Sherah," she said when that young woman arrived with her early morning bread, "if you should see my nephew when you go to the well, would you tell him about his new cousin?"

"Of course, Susanna, I'd be glad to—if I see him. I rarely do, however." Sherah stayed to put honey on the warm bread. Susanna had the feeling that her friend wanted to talk about something, but had no idea what it could be.

She tried several topics, but finally there was silence between them, until Sherah managed, "Susanna, is it . . . worth it?"

"The pain of having the baby? Yes, oh yes," she said, involuntarily drawing the infant closer.

"But I heard you groaning and crying, and several times there were screams."

"I tried to hold them back as best I could."

The young face showed puzzlement or perhaps something different. Was it distaste? Fear? It didn't seem like that. "I have no father or brother to arrange a husband for me," she finally began. "I know I'm not beautiful like you, and I'm sometimes bossy—and I have no dowry. Even though I've been a woman for several years, until now nobody has asked for me as a wife, though some of the travelers have asked for me in other capacities," she added with a wry grin.

Remembering her terror when she had been accosted, Susanna was grateful Sherah could joke about it. "Would you like Taharka to make some inquiries, to let it be known you might be interested in marriage?" she asked softly.

Sherah's blush could be seen by the light from the open doorway. "That's not what I—had in mind. You see, last night one of the men with Mibzar's caravan approached me and told me he was going to see Taharka the next time he comes—about taking me as his wife. But I don't *want* to be his wife!" she stated emphatically. "He must be at least fifty years old, and his teeth are rotting, and he doesn't bathe, and—and I would be miserable living with him!"

Susanna reached to take her hand. "Sherah, my own dear friend, you don't have to marry anyone. You can stay here where we all love you and—"

But the shaking of Sherah's head made Susanna realize she must have misunderstood. She waited for Sherah to explain. "It's not that I don't *want* to get married. Every Samaritan woman wants that. But I don't want to marry the Syrian non-believer. I want to—to marry someone else."

"I assume there is a specific 'someone else,'" Susanna said. "Do I know him?"

She nodded, eyes remaining focused on the baby. "Yes."

"Does he feel this way about you?"

"Yes, he does." Again she paused before blurting out, "But he is a fourth son, and there is no inheritance, and the only work he can get even helping his father and eldest brother will not make it possible for us to marry unless we're willing to live in the same two-room house with his parents and three married brothers."

There were tears in her eyes. "I fear I am spoiled by being allowed to continue living in the room my mother and I formerly shared. I don't *want* to live in his house with fifteen other people ranging in age from a baby to a great-grandmother!"

"I wouldn't like that, either," Susanna sympathized, remembering how grateful she'd been for the tiny lean-to at her brother's, which had given her some privacy. "What does your . . . loved one suggest?"

A sigh preceded her reply. "He didn't want me to ask, but I—I have to, Susanna. He isn't needed at his father's, and he is very handy and quick to learn." Susanna hid a smile, remembering she'd used that expression in the past when referring to Sherah. The girl quickly went on, "Is it possible that Taharka and you would consider letting him work here? After our marriage, we could share the room I now use."

Wondering if she knew him, Susanna asked, "Who is this man?"

147

Sherah's face was a study of eagerness and pride. "It is Mahlon."

Mahlon? The child-man who had been healed by Jesus almost two years ago? That explained his being around so often, helping in many quiet ways. "I didn't even suspect. I've never seen you together."

"We've been careful, for we wanted no gossip. But we do love each other," she added quickly. "We really do."

"I can tell that from the light in your eyes when you say his name." Susanna patted the side of her bed, indicating her friend should sit beside her. "Tell me about him."

Sherah needed no further invitation to extol his virtues, among which were gentleness, kindness, eagerness to please her, and willingness to do whatever needed to be done, no matter how insignificant or great.

"Come back at noon," Susanna finally said. "Bring your lunch, along with Taharka's, and a bowl of soup for me. I would like you to eat with us and tell my husband of your request."

"I was hoping perhaps you'd speak for us."

"Don't be afraid, Sherah. Taharka is a good man and truly cares for you, as well as all others who live here. You can always talk to him."

~~~~~

Taharka learned of the dreams of the young couple and two days later met with Mahlon during the early afternoon. For the next two days Taharka left the inn for several hours in the morning but volunteered no information concerning this.

Susanna no longer minded his silence on specific matters, for he was more than usually talkative and joyful with her and their new son. There had been a number of names suggested for the baby before his birth, but there was no longer any question as to what it should be. Certainly Susanna's conceiving and bearing this child and Ephrathah's arriving when she was needed—well, everything pointed to the fact that Yahweh wanted this child to be born to them.

The name to be given at the time of the circumcision was "Jonathan," meaning "gift of Yahweh."

Sometimes in the privacy of her own room Susanna would whisper the name. She found that it rolled joyfully across her tongue, but she didn't refer to the baby by name even in front of Taharka, for this was not allowed.

It didn't seem possible that their new son was now eight days old. He was a good child, eating and sleeping well and crying little. Susanna watched as her husband left that morning for the synagogue, his cap on his head, tasseled robe worn with dignity. She almost wished the priest would not be returning with him to perform the ceremony that, though making their son a Child of the Covenant, would also give much pain.

She got out of bed slowly, having found that she became dizzy if she rose quickly as she formerly had. She washed herself and put on a straight, simple gown of pale blue over which she would wear her dark blue mantle when welcoming everyone into their home.

Then she gave the baby his bath and cuddled him closely, wishing she could nurse him. If only she could spare him the coming suffering! She found it hard to believe that he would not feel or notice the pain as much if he was very hungry, as everyone said.

Taharka arrived with the priest and the sandak—the man who would hold the baby during this rite. Susanna could no longer put off the duty of handing her child to the priest at the doorway of the decorated room to be placed on the pillow on the sandak's knees. Susanna had wished that she, who loved him so much, could be the one to hold the baby, but now knew this was better.

She could not watch.

It was bad enough to visualize the priest grasping the foreskin with his left hand, fixing the shield, and with one long sweep of the double-edged flint knife along the shield, cutting away the tissue.

Screams of agony replaced the cries of hunger. Tears came into Susanna's eyes, and it was all she could do to keep them from falling; but she *must* not shame the man she loved by weeping over this ritual.

The crying infant was handed to his father, and the priest, holding a goblet, recited a benediction for the wine and another one praising God, Who established this covenant with His people, Israel. The priest then led in prayer for the welfare of the baby, and Taharka announced Jonathan's name.

The guests, friends from the community and everyone from the inn, replied, "Even as this child has entered into the covenant, so may he enter into the Torah, the nuptial canopy, and into good deeds." And then they gave gifts to the family of Taharka.

Family—what a wonderful word! Not long ago it had been just her, and then Tarharka and his wife. Now they were a family.

She welcomed Jonathan into her arms and excused herself to nurse him in privacy, offering her breast as much for comfort as for nourishment.

"Jonathan, my dear, suffering son, the light of my life," she crooned as her body gently rocked him. "I am so sorry for your agony. There is no way I can show you how much I am hurting for you, but I promise to try to keep you from pain as much as possible from this day forward."

She almost resented the seeming lack of sensitivity as the men laughed and drank wine together, but she told herself she still did not fully understand the ways of men.

The meal which followed was festive and enjoyable and Taharka presented the guests with special sweets that he had procured. The hymns sung for the occasion were appreciated by Susanna, as was the prayer for the blessing of the parents, the priest, and the sandak.

~~~~~

If only Taharka could be in bed beside her, she would have been completely happy. However, the Law specified forty-one days of uncleanness following the birth of a son, during which the husband could not sleep with the new mother. She smiled, though, realizing that, although she was alone with the baby, she was not lonely.

It was comforting to know that Taharka missed her as much as she did him.

As she got stronger, she took Jonathan with her to the weaving room, where her first projects were to make the long, narrow strips of cloth to wrap around the waist as girdles, and also some head cloths. The looms used for these were not as large, nor did they require as much physical strength.

She wandered through the entire inn, even into places in which she had spent little time before. In one closed-off area on the gallery she came across an assortment of cured hides about which she asked Taharka while they were eating their midday meal.

"Long before you came, we had an elderly man living here who made sandals and leather pouches as well as wine and water skins. He took care of the needs of everyone here, and we even sold some of them.

"However, his eyesight failed, and it got to the point where he could not even make the simplest of items anymore."

"What became of him?" Susanna asked, looking concerned.

"He went back to live with a son in Shechem. I understand he died soon afterward."

"Oh. That's sad."

He looked at her tenderly and reached across the table to lay his hand on hers. "I didn't send him away, dear."

"I never thought you would, Taharka," she protested. "I know how you care for everyone."

"I'm glad you came across the leather today," he went on. "I've been trying to find something constructive for Mahlon to do, something that could make him feel he was contributing to our well-being. Because he has experience caring for sheep, I've been checking at the synagogue to see if anyone has need for a paid shepherd. However, each has enough sons, not enough sheep, or too many servants already. I've just remembered that when I talked with Mahlon I remarked on the fine leather girdle he was wearing. He told me he'd dyed and embossed it himself and that he not only made the sandals he was wearing but also most of those for his family."

Susanna's excited voice interrupted, "So maybe he could help Putiel and spend the rest of his time working with the leather!"

"That is at least worth considering," he agreed, leaning back in his chair.

They had assumed Sherah would want a betrothal party and the usual lengthy period of waiting before a marriage. However, when they called her in to ask when Mahlon would be free to meet with them to make these arrangements, they found that Sherah and Mahlon had already decided they would like to be married immediately.

"But *why?*" Susanna asked.

Standing straight and looking Susanna in the eye, Sherah said simply, "We love each other. We do not need people drinking and dancing to make our union blessed. Besides," and she grinned conspiratorially, "I'd like to be married before Mibzar's caravan returns from Damascus, and that will be soon."

So this marriage was even more simple than Susanna and Taharka's had been. In addition to the people from the inn, only Mahlon's immediate family attended.

Two days later Mibzar entered at the wide gates. The man who had desired Sherah received good-natured teasing, but he shrugged his shoulders philosophically and announced that perhaps he'd try for that twenty-year-old widow he'd met in Bethlehem.

This time Ephrathah brought word of Jesus' feeding some four or five thousand men, "Not counting the women and boys and girls," she added with excitement. "How I wish I could have been there, but I was too late. As we were coming through Chorazin on our way to camp near Capernaum, we heard that Jesus was on the northwest shore of the Sea of Galilee. Several others from the caravan joined me as we left and hurried down to where we expected to see Him, but before we got there He had taken a boat and crossed to the other side."

"Oh, I'm sorry," Susanna exclaimed.

"What I didn't know was that many people went hurrying around by the shore and got there even before He did. It seems that He taught, preached, and healed, and everyone stayed and stayed, not paying any attention to the time of day."

"Where was this?"

"Over near Bethsaida."

Susanna remembered the day on top of Mount Gerizim. "Several of Jesus' disciples are from there."

"Yes, I know. That's why I sent some of our men to find Andrew. He's the one who told me about what happened. He said that the people with Jesus were like sheep with their shepherd. They hung on every word and had no desire to leave, even when it got late. Finally the disciples became concerned and talked to Jesus about the problem.

"Jesus looked right at Philip and asked, 'How are we to buy bread, so that these people may eat?'

"Philip looked around at the masses of people and declared that the wages from two hundred days' work couldn't feed everyone there.

"Just then Andrew went to them and said that the only food he'd been able to locate was a boy's lunch of five barley loaves and two fish, which, of course, would be of little value here.

"However, Jesus told His disciples to circulate through the crowd and tell people to sit down on the grass in groups of fifty or a hundred. As soon as they had done this, Jesus took the bread and fish that the boy had given to Him, looked up to Heaven, prayed, and started breaking the food into pieces.

"Susanna, you're not going to believe this, but the more He broke, the more there was to be broken. He kept at it, and the disciples distributed the food until every single person there was not only fed but unable to eat another bite—as Andrew put it, they were completely satisfied."

Susanna had listened to the account, hardly able to breathe. "I *do* believe that, Ephrathah."

Her friend smiled. "And, Susanna, one of the things I thought especially interesting was that, although He is obviously able to make as much food as He wants to, He's just like you and me in some ways. He couldn't let anything go to waste, so He sent these twelve men of His out with baskets to gather up fragments of the barley loaves and the fishes, and they came back with twelve whole baskets full!"

Susanna mused aloud. "So, if they ended up with so much more than they started with, in addition to all that was eaten, nobody could claim that the people had been so excited, so involved, that they just *thought* they had eaten—or forgot they hadn't eaten, or something."

"Oh, there was no thought like that at all. When they saw this miracle He had performed, they all began talking among themselves there in their groups on the grass, and they came to the conclusion that this *had* to be the prophet who is to come into the world!"

"I *knew* it!" Susanna enthused. "He has to be the one!"

But Ephrathah had more to tell. "The people decided that if He could do this, He would indeed be the right person to be made king. In fact, some wanted to insist right then and there that He accept the crown. When He realized this, however, He went off by himself into the hills.

"Jesus must have told the disciples to go on without Him if He wasn't back by evening, for they had started for Capernaum by boat when one of those terrible storms came up. Even though some of them have been fishermen for years, the disciples had an awful time with the rowing, for the wind was against them.

"They were frightened when they weren't able to get where they wanted by rowing, but that was nothing to their terror when out of the blackness surrounding them they saw someone walking on the surface of the water, right toward them. Thinking it was a ghost, some actually cried out with fear.

"Imagine their relief when they recognized Jesus' voice calling over the storm, 'It is I; do not be afraid.'"

Susanna's eyes were wide. "Jesus was walking on the *water?*"

Ephrathah started to laugh. "Something funny happened then, though I guess I shouldn't be amused. Peter called out, 'Lord, if it *is* you, bid me come to you on the water.' So Jesus commanded him to do so, and the fisherman clambered out of the boat and walked right over to Jesus. When he got there, he looked around and saw the waves and the boat with the eleven doing their best to row, and suddenly he got scared and started to sink."

"Even though he had done what Jesus commanded? That doesn't seem fair," Susanna said.

"Jesus reached out to him even as Peter was going down. He pulled him back up, and the two walked over and got into the boat. Immediately the wind ceased."

"Really?"

"Really! And Andrew told me that all of them in the boat worshiped Jesus, saying, 'Truly, You are the Son of Yahweh.'"

"They could have believed nothing less," Susanna declared.

"Neither they nor those where they landed. Word was sent into the surrounding villages and throughout the area, and people came, bringing everyone who was sick, weak, or crippled. There were so many that He couldn't talk to each one or even touch all of them, so those lying beside the paths reached out and touched the tassels of His garment. And as many as even touched those were made well."

Susanna sat in her favorite cane chair, her gaze leaving her friend to turn toward the darkness outside the door. "If only my brother could have been one of these," she sighed.

"Have you heard anything from him?"

"Nothing since the last time you took him food and clothing." And then she asked, "Do you know, have you heard yet if Jesus has healed leprosy?"

Ephrathah frowned. "I haven't heard. But I promise you, my friend, that I'll continue to make inquiries throughout Judea and Galilee."

While Susanna awaited Ephrathah's return, her days were full and passed quickly. Little Jonathan was the light of her life and a joy beyond any she had ever known. The days of her uncleanness were finished, and Taharka came back to the room they happily shared again.

She returned to helping Taharka with the record keeping and even wrote some of his letters, but business at the inn was continuing to decline. She had been fairly sure this was the case just from observing day-to-day activities, but on checking back she was dismayed to see what a drastic reduction had taken place in the past two years.

In the silence of her room, while carrying water, or while carving mutton, she silently repeated the same question, "Why, Yahweh, when Taharka has willingly become a Samaritan, gives his allegiance to You, and brings his tithes faithfully to the synagogue, why does his business have to suffer so? How long can he *stay* in business if he is prohibited from conducting it for two out of the seven days? Isn't there some way, *some* way . . .?"

eighteen

Susanna had forgotten to ask Ephrathah if Andrew had been taught to heal yet. It seemed likely. After all, Yahweh had answered when Ephrathah and Taharka had prayed in Jesus' name for help in turning Jonathan within her womb. Being with Jesus all this time, Andrew would certainly have learned this lesson before they had.

Her feet came to a complete stop perhaps a hundred feet from Jacob's Well, and she drew in a startled breath at the sudden realization that she *hadn't* learned the lesson well. *Forgive me, Yahweh,* she prayed. *I've been asking over and over again for Jesus to come so I could take Him to heal Jonah. But Yahweh, I don't really care whether I'm involved. Just please, somehow, some way, let Jesus be in the countryside near my brother.*

Let Jonah learn of His being there in time so that, even though he doesn't run and walk as he used to, he can get to Jesus and—and at least have the chance to touch the hem of His garment. In Jesus' name I ask this. Your humble servant, Susanna.

She felt better after this prayer, but variations of the same message were included every day, along with those used in the synagogue and the one Jesus had taught His disciples. She also included others she made up herself, prayers of praise, wonder, and supplication.

Of the group learning arithmetic, only Sherah, Peter, and Rachel showed enthusiasm for lessons in reading and writing. With such a small class, Susanna could give individual attention and was amazed at how quickly and eagerly they grasped even the slightest variations between letters.

Sherah volunteered to smooth the slates in preparation for each class, and Susanna watched as they were carried carefully to her room after the lessons. What a fine woman Sherah was to take on this extra task in addition to all her other duties!

Following the alphabet, then simple phrases and sentences, Susanna was uncertain what to use for reading material. The precious scrolls were too valuable to be passed around, so Susanna finally decided to copy selections.

The first scripture passage to be presented should be the Ten Commandments, so for the first weeks she wrote portions of them on her dark rock. She soon realized the students were memorizing them, and was delighted. They were taking advantage of this opportunity to learn the Commandments word for word.

Hearing of their interest, Taharka came in one day, gave each of the students a sheet of papyrus, and told them he'd permit them one at a time to make individual copies from his scroll.

Susanna's heart swelled at the generosity of this wonderful man who was her husband, and that night as she held him tightly she whispered, "That was one of the kindest things you could have done. Did you see Sherah crying for joy?"

His lips caressed her cheek. "But whose kindness was it that made it possible for them to learn to read and write, my beloved? And who is teaching them the Ten Commandments and Bible stories?"

She couldn't understand why he thought this commendable. She loved reading and writing so much that she *had* to share this blessing with others.

She was surprised Mahlon did not show more interest in Sherah's accomplishments or in other things taking place at the inn. Several months after he'd married Sherah, Susanna stopped him one noon as they passed in the courtyard. "Mahlon, are you happy here with us?"

He was startled. "Very happy, Susanna."

"You don't talk much to anyone, and you are very quiet."

He shuffled his feet and looked around as though searching for Sherah. Slowly his gaze returned to Susanna's. "As long as I can remember I have been . . . different. When I had a spell coming on or just after it passed, I would see only fear or ridicule—or superiority—in people's eyes. During my whole life, until Jesus healed me, I never had a friend."

A tightness in her throat gave her difficulty with speaking. "But that is changed now, Mahlon," she said gently. "You have been made *whole*. You have a real talent for leather working and you have a good mind—and you have the love of a wonderful woman."

The smile lighted his face with radiance. "Sherah is the most wonderful woman in the whole world—begging your pardon, Susanna."

"I'm glad you think so. But, Mahlon, can you talk with *her*? Can you tell her how you feel about things? What your hopes are? Your dreams? Your . . . ambitions?"

It seemed terribly difficult for him to express himself. When he answered, it was with a simple yes.

Reaching for both his hands, she said softly, "Then I'm not going to worry about you, Mahlon. I am glad you married Sherah, and I'm glad you're here. But if there's anything you'd *like* to talk to either me or Taharka about, please let us know."

He swallowed hard. "All right. And—and thank you." He stood still where she left him until, as she went into her room, she looked back and smiled.

It was the following day he met her as she brought water from the well. He walked beside her across the courtyard and reached to lift the jug from her head and dump it into the container. Even though she was sure he wanted to speak, she had no idea how to encourage him other than thanking him for this considerate act.

Finally he stammered, "You said I could talk with you if . . . if . . ."

She gave him her full attention. "This would be a good time, Mahlon."

"Sherah says—she told me you ask people from the caravans if they have news of the man who healed me."

"I'm interested in Jesus for many reasons," she said as he paused.

"I want so much to see Him and tell Him how grateful I am! I didn't get to know Him at all before He healed me and then, afterward, other people were around. I never learned to talk with anyone but my family, and, though I did ask if I could go with Him, nobody took me seriously."

"I'm sure *He* realized you were sincere, Mahlon."

"My family couldn't believe I was totally healed, and they wanted me home with them. As I'd never done anything on my own, I didn't argue, of course."

"Of course," she agreed. "But now?"

"Now I have this *need* to know about Him, to know who He is and what He's done and what He is doing. I understand He's a teacher as well as a healer, but I hear He's a Jew instead of a Samaritan and . . . and I don't know what to believe."

She noted from the short shadows that it was nearly time for the midday meal. "Right after we eat I have the time of teaching, Mahlon. Why don't you come to my room immediately after that, and I'll tell you some of the things I've learned about Jesus."

His breath was expelled in a deep, contented sigh, and his wide, intelligent eyes partially closed in a genuine smile. "I'd appreciate that very much. Thank you."

"I love to talk about Jesus, so this will give me an excuse to do so."

The class was conducted differently that day. She always brought Jonathan into the room with her, and usually, having nursed immediately before, he slept soundly or, if awake, was content to suck his thumb and look around with wide dark eyes.

Today, however, he was fretful and seemed to need the warmth and security of his mother's arms. She walked around trying to calm and comfort the baby and sent her students one at a time to write on the flat rock the words and phrases she dictated out of context.

They surprised her with their knowledge, for she remembered from her own experience not long before that it was much easier to learn reading than writing.

The faintest of breezes was present in the doorway, so she was standing there with the baby when she saw Mahlon coming. She smiled an invitation but did not interrupt Rachel, who was struggling to write "Mount Gerizim." She could not help noticing Mahlon's keen interest in the proceedings, and a little later she was sure she saw him shake his head a little as the next student made a spelling error.

She would have dicontinued the lesson at that time but was intrigued by Mahlon's reactions. Later, when they were alone, she asked him directly, "You know how to read and write, don't you?"

He looked stunned, guilty, as though she wouldn't approve. "Only a small amount."

"But you told us when you came that you'd had no schooling."

"That was true."

"Oh?"

He drew in a deep breath and hung his head forward. His right sandal scraped across the packed earth floor. "Please don't be angry with me—or Sherah."

Why she should be angry or upset with either of them she couldn't imagine. "I'm sure I won't be."

"I've always longed to have some learning, but because of my illness I missed being sent to the synagogue school as my brothers were. When Sherah and I first became friends, long before she came to love me, she taught me the number game. As you taught her to multiply and subtract and everything, she passed this on to me. And now, she's teaching me to read and write."

How was this possible? There was no paper on which to practice, and Susanna had the only dark rock. It was not winter, the rainy season, so they could not even use mud and a stick with which to practice.

The network of puzzle-wrinkles cleared from her forehead. Of course! "She's using the slates she takes home to smooth?"

He took a step backward. "We don't hurt them—we take very good care of them," he said, his voice and outstretched hands pleading for understanding.

"You read from them and write on them?"

Her questions were upsetting him further, "Oh, *please,* Susanna! If what we did was wrong, I'm sorry. Please, though, don't blame Sherah. It was my influence that made her offer to bring the slates home to smooth. It was because of her love for me and not for her own gain."

Susanna shifted Jonathan against her left shoulder so her right hand was free to reach out for this earnest man's hand. "Mahlon, I'm not angry. In fact, I'm *glad* you found a use for the slates during the hours we're not using them. For that matter, your wife has done a much better job of making them perfectly smooth than I did." Seeing the hint of a smile, which was immediately repressed, she asked, "Or is it *you* who makes them so perfect?"

"Sherah has so many other things to do," he murmured.

Susanna knew that to be true. "I'm afraid we take advantage of her."

"I didn't mean that," he protested. "She never complains about her work here."

"She's an exceptional woman."

"Yes, she is . . ."

~~~~~~~

Before long some of Mahlon's handwork was being sold. When one of the caravan masters asked Taharka if he could have a large number of sandals and pouches ready to be picked up the next time he passed through Sychar, Taharka called Mahlon to his office. "What do you think? Could you make that many within the next six weeks?" he asked.

The young man's face showed his concentration as he considered the procedures and the time needed for each. "I'd have to give at least five hours a day to this work, in addition to my helping here when the caravans come—and also when they leave in the morning."

"Would you like to work that long and take on this order?"

"If you'd like me to," Mahlon acceded. "Whatever you think best."

"That's not what I was asking," Taharka interrupted. "I may have pushed you into leather working when you married Sherah. I don't know if it's something you find pleasurable or challenging or if you'd rather be caring for sheep or spending more time with Putiel, working for the inn itself."

Mahlon nodded. "I do like this work, and it's something I do well," he said matter-of-factly.

"Would you like to continue with this, or would you prefer something else?" Taharka persisted.

This time there was appreciable hesitation. "There is only one thing that might be better, but I'll probably never be able to achieve it. So, yes, I could be happy continuing to work with leather."

"What might you prefer doing?"

"You'll think it stupid."

"If I didn't want to hear, Mahlon, I would not have asked."

"Well, I have this dream, this hope, that . . . that someday I will be able to learn to write well enough to become a scribe. But that's probably foolish."

"It's foolish only if you dream but do nothing to make it come true. I understand from Susanna that you and Sherah are working at your studies. You may attend Susanna's lessons if you would like, even though that takes time from your leather crafting. Get wood from the pile of lumber Putiel keeps for repairs and make a wax slate at least three times as large as the ones you now use. When it is completed and the wax applied, bring it to me."

Mahlon had been using the leather that had been stored at the inn, but as more was needed Taharka insisted he keep records of all costs and from whom supplies were purchased. Also he was to mark down how much time he was spending on each project. When Taharka had him help determine selling prices based on this information, Mahlon looked shocked. "But that's more than what has ever been charged here," he protested. "People won't pay that much."

Taharka said drily, "Then they will do without. However, if your quality remains as good as it is, you'll have no trouble disposing of all you make."

This proved to be the case. When the caravan master who had asked for the original large order refused to accept it at the new price, Mahlon was discouraged, sure they would be unable to sell them at all. However, a Babylonian factor bought every item when he passed through two weeks later, and asked for more to be available when he came again.

～～～～

Stories concerning Jesus became favorites among those who made their home at the inn. Even though they'd been heard many times before, Susanna was often asked to repeat one or more of them as everyone worked together preparing the evening meals. They rejoiced at the reports they heard of the confrontations between Jesus and the Pharisees, for, at least according to those bringing the accounts, Jesus was more than a match for their legalism.

Taharka called Susanna to hear the account brought by a tent-maker, Jemuel, traveling with one of the Ethiopian caravans. When Susanna found what a good storyteller he was, she asked Jemuel to come with her. The workers were surprised and delighted at having a stranger in the cooking area, and listened attentively.

"When I was recently in Jerusalem I visited with a man named Isaac, a cousin of my wife," he began. "Unfortunately, he was born blind, but his family took care of him and helped him learn his way around the city so he could beg for a living.

"One Sabbath day Isaac heard a group of people coming toward him and cringed when he realized he was being talked about. One man asked, 'Rabbi, who sinned, this man or his parents, that he was born blind?'

"The answering voice had to be that of the teacher, explaining that it was nobody's fault, the blindness being so that Yahweh's works could be shown through him. It seemed unfair to Isaac that Yahweh might want him to be blind, and he was trying to decide whether to ask for alms or turn and shuffle away when he heard someone spit on the ground and felt gentle hands placing something warm and wet on his eyes.

162

"He wondered if this could be another of the cruel jokes frequently played on him. But the person did not seem unkind, so when the voice of the man they called Jesus told him to wash in the pool of Siloam, he decided to do so. Feeling his way along familiar buildings, he made his way to the pool, leaned over, scooped up water, and washed the mud away."

Jemuel looked around, obviously enjoying the total involvement of the listeners and his own role as narrator. He went on, "Isaac described to me the amazing sensation of brightness, of something he could only guess to be that which people referred to as 'light.'

"His eyes opened slowly and his hands flew up to shade them as the searing afternoon brilliance struck eyes never before having seen it. By squinting, he made out sights that, when he closed his eyes and listened, he recognized as people, dogs, and even a donkey.

"He feasted his gaze on these things so different from what he had imagined them to be. Then, remembering Who had performed this miracle, he went to seek for Him. People could not believe this was the man who used to sit and beg, but he assured them he was the person they had known and answered their questions by telling of meeting Jesus and of washing in the pool of Siloam.

"He was told to accompany some of them to the Temple and, being grateful for the miracle, gladly accepted this opportunity for giving thanks. Almost everyone rejoiced with him, but the Pharisees asked *how* he had received his sight and he told them. Some began arguing that Jesus could not possibly be from Yahweh or He would know better than to break the Law by healing on the Sabbath, while others protested that if He were a sinner, Yahweh would not permit Him to heal.

"Finally, some asked Isaac his opinion but became furious when he stated he considered Jesus to be a prophet. They accused him of having faked blindness all these years so he could get money by begging. His parents were even brought there to verify that Isaac was their son, blind from birth.

"Aware that the Pharisees had decided that anyone confessing Jesus to be the Christ should be put out of the Temple, my sister and her husband told the Pharisees not to ask them but to ask their son, who is an adult, how this miracle had been done. When they called Isaac back, the Pharisees demanded that he give praise only to Yahweh and not to Jesus, whom they claimed was a sinner.

"Isaac's response was that the only thing he knew was that he used to be blind but could now see. When he had previously asked what could be done to give him sight, the Pharisees had informed him that never since the world began had anyone opened the eyes of a man born blind. If Jesus was not from Yahweh, Isaac insisted, He could do nothing. The Pharisees became so angry they threw him from the Temple.

"Being banned from the Temple is the worst thing that can happen to a Jew, so what had been his happiest day was now his worst. While he was beginning to think that perhaps he should not have spoken out so strongly, somebody came to walk beside him and spoke in that voice he could never forget, 'Do you believe in the Son of man?'

"Isaac recognized the term from prophesies he had heard read in the Temple, but asked to whom it referred. When Jesus said it was He who was speaking to him, Isaac knelt in worship of Him right there on that dusty street and declared, 'Lord, I believe!' "

———〉〉〉〉———

As the Ethiopian stopped speaking there was a collective sigh from those who had been listening. Huldah hurried to retrieve from the oven the bread she had forgotten; Naomi went back to shaping loaves; and Peter quickly turned the spit, obviously grateful to find the mutton not charred.

Several people asked questions, and then Susanna thanked Jemuel for sharing this account and walked with him to the court-yard. She had to find out one more thing before parting. "May I ask? Are you a follower of Jesus?"

He looked around surreptitiously. "I have not met Him person-ally. From what I've heard, however, a man would be a fool not to have faith in Him." His smile revealed teeth surprisingly white in contrast to his skin. "Ask me the next time I come."

Later, as her husband was unrolling the scroll in preparation for their scripture reading, Susanna said, "Taharka, I keep remembering that a number of Jesus' miracles have been done on the Sabbath, and He always defends His right to do this. Please don't be upset if I suggest that our having the inn open on that day *could* be His will. I know the Law states we are not to do work then, and I know those traveling on the Sabbath are not Samaritans or Jews in good standing. But might it not be obeying the laws of hospitality to have the inn available for them?''

She had half expected a rebuff for this interpretation of Jesus' words, but Taharka leaned forward, elbows on the table, bearded chin resting on his fists. "I really don't know. I would like to think that, but the hospitality mentioned is to be without pay, of course, and we can't afford to do that."

She tried to decide how to express herself. "When Yahweh made the world, He worked six days and rested the seventh—and yet He doesn't let the sun and moon fall out of the heavens on the Sabbath, or forget to continue the waters flowing, the crops growing, or us breathing. Maybe what He wants is for us to use our Sabbath to help others and keep *our* part of the world running smoothly, or . . ." She despaired of making sense of her thoughts. "I still don't have it worked out in my mind. I shouldn't have brought it up."

He smiled encouragement, but his eyes were still troubled. "You should indeed share your thoughts. I have been thinking, worrying, and praying about this for a long time. The words coming to my mind are those of Jesus that Ephrathah told us. Remember when He and His disciples were walking down the road, and the Pharisees denounced them for 'harvesting' or working on the Sabbath as they pulled off heads of grain and rubbed them between their hands so they could eat? 'The Sabbath was made for man,' He said, 'not man for the Sabbath; so the Son of man is lord even of the Sabbath.'"

"Oh, I wish we could talk with Him! If only He would come this way again soon!" Susanna cried. "I've thought that perhaps you could go and try to find Him, but if you went to Nazareth, He might be in Jerusalem, or if you went there, He could be at Bethsaida or up near Tyre."

"Or that might be when He came to Sychar again," Taharka added.

Susanna sighed. "There are many people who know we want to see Him and have promised to let us know if He's anywhere nearby. We will have to wait until we hear something."

She certainly did not expect to hear the news brought by a southbound caravan ten days later.

nineteen

Usually she approached the office quietly, knocking to announce herself, or silently retreating if someone was with Taharka. This day, however, Susanna ran down the passageway, calling, "Taharka, you'll never believe the stupidity, the inhospitality, the *cruelty* of some of our people!"

He looked up from the accounts, his finger marking his place. Seeing how upset she was, he asked, "Our people here at the inn?"

"No. No, of course not—they wouldn't be so stupid." She flounced into the room and around the table to drop into a seat across from her husband. Her eyes were as stormy as her disposition. "I just heard that Jesus and His twelve disciples were on their way here. Maybe they were planning to stay with us, as we had invited them to do when they came through Samaria."

"What happened! Why *didn't* they come?"

"He sent several of His men ahead to make arrangements for food and a place to stay. But when the people in the village realized these Jews were on their way to Jerusalem, they'd have nothing to do with them. They wouldn't sell them food or give them accommodations, or *anything*."

"So what did they do?"

"They apparently returned and asked Jesus to be allowed to send fire down from Heaven to burn up the city, but He scolded them for such thoughts. Even though they were tired, they went on to another village where they were able to stay."

He reached across to take her hand in his warm, comforting one. "I'm sorry, dear. We both were so hoping that He would come."

"The place they spent the night was over near the Jordan River, so they continued south using the road through the Decapolis and Perea." There were tears of frustration and anger in her eyes. "*Why,* Taharka? Why, when we've prayed and prayed for Him to come, why couldn't He have made the trip by way of Sychar? He must have been within a mile of Jonah and less than a day from here."

He sighed. "There must be some reason."

"A reason for Jonah's continuing to have leprosy for another day or month or year?"

"I don't know, Susanna. Maybe the time isn't right. Maybe he'll be healed some other time."

"But I want him healed *now*," she wailed. "I love him and want him back. And David and Mikal need him—as does Leah, too. Jesus will probably hate all us Samaritans forever and ever."

Taharka's slight smile showed her the irrationality of her words, but she was still upset until he assured her, "The Jesus we know and have been hearing so much about is not a man to carry grudges, Susanna."

"Well, I hope not! I will never forgive the people of that town if my brother is not healed."

His voice softly quoted, ". . . 'And forgive us our debts as we forgive our debtors.'"

Her lower lip trembled, and, though she struggled to restrain the tears, they spilled over and ran down her cheeks. Through her sobs, which were uncontrollable, she managed, "Oh, Taharka, I'm so miserable. I'm not a good person and—and I'm hateful—and, though I pray Jesus' prayer, I don't even want to practice it sometimes."

He got up and came around the table. As easily as though she were a child he lifted her into his arms and sat down where she'd been, with her on his lap. "It's all right, dear," he soothed. "I know how much this means to you, and I don't blame you for being upset. However, we will continue to pray every morning, evening, and many times between for your brother's healing. And we will pray for forgiveness for the people of that village."

Her voice was muffled. "I don't think I can, not right now."

"But you've forgiven Leah her unkindness."

Susanna wished he had not mentioned Leah just now. Huldah had just told her this morning that gossip around town reported Leah was seriously considering getting a divorce from Jonah so she could marry a widower with three children who lived in Shechem. There were only two grounds on which a woman could get a divorce: infidelity and leprosy. Her husband had been a leper for almost three years now.

She buried her face against Taharka's chest, and he could hardly hear her words. "Most of the time I think I have forgiven her, but right now I'm still angry at her and at Mara, and at the disease that has hold of Jonah."

He gently brought the subject back. "If you *don't* forgive the Samaritan village, how can you ask that Jesus forgive the country of Samaria and come this way?" he asked.

She pulled back a little so that, leaning on his arm, she could look up at the strongly handsome face she loved so much. She ran a finger across the high cheekbone then down along the edge of his beard to his lips, which she traced gently. "I love you even when you're logical and make me feel so stupid."

His lips pursed to give her finger a kiss. "You're usually so sensible and happy and friendly and dear. Perhaps you're entitled sometimes to cry out against things that don't seem right."

Feeling ashamed of herself, she struggled to sit up, but he held her securely. "Not yet, my love. I'd much rather have you in my arms than work with the records."

She was contrite. "Since Jonathan is having such trouble with cutting his tooth, I haven't been of much help to you," she apologized.

"You're his mother. You should be with him when he's fretful."

~~~~~~

Although she prayed frequently, Susanna was still worried that Jesus wouldn't have anything to do with Samaritans or try to come through Samaria again after the ill treatment He had received. It was with relief and joy that she heard a couple of months later that He'd told a parable about a Jew who was going from Jerusalem by the road that Jesus must usually travel down toward the Jordan River. He'd approach Jericho by way of a steep, rocky, deserted area that abounded with thieves.

The Jew of the story was attacked by robbers who took everything he owned, including his clothing, then beat him and left him along the road to die, or perhaps they thought him already dead.

A priest came along, but, although he saw the man, he didn't approach him. Taharka reminded her that if the priest were to touch a dead man he would become unclean for seven days, so perhaps that was why he didn't stay and help, but Susanna didn't think this a very good excuse.

The next person to come was a Levite. Certainly he would help the man, she thought—but that was not to be, either. He looked at the victim from a distance, walked by on the far side of the road and hurried on. Susanna wondered if he might have been afraid this man was a decoy for robbers who could be hiding nearby to jump out and overpower him if he let down his guard. She could just imagine him scurrying on his way as fast as his legs could carry him.

After a while a third individual, a Samaritan businessman, approached. This man had the least reason for helping, but, seeing the beaten, bleeding man, he was filled with compassion. He went to him immediately, cleaned and bound his wounds, then gave him nourishment, after which he helped him up onto his own donkey and led the animal to the first inn they came to.

He arranged for a room and stayed with the man all night, attending to his needs. By morning, however, the injured man was still not fit to travel, and the Samaritan had to be on his way. Therefore, he took out money enough to pay a laborer for two days' work and gave this to the innkeeper, saying, "Take care of him; and whatever more you spend, I will repay you when I come back."

Susanna especially liked this part, for it showed the innkeeper must have had faith in the Samaritan, since he promised to do as requested.

But what was even better than this was Jesus' reason for the story. It was to illustrate that what made men neighbors or friends was the showing of mercy and love for one another.

Susanna sighed contentedly when the story was finished. "Jesus really doesn't hate all us Samaritans," she said with relief.

Taharka grinned. "If He hated a whole nation because of a few people, He'd be very lonely. With so many of the Jewish leaders against Him, He'd have to hate all the Jews, even though He is one himself."

"Well, I'm still praying for Him to come," she declared.

~~~~~~

Even the many weeks of rainy weather didn't make the winter drag for Susanna. The nights were cool but the days still warm. Little Jonathan, a delightful, happy child who made friends easily, had begun walking early and was by now running on chubby legs through puddles and into everyone's way. Since many people traveling with caravans were away from their families for weeks or months at a time, a number of the men and most of the women made a fuss over him.

With spring, the grain began to fill, and the rains dwindled to showers, then stopped completely, so weeks passed without precipitation. Jonathan no longer was willing to be carried by his mother when she went for water, but his legs were too short to keep up with her when she went to Jacob's Well. So she went there early in the morning before he was around or would make the much shorter trip to the well in the center of town.

Jonathan accomplished what her efforts had failed to do. With his outgoing, loving disposition, the way he greeted each person with a radiant smile and his own version of conversation, he soon had all the women calling him by name and sometimes even bringing him honey cakes or pieces of fruit.

And she, as his mother, also received smiles and greetings. Even Mara behaved better, although Susanna would never quite trust her.

She was returning from one of these water collections when she snatched her son's hand to keep him away from the flashing hooves of a big brown horse being ridden at a gallop into the courtyard.

The rider leaped off and said to Mahlon, who was helping to clean up following the exit of the last caravan, "I have a message for Taharka or for his wife. Where are they?"

Mahlon's glance slid toward Susanna, who almost imperceptibly shook her head, preferring her husband to handle any business. "My master is in his office."

Then, seeing Susanna's intense gaze watching the short, slight newcomer run in the direction indicated, Mahlon reached up and removed the jug from her head. "I'll empty it," he offered. "Come with me, Jonathan."

As the toddler ran beside Mahlon, whom he'd come to love, she turned to follow the stranger. Was it bad news? A single rider often came to make arrangements for a caravan, but not this early in the day, and the man seemed in a great hurry.

". . . And I was to stop no longer than to rest my horse, for I must get here at once," the courier was saying as Susanna slid through the door and stood close to the wall. "Jesus and some of His followers are heading east down the valley of Bethshean, along the Galilee–Samaria border. They are stopping along the way to visit several people."

"When did you see them last?" Taharka asked.

"Last evening. I would have left immediately, but it isn't safe to sleep along the road alone or to travel through the night, so I slept in Galilee and started this morning before daybreak."

Taharka was on his feet, taut with suppressed excitement. "How soon can you and your beast be ready to start back? We could leave very soon."

The messenger, Uzziel, nodded. "As soon as we have food and water," he assured them.

How they got everything taken care of in that short a time Susanna never quite knew. They had hoped and dreamed of this for so long, but their plans had not had the immediacy of this moment nor included what she was about to do. It was only now she realized she must take David with them.

Leaving Sherah to gather together food and drink, she ran through the streets of Sychar. *Oh, Yahweh, please let Leah be there when I arrive. Let her agree to our taking David with us to see his father. Please help me have the words I need, and keep her from refusing.*

Surprisingly, Leah didn't ask for all the details or a guarantee of when they'd return or any of the things Susanna had feared would take too much time. *Yahweh must indeed have heard my prayer,* Susanna thought as she accepted a small bundle containing David's blanket, in which, if need be, he could be wrapped for sleeping that night.

"We'll take good care of him," she assured Leah and then did impulsively what she'd never have done had she thought about it beforehand. Going to her sister-in-law, she put her arms around her and hugged her tightly. "Thank you for entrusting him to us," she whispered.

There were tears in Leah's eyes. "Go with Yahweh," she said softly, and Susanna smiled. Surely Leah still loved Jonah. If she *was* thinking of divorce, she must be desperate financially, or her brother must be pushing her.

"Let's have a race, David," Susanna challenged. "Let's see who can get to the well first." They ran side by side through the streets.

She'd expected to have to hold herself back but found that, although at first she easily could have outrun him, she was breathing heavily before they got to the square, while he was hardly winded. She stopped long enough to get a dipper of water for each of them from the containers left for passersby, and then rechallenged him for the race to the inn.

They arrived as Taharka was fastening the last of the bundles to the back of a horse. "Horses?" she asked. "I've never ridden a horse, Taharka."

"I know," he said, looking concerned. "But I'm afraid we'll be too late if we use donkeys."

Putiel encouraged her. "You will do well, Susanna. Hareph has assured us these horses are gentle and obey readily."

"I'm going with you to care for them," put in Hareph, the middle-aged, bowlegged man who lived on the other side of Sychar and rented horses, donkeys, and carts.

He showed her how to mount from the horse's left side, but she knew she could never keep from sliding off with both legs on the one side of her steed. "I can't *do* it!" she cried, dismay mingling with panic as the horse sidestepped.

"You'll have to," Taharka stated firmly. "There's no other way."

She held onto the mane as Hareph led them a few steps, and bit her lips to keep back cries of terror. The mare tossed her head as they made the turn at the cistern, and Susanna began to slide. "Taharka!" she wailed.

Catching herself, she glanced at her husband and saw what looked like exasperation in his eyes. "Hareph, wouldn't it help if I rode with one leg on each side, like you do?"

The man looked from her to Taharka and moistened his lips before answering. "But women don't ride like that."

"I can't go all that way like this," she protested, "especially if I'm carrying our son." And then she silently thanked Yahweh when Taharka's manner changed with mention of Jonathan. He came at once and helped her down, then assisted as she "girded her loins," as a workman would refer to it when he'd pull the back of his long tunic forward between his legs and tuck it into the front of his girdle.

She felt indecent with her legs exposed like this, so she pulled a fold of the horse's blanket over her limbs when she was helped back up again.

It was possible now to grip the body of the tall animal between her knees, and she concentrated on learning how to hold the reins firmly as she was instructed. She insisted on riding around the courtyard and making sure her reddish mare would obey before she accepted Jonathan into her arms.

David, large-eyed and sober, was lifted into the care of this uncle he had never known, and the other two men vaulted easily onto their animals.

Mahlon stood beside Susanna's steed, rubbing its smooth neck with the palm of his hand. "If you—*when* you see Jesus, tell Him I remember Him in my prayers each day and I thank Him."

Her hand rested for a moment on the black hair. "If I have the opportunity, I'll tell him—about you and Rachel and all the good things that have happened because He came here." She looked at Taharka and then at Jonathan as she finished speaking.

They left the inn and were soon going out through Sychar's gateway and onto the road leading north. It was a strange feeling to be riding a horse with its front-to-back movement instead of the side-to-side rocking of a donkey. Insecure with the newness of the experience, she was unable to pay attention to her surroundings at first.

After they had passed Mount Ebal, however, her interest became more keen, and she pointed out to Jonathan and David various rock formations, strangely shaped trees, vineyards, and shepherds with their flocks.

She shifted position frequently, for riding was not without discomfort. Taking her place at the rear of the small group, she nursed Jonathan, and he went to sleep, not waking until they stopped to let the horses drink from a brook while the riders walked around, drank from their water skins, and ate some of the bread left from the morning meal.

They were soon back on the horses again. David, who had never been on a horse and only seldom outside the walls of Sychar, marveled over everything. He asked questions, made comments, and was as enthused about a small fish in a brook as about the wild hart leaping away from them.

She knew she would prefer walking if given the choice, and she'd probably be sore for days, but it had been wise for Taharka to make arrangements for these horses.

If only they could get to Jonah before Jesus passed that way! *Oh, Yahweh, please, please let us be in time!*

She remembered Mahlon's wistfulness and realized how greatly he'd have liked to accompany them. She wished he could have, but with her and Taharka gone, Putiel would need help with the work this evening and tomorrow morning. She would certainly make every effort to speak to Jesus about him, Rachel, and Putiel.

Taharka rode beside her during the afternoon, and they talked of many things as both children napped. "When we came this way before, I dared not let myself be alone with you," he said.

"Oh?"

"I loved you so much, but I didn't want to do or say anything about it until I spoke with your brother, as the head of your house."

"And you found he was willing."

"He said he was sure you loved me, also, though you hadn't put that into words." He fanned away the large fly trying to land on David's face. "And that night under the stars I was awake most of the time. It was so overwhelming to have you sleeping near me that I feared I might in my sleep reach out and draw you to me."

Her eyes met his, and they needed no contact of hands or bodies to unite them. "I could not have refused you, my beloved," she declared softly.

"Perhaps we wasted too much time," he suggested, then added quickly, "but I think not. We became dear friends before becoming lovers."

"Which is the very best way," she affirmed.

A little later Uzziel called back to them, "Just over this hill is where the lepers live."

She hadn't expected this tightness in her throat and her fast heartbeat. They were so near to Jonah, yet she had found no way to prepare her nephew for what he was about to see. All they had told him was that he was going to meet his father, whom he barely remembered.

She suggested, "Taharka, would you like to ride on ahead with David while I speak to my brother?"

"I've been wondering, might it be best not to build up Jonah's hopes till we know Jesus is still in the area?"

"But he has to be prepared—so he won't miss Jesus, even if we should."

There was a brief silence, followed by Taharka's offer, "Do you want me to go down? We don't know how bad Jonah may be by now."

She appreciated his trying to spare her, and felt much less brave than she hoped she sounded as they neared the top of the slope. "I must be the one to tell him. Don't worry, Taharka. I will be strong."

As she left the men, children, and horses at the road and clambered down toward the brook separating her from the caves of the lepers, she shivered involuntarily. What would she find?

Deciding that reality could be no worse than her imaginings, she raised her hands to cup her mouth and shouted, "Jonah, your sister, Susanna, has come to see you."

After waiting for a time, she called again. There was no echoed response, and she was dismayed that the only motion she saw was a short old man moving from one cave to another. Was their journey for nothing?

She had to try again. "I am here to see Jonah of Sychar. Would somebody please get him or bring word of him?" She added the last, fearing he might have died and she'd not heard of it. *Oh, Yahweh, please* . . .

There were now two figures at the opening of the cave, the man she'd seen enter and a slightly taller, bent figure exiting with him. The second man was using a crutch and a cane and was moving slowly, with a peculiar shuffling, close-footed gait.

This could not be her beloved brother. He was too short, too aged, too stooped. Perhaps he was their leader or a friend, coming to give her a report.

Or perhaps he was about to beg for food or alms.

When he had hobbled a third of the way to the creek, the man said, "Susanna!" and there was no longer doubt. This man, this wreck of a man, was what was left of the brother she loved!

She would not cry! She would not hurt him or shame herself or Taharka, who had so loyally offered to bring the message.

"Is my family well?" he called, apparently fearing her coming meant bad news.

"We are all fine," she told him. "Taharka is up at the road with your son and ours."

His rough wooden supports were needed even more now as he stood still, staring at her, horrified. "David is *here*?"

"I thought you'd want to see him. He's a handsome six-year-old, strong and healthy and intelligent, just as his father was."

She could have bit her tongue as he cried bitterly, "'Was' is correct. But look at me now! I am nothing. I am worse than dead!"

"That's why we're here, Jonah," she interrupted. "We received word that Jesus is coming this way, and we want to make sure you will meet Him and be healed."

"Nothing can heal me," he declared morosely, and she realized with a pang that he had not even welcomed her or said he was glad to see her.

He probably wasn't, either, she realized. He would have to be shaken from his depression and discouragement. "We're leaving now to look for Jesus, as He may be in any of the houses or villages in this area—if He hasn't gone too fast and is already east of us," she added. "I can't promise we'll find Him, but we're going to do the best we can. In the meantime, I want you to cross this stream, climb the bank, and start up the road."

"Susanna, you don't understand! This is the farthest I've walked for this entire month." His words were a cry of despair.

"Well, *try*," she pleaded. "I'd stay and help you if I could, but . . ."

"Don't be a fool, Susanna. I wouldn't *let* you touch me. I'd die if I gave this curse to someone I love!"

"Will you try to come?" she begged.

His laugh was almost a croak. It had probably been so long since he'd had anything to laugh about that he'd forgoteen how to do it. He pulled the tunic up above his knees, showing his deformed legs, which were sore-covered and filthy. Her stomach heaved at the sight, and she looked away then struggled to keep from staring at his nose, which was curiously flattened. His face, though emaciated like the rest of him, no longer had the prominent high cheekbones she remembered so well.

"I promised your son he would see you, Jonah," she reminded, "and I'll keep my word. I hope by that time you will be healed. But now we must go look for the Master."

She turned and scrambled up the bank. Hot tears were collecting, but she *would* not cry! Not for her sake, for young David's, for Taharka's, or for Jonah's.

She pointedly ignored Jonah's protestations from behind her that he was unable to follow her and to seek Jesus.

"Susanna, where's my father?" David asked before she got near the road. "Why isn't he with you? When am I going to see him? What did he say?"

She tried to be cheerful as she told him his father wasn't feeling well and they would have to wait until later for David to meet him.

Taharka's quiet face revealed that he realized her interview had not gone well. As he handed Jonathan to her after she got on her horse, his hand pressed her thigh firmly and, his eyes holding hers, he whispered, "Keep praying, beloved."

She blinked to keep back tears, and her quivering lips turned up just a little in the bravest smile she could manage. "I am."

Taharka remounted his horse and rode forward to get David from Hareph, who had entertained him during the time Jonathan was with his father.

Within minutes they were in the valley of Bethshean. As they permitted the horses to walk in the shade of olive trees on the left side of the road, Uzziel stated, "I shall continue on this road until I check at each house within a mile. If Jesus has been in the area, someone must know of it."

"I doubt He's got this far, considering that people constantly stop Him to ask for healing or for blessings on the children," Taharka said. "Since we think Jesus is still to our west and you're trying to get help for your brother, Susanna, we thought it best for you to go that way, while I check with everyone I can find in this little village."

"And I am going with you, Susanna," Hareph stated simply.

Susanna drew a deep breath as she looked at these three men trying so hard to make her dream come true. How good it was of them to arrange things so that the owner of the horses would be traveling with her! "Thank you—all of you," she said, the words sounding inadequate to her, though they expressed her sentiments.

They separated at once, with David unhappily wailing as his aunt went off in a different direction from that he, Taharka, and the red horse were taking.

"Hareph," Susanna asked, "from what you've seen and heard, do you believe that Jesus is the promised Messiah?"

"It's hard to know. He could be, I suppose, but I can't believe the Messiah would be some homeless, traveling preacher-magician."

She would have to tell him later what she knew of Jesus, but there wasn't time now. "If Jesus stopped at midday, He should be about to start again now," Susanna mused, noting the length of the shadows.

"I would think so," Hareph agreed. "From what your husband said about everyone congregating around Him, I doubt He could be in one of these two very small houses here."

"I'd doubt it, too, but we must make sure. There must be no chance of missing Him."

Hareph slid down from his horse and went to the door of each dwelling, but received no answer to his knocks or calls. "Maybe He *is* near," Susanna said, and the thought sent a shiver of expectancy up her spine. "To have nobody home at this hour in one house might not be unusual, but for no one to be about at *two* homes must mean something special."

As Hareph nimbly mounted his brown-and-white stallion, they moved farther west. "What do you think?" she asked. "Shall we try the group of houses off there to our right, or go first to those seven on our left?"

He shrugged. "Could be either or neither."

She studied them carefully as she and Hareph approached the paths leaving the one they were on. "Maybe it's because I'm a Samaritan," she began with a slight smile of deprecation, "but I'd like to go first to those on the left. Listen! There's laughter and lots of talking and—and there seem to be many people."

Within a minute or two they were riding into the area fronted by all the homes. A young woman came running out, crying "Welcome, welcome! Get down from your horses and come meet the other guests!"

"Is Jesus here?" Susanna asked of the tall, happy young woman in a flowing linen gown of palest blue.

Her eyes almost closed when she laughed, and the deep dimples gave her the innocence of a child, although her figure was definitely that of a woman. "Everyone must be here! Come, don't waste a moment."

Susanna looked toward the well. "May I ask a favor? We've been riding since early morning, and it's so very hot. Could we have a drink of water first?"

As Susanna slid down gingerly from her mount and Hareph took hold of the bridle, the golden-haired woman held Jonathan. She handed him back after giving him a quick hug. "There is wine inside, but I agree, nothing quenches sun-given thirst like fresh well water."

She drew a bucketful and handed Susanna and Hareph cups filled to their brims. She asked their names and introduced herself before taking Susanna in to the crowded, packed room where everyone seemed to be talking, shouting, questioning, greeting, and hugging one another.

"But where is Jesus?" Susanna finally asked. "Or Andrew or Peter or Nathanael?"

"I don't think I know any of those," her hostess said. "Perhaps they'll be coming with my bridegroom right after sundown."

Susanna's brow furrowed for a moment and then awareness came. This was the day of a wedding, and doubtless the girl who had met them was the bride. Many family members and friends had arrived, and she must have thought Susanna, Hareph, and Jonathan were a family coming from a distance to attend the festivities.

Susanna tried to explain her dilemma, but other guests whisked away the lovely young woman, who said in parting, "I'm sorry I can't introduce you. Make your way around and meet everyone. The food's over that way." And she was laughing and talking with others.

Susanna tried as quickly as possible to make her way to the door and out to Jonathan and Hareph, but she didn't wish to be rude to the friendly people who were stopping her and wishing her well—and doubtless trying to figure how she fit into the family relationships.

As Hareph saw Susanna hurrying toward him, he scooped up Jonathan, who had been playing with pebbles in the shade of a fig tree. "It's the wrong house," she whispered, exasperation, embarrassment, and even a little humor mixed into her tone. "Everyone's eating and drinking and visiting while they await the coming of the groom!"

He apparently couldn't help grinning at her discomfiture but then sobered as he realized what she must be thinking. Perhaps they had missed Jesus! He helped her onto her horse, handed Jonathan up, then, after leading both animals around the corner of the house, remounted.

"Oh, dear," she sighed, "could *that* be Jesus' group?" She pointed in the direction from which they had come a short time earlier. "They must have been visiting in those houses over there!"

They could not race the animals. Susanna had managed to stay on with her horse walking, but that would have to suffice, especially since she was carrying Jonathan. Hareph did nudge his animal into walking faster, however, so Susanna's mount did likewise.

They were gaining on the band, which was now almost to the crossroads leading to Nain or to Sychar and Jerusalem. Because of the small orchard to the right of the intersection Susanna could not see if anyone was there, but nobody was in view farther south. If Jonah had not started right away, he might not get here in time. If only he had—if only he did . . .

If only she dared ride faster! Looking off to her left she could see dust raised by a lone horseman. "Is that Uzziel?"

Hareph shielded his eyes with his hand. "Yes, that's Storm he's riding."

As Uzziel was too far away yet, she considered sending Hareph on ahead to find out if Jesus was among this group and, if so, to ask Him to wait. But just then they moved slightly to the left, toward the small village Taharka said he would be checking.

Well, at least she should be able to catch up with them there, she thought, shifting Jonathan to lean against her left arm.

There was so much laughing and talking among those before her that she was not aware at once of other sounds and activity. She noticed individuals nudge one another and point and, looking to her right, Susanna beheld a motley assortment of men plodding toward the intersection. Jonah *was* here! She could identify him by his cane and crutch and his strange, slow shuffle, which was obviously painful.

"Jesus, Master, have mercy on us," Jonah called, and then his words were taken up by others in his band until all ten were begging, pleading the same prayer, which Susanna knew would never leave her mind.

They came only to the edge of the east-west path that Jesus had just left. They were keeping the prescribed distance, even though they were chanting their plea instead of calling (as was required), "Unclean! Unclean!" to indicate they were lepers.

Susanna expected Jesus to go to them even though they were afflicted. Maybe He would lay His hand on them or spit and make mud to put on them or pray over them as He had Rachel. Any of these things would have pleased her.

What He did was a complete disappointment.

He stood and looked at them for a long moment and then, in a voice ringing with authority, commanded, "Go and show yourselves to the priests."

That was all.

Susanna had a sinking sensation somewhere in her chest. The last time Jonah had shown himself to the priest he'd been sent away to live a life worse than that of a wild animal.

The men were moving, not staying to even say farewell to one another. Jonah turned and hobbled with his cane and crutch back the way he had come, while two of the men headed down the path toward the Jordan River, four toward her left, into central Galilee, and the other three toward her.

She nudged her horse clear of the road, wanting to stay as far away from the lepers as possible, and she noted Hareph did likewise. Six feet was the absolute minimum commanded by the Law, but she'd prefer a much greater separation. Her brother was hidden behind the olive trees, so her eyes were riveted on those coming toward her. They didn't seem as bad now that they were nearer. In fact, their condition was nowhere near as bad as Jonah's. Maybe what they had needed was exercise or something, for even the short, stooped, gray-haired man she'd seen go to Jonah's cave was more erect now.

The men were hurrying, and were near enough that she could see that the hair of the man she'd thought so old was streaked with black. *It's strange I didn't notice that before,* she thought. And the skin on his arms that had appeared to be covered with sores—was it just dirt? But *if* it was dirt . . .

She stared at them frankly, trying to see just how serious a case of leprosy each had that he'd been banished to holes in the earth.

The oldest man must have seen her expression but was so used to people gawking at him that he could ignore it. He looked down at his bare arms and then, stopping in mid-stride, bent to examine his knees and legs. "Yahweh be praised!" he breathed, and then, tugging at the tunic of the middle-aged man beside him, commanded, "Look at yourself—look at me!"

They stood there, three grown men, examining their hands, arms, and fingers with the intensity of babies just discovering these body parts. The youngest of them used his right thumb to press down hard on each fingertip of his left hand, and then ran his dirty fingernails across his palm, the back of his hand, and on the firm flesh of his forearm. "I can feel—I can *feel* again! I haven't been able to feel anything for seven years!"

"And my skin is smooth. Look at my skin!"

The other two were also exclaiming, and suddenly the youngest cried, "I've got to get home. If I get to my priest before sundown, maybe I can get the paper stating I'm clean, and can spend this night in my village."

"That's right," the middle-aged one agreed. "And I have even further to go than you." He started running with his companion.

The older man stood, uncertain for a moment, looking back toward Jesus, then down at his obviously healed legs and feet. He glanced up at the sun, apparently reckoning the time he had before the day was over.

And he hurried down the road, his shadow behind him.

~~~~~

Susanna's gaze went back to Uzziel, at the far edge of the village, then searched for Taharka. Although he must be among the villagers who were congregating or with those who had come with Jesus, she could not see his tall, erect form.

But there was Jonah, a lonely figure going up the long hill beyond where he had lived in the cave for three years. She wished it were possible to see clearly that far away, but it did seem remarkable that he had covered that distance in this short a time.

Maybe he wasn't so crippled anymore. Even squinting, she could discern nothing in his hands. "Hareph, look at my brother. Is he using a crutch and cane?"

"I was about to ask you that. He *seems* to be . . . walking, almost running, if that's possible."

Their eyes met. "You saw the lepers who were right here," she said. "If they were healed, wouldn't he be also?"

She wanted to go to Jonah, but other things came first. "I need to find Taharka, and I must talk to Jesus for even a few minutes. Then we should start for Sychar if we are to arrive before dark."

He nodded, and they rode side by side, strangely silent. Had the miracles they had just seen included a healing for Jonah? What if he had not been healed?

"Susanna!" It was a welcoming, pleasant masculine voice that she recognized immediately.

"Andrew!" She eagerly turned toward the tanned Galilean threading his way toward her.

His eyebrows rose as he looked at the bright-eyed child in her lap. "Much has taken place since last I saw you."

They had come to a halt because of the number of people between her and Jesus, so she slid down from the horse after handing Jonathan to the disciple. It took a while for them to even begin to get caught up with each other's recent activities, but at last she remembered to check, "I've wondered if you have been given the power to heal."

He beamed at her. "Yes, but it only takes place when we pray in *His* name."

"I know."

"You *know?*" he repeated. "How do you know?"

"We wouldn't have Jonathan were it not for that. Ephrathah, who has become a follower of Jesus, told us that if two or three are praying in Jesus' name, Yahweh hears and answers. So Taharka prayed with us, and Ephrathah, with Yahweh's help, turned Jonathan within my womb so he could be born."

Andrew gathered the youngster close and kissed him on the forehead before handing him back to his mother. "You have been much blessed."

She smiled through a film of tears. "I know, and I praise Yahweh every day and thank Him."

Andrew was called away, but he parted with a blessing just as Susanna saw Taharka and waved to him. "I've been talking with Jesus," he announced when he and David got to her. "Everything's making sense at last."

"About the inn and the Sabbath?"

He nodded. "The way I understand it, Yahweh wants us to realize we need one day of the week for coming closer to Him. When the Law was first given, the children of Israel were nomads, and travel was part of their everyday lives. Therefore, to not travel was for them to have a time to pray and be closer to their Lord. There are still people who, traveling, need accommodations. If people like us close our doors to them, that makes for hardship. We will continue to pray about exactly how to do it, but we really *can* make this day a special one for everyone. Each person must have the opportunity for fellowship with Yahweh, so the half of the people working each Sabbath will have a day off during the week. This will give time for going to the synagogue, for learning more about Yahweh, and for rest."

"That's fairly close to what you'd been thinking about before," she ventured.

He smiled wryly. "But I was afraid I might be talking myself into this—that it wasn't really Yahweh's will."

A young man in a short, unbleached woolen tunic came toward them and stopped beside Taharka. "I have done as you requested," he said formally.

Susanna looked at the two flapping, fluttering pigeons in the man's left hand. She didn't realize at once their significance, but

Taharka said, "Excellent. You made good time." He reached into his girdle and pulled out his purse. "They are completely without blemish?"

The Galilean nodded, looking pleased when he saw the coin Taharka was giving him. "I checked them carefully. There is no imperfection on either of them."

As the satisfied man walked away, Taharka examined the birds. "When we catch up with Jonah, he may wish to stop at the first town he comes to and have the priest there examine him and pronounce him clean." How Susanna loved and admired her husband! She had been going to tell him about the healing, but he had believed and acted on the expectation of their prayers being answered.

How could she ever thank him for remembering? They had often read these passages together and marveled that even though they'd never heard of anyone being healed of leprosy, Yahweh had made provision in Leviticus for ceremonial cleansing, and this would require two perfect pigeons.

The priest would have to come outside the town to check Jonah and, if finding no signs of leprosy, proceed with the cleansing. He would order one of the two sacrificial pigeons to be killed over fresh water in a clay pot, and would dip the other bird, cedar wood, scarlet yarn, and hyssop into that blood. Seven times he would then sprinkle Jonah with the blood before letting the living bird fly into the open field.

Jonah would be required to wash himself and his clothing thoroughly and shave off all his hair before being allowed to come within the walls of Sychar to sleep. He would not, however, be allowed to go into any of the homes there for an additional week.

On the eighth day he would return to the synagogue with his sin offerings and guilt offerings and be anointed with oil to make atonement before Yahweh. And then, being declared totally clean, he could return to his wife and children and take up a normal life again.

There was a commotion at the edge of the crowd, over where Jesus was standing. "What is it?" Susanna asked, unable to see over the heads.

Taharka's face was wreathed with smiles as he lifted David to his shoulder and indicated she and Jonathan should follow.

There came Jonah, running, leaping into the air, and swinging his arms. Perhaps some might think him crazy, but she knew that he had been completely healed and was so overjoyed that decorum was beyond him.

"Yahweh be praised!" he shouted. "He does all things well. Though we do not know His reasoning or His time schedule, yet He works His deeds so everyone may see. And today, today I am healed!"

The crowd parted before him, but he was not aware of the individuals as he continued right up to Jesus and fell at His feet, crying, "Thank you, Jesus! Thank you for healing me, the least among Yahweh's subjects. Thank you for hearing our pleas."

Susanna's gaze rose from her brother to Jesus. He had told her to rise when she had knelt before Him that evening, but now, in loving sadness, He looked around at the people and beyond them, past the village. "Were not ten lepers cleansed?" he asked softly. "Where are the other nine?"

Susanna ached for Him. It must be sad to do so much for people and find them ungrateful, willing to accept yet unwilling to put themselves out even long enough to give thanks.

"Was no one found to return and give praise to God except this foreigner?"

Susanna winced. She had seldom been outside of Samaria and found it hard to think of herself as a foreigner, even though she was now several hundred paces within Galilee. However, He was not insulting them; He was making a point with those surrounding Him, who were all Jews. He was saying that just because they thought of themselves as the Chosen did not mean that their eyes were open spiritually.

The healed Samaritan had returned to give thanks. Jesus felt that what Jonah had done was worthy of being pointed out to these Galileans.

Was this what Ephrathah was telling her about—Jesus using everyday occurrences, feelings, emotions, and actions that were universal, to get His message across to His listeners?

David nudged her on the shoulder. "Aunt Susanna, is that my father? Why is he on the ground? Why doesn't he stand up?"

She held his hand tightly in hers. "Remember this day, my darling. It is the day that Jesus, the Messiah, healed your father. Look, He's helping your daddy to get up. Hear what He's saying."

The smile on Jesus' face was radiance, was warmth, and His voice rang out with assurance and approval. "Rise and go your way. Your faith has made you well!"

Jonah was on his feet, looking around with joy at a world that in eight more days would fully accept him back among the living. Taharka carried David toward him, and Susanna followed.

These were the men she loved, whom she would gladly live or die for: Jonah, who had cared for her since she was a baby; David, the adored child of her brother whom she had also lost for a time; Taharka, who loved her so much he had married her for the sake of that love; and Jonathan, the blessed child of their union.

But the greatest of all was Jesus.